GOYA'S GLASS

MONIKA ZGUSTOVA

TRANSLATED BY MATTHEW TREE

THE
FEMINIST PRESS
AT THE CITY UNIVERSITY
OF NEW YORK
NEW YORK CITY

Published in 2012 by the Feminist Press
at the City University of New York
The Graduate Center
365 Fifth Avenue, Suite 5406
New York, NY 10016

feministpress.org

Originally published as *Grave cantabile* by Odeon-Euromedia Group in Prague in
2000, and *La dona dels cent comriures* by Proa in Barcelona in 2001.

First printing July 2012

LLLL institut
ramon llull
Catalan Language and Culture

The translation of this work was supported by a grant
from the Institut Ramon Llull.

Cover design by Faith Hutchinson
Text design by Drew Stevens

Library of Congress Cataloging-in-Publication Data

Zgustova, Monika.
Goya's glass / by Monika Zgustova.
p. cm.
ISBN 978-1-55861-797-1
1. Alba, María del Pilar Teresa Cayetana de Silva Alvarez de Toledo,
duquesa de, 1762-1802—Fiction. 2. Goya, Francisco, 1746-1828—
Fiction. 3. Nemcovâ, Božena, 1820-1862—Fiction. 4. Berberova,
Nina Nikolaevna—Fiction. I. Title.
PG5039.36.G87G68 2012
891.8'6354—dc23

2012015164

CONTENTS

Passages in this novel attributed to
Francisco Goya, Božena Němcová, and Nina Berberova
are derived from historical texts.

GOYA'S GLASS

or the last time. For the last time, meaning never again.

For the last time. How many times have I pronounced these words as a threat? I used to think of them as words like any others, insignificant, featherweight. I played with them as a child with her doll, like a lady with her fan. Only on that one occasion, when I said them in front of him, did these words become the chimera of a nightmare, a monster with bat's wings and donkey's ears, with a beak and claws designed to inflict punishment, and when it has finally abandoned its horrible task, flies off with a heavy heart, as if reluctantly leaving a trail of incense and sulfur.

For the last time . . . There was just one candle lit. The light avoided the corners, the walls dripped with humidity and darkness. I thought that I had come in vain. The emptiness without his presence frightened me at first, but then left me feeling relieved. I had made the journey to his house on foot at a hurried pace, stopping every now and again, determined each time not to go one step further. I had gotten rid of my carriage because I couldn't simply sit there without doing anything, just shouting at the driver to go faster and thinking, heaven help me, let him run over whomever in the happy crowd might be blocking our path. The happiness of others struck me as unbearable, out of place, and I jumped from the carriage so as to go ahead on foot. I was desperate.

I reached his house without feeling the pain in my feet. Of course, Venetian slippers covered in emeralds are not made for trotting through the badly paved streets of Madrid. I climbed up to the third story with my skirt raised up above my knees. I cared not if the neighbors saw me. Desperation and anguish made me run as if I were fleeing from a gaggle of cackling geese.

Darkness reigned in the spacious room of stone and the little flame of the candle lit up only the small space immediately around it. Wherever you looked there were half-painted canvases, like white monsters, full of folds and wrinkles. Little by little I grew accustomed to the shadows, and amid all the folders, paints, and pots, I found a carafe of wine and poured myself a little. In the candlelight, the Manzanilla looked like honey in its glass. At that moment I smelled the familiar odor of bitter almonds and heard the creak of a bench from which a man was rising drowsily. In the shadows, the barely visible figure tied up his shirt and trousers. Before entering the circle of light from the candle, I smelled his odor as he shifted in his sleep. So he was there! I was overcome by a feeling of relief, just as his absence had been a relief to me a moment ago. So powerfully could he move me! Suddenly something whispered to me that I should punish him for making me suffer in this way, that I should show him who I was. He didn't give me time to do anything but took

4

hold of me with his large hands that sunk into my back like claws. We were standing, sitting, lying, sitting again, he with his claws forever dug into my face, in a sweet violence that made me feel lost. And when I came to again, he was bending over me, nursing the wounds that the long race through the streets of Madrid had left on my feet, licking off the blood as a mother bear does with her cubs.

For the last time . . . These words came back, they grew between us, a monstrous bat that beat its wings blindly against the walls. Was it he who spoke them? No. I myself released the monster from its cage. The need to punish the man in the unlaced shirt was uppermost in me. But the bat flew out of the room of stone; it followed me when I went down the stairs, when I was fleeing. Fleeing? And the man with the creased shirt stood at the threshold of the door. His wide shoulders slumped; his hair, twisted like a nest of snakes, hung lifeless. I turned around, per-haps to tell him something, perhaps—yes, that was it!—to take back those words, to withdraw them, to cancel them out, but he had already closed the door after saying, with indifference: Go, and don't catch cold.

I simply cannot stand healthy people. The maids and chamber-maids run up and down, and what is it with them that they don't realize that I have no wish to see their pale delicate legs? That I don't want them to bring me hot chocolate with ladyfingers in bed because I simply cannot bear the sight of those flexible, smelly hands of theirs, with their pink nails? I don't want roses or gladioli, I don't want anything that is beautiful and bursting with health, when I, here in my bed, smell the rancid, sweetish smell of my body, which has surely begun to decompose even though it is still full of life. People's day-to-day pleasures have always irritated me and I would now quite happily tear the Venetian crystal vases full of flowers from the hands of the chambermaids; I would smash them against the floor until they shattered, then I would grab the girls by their hair and drag them so that the pieces of glass tore at their pretty, healthy faces, so that the scars would remain engraved on their faces forevermore in memory of the Duchess of Alba.

But I cannot do it, I cannot get up, and when I want to write a few lines or read for a while, two maids have to hold me up like a dead weight so that a third may place some large cushions behind my back. Yes, all these pretty girls will still be around after the Duchess of Alba has taken her leave, just as, some time ago, her father ceased to be, and then in turn her stepfather, her mother, and worst of all her grandfather. I am still looking for him, even today. The woman who everyone has desired—all men, without exception—will disappear. Once a year has gone by, who will remember what *le chevalier* of Langre, that unbearable Frenchman, wrote about me, when he said that each one of my hairs gave rise to outbursts of passion? And that when I walked along the street, the people, stunned, leaned out of their windows, and children stopped playing to observe me? All of that has finished forever. The coveted woman will die, she and her passions, her pains and her satisfactions, and with her a whole world will disappear. Nothing of it will survive; the only thing that might remain are his pictures. Yes, it is in them that I will live forever: the duchess, the perfidious beauty, the vice-ridden duchess, the duchess-harlot, converted into the witch who flies above the heads of men. That is what will remain of me, that and nothing else.

And now what are you bringing me, darling? The thing is heavy; watch out you don't slip on the carpet. You are smiling at me. Come close, yes, yes, closer, closer. Ah, a deep crystal bowl full of rose water and water lilies: Are you bringing it so that the odor of my body should become even more obvious? Is that what you want?

Now she has turned to draw the curtain of the bed. All I would have to do is to pull on the cloth covering the bedside table, like this, yes, just a little more . . . now! What a wonderful thing, all those slivers of glass, like an explosion of ice! Large and small pieces that shine on the wood floor and on the carpet, what a wonderful image of destruction, ruin, and perdition! While she picks up the shattered glass, the girl sobs and tries to say something. Yes, make me dizzy with your excuses, you little snake! I can't throw anything at you; I haven't the strength to do it. But I can push you under with the weight of my body . . . Like this! Aaah! Help! Help! That is what I wanted, to sink that pink little face into the glass, like this, darling, like this, and may your injuries become infected, and pus take over your face.

For my eighth birthday I was given a new dress, which I had very much wanted. When I tried it on, I didn't even prick the dressmaker with the needles, as was my wont. The dress was of sky blue silk, with lace around the décolletage and the cuffs, and I wanted it really tight around the waist. When I tried it on, I held my breath so as to hide my belly. My mother's waist was as narrow as a wasp's; all the ladies admired her waist. And I wanted to be like Mama! Oh, and what ribbons adorned my new dress! One on the décolletage, three on the skirt, one in my hair, and all of them as pink as geranium flowers. No, more like tender carnations. That day I barely touched my lunch, I was so anxious to start getting ready for the party, which was to be held in my honor: to have a perfumed bath, to wash my hair, to anoint myself with rose water, and then, when I was finished, to put on that dress. I was ready by five in the afternoon, although the dinner did not begin until eight o'clock. There were three hours until Mama would see me with my new dress. I wore my hair loose, and at that time it reached down to the ground and was as curly as a bunch of eels. I got it into my head that I wanted to look like my mother's little sister, or a younger friend. I couldn't stop imagining how she would invite me to preside over the table to show all her guests how proud she was of me, how when the time came to serve drinks she would say to the serving maid: *d'abord* to the little duchess Maria Teresa, *s'il vous plaît*. And the maid would walk right around the long table, past dozens of seated guests, and serve me a little bit of the sweet wine that would pour slowly from the bottle, like a garnet necklace, into the tall wine glass, and dye it the color of blood. I would spend the entire evening sipping that blood like a great lady. When I was dressed and powdered, coiffured and perfumed, I walked from one end of the house to the other. I went up and down the palace stairs; I contemplated myself in the mirrors on the landings and in the halls; I bowed and curtsied. I had never before worn such a tight-fitting dress. Later, I watched the maids lay the table. Right in the middle, on the pale rose-colored tablecloth, they had arranged a centerpiece of lilacs, which at that time of year were starting to bloom in our garden. It was of the same color as my dress, sky blue, no, lilac blue, and they had decorated it with pink ribbons like those on my dress. My dishes, and mine alone, were decorated with little clusters of lilac.

Finally the guests began to arrive, wishing me many happy returns and kissing me while I fretted that the white powder would come off my cheeks and the perfume of rose water would fade. I kept a lookout for Mama although I knew that her triumphant entrance would put an end to my pleasure at being the center of attention. And the fact is that Mother always became the focus of attention because she was the most beautiful, the most elegant and refined, the kind of woman for whom, when she entered a salon, the musicians stopped playing, so dazzled were they. And then I made a firm resolution that would be the aim of my life: to stop the music playing when I entered a salon.

My grandfather bid the guests welcome. He was all dressed up, his chest gleaming with orders and medals: a military man who had earned his merits, *Capitán General*. He looked so fine! How proud I was to have him. I thought that when I was grown-up, I would marry only a general, strong and good-looking, who would proudly wear the uniform that makes men look so beautiful. But quite the opposite happened: they married me to a man who was neither strong nor good-looking, and who wore no uniform. I think that if my grandfather wore his gala uniform on the day of my birthday, it was only to make things pleasant for me, to make me happy, because as a rule he never dressed with the pomp that was customary in Madrid, but in a simpler fashion. I suppose that this was out of respect for the authors who were banned in Spain, and who I also imagined dressed in a simple, humble fashion, all those French encyclopedists: Diderot, d'Alembert, Voltaire, and, above all, grandfather's great friend Jean-Jacques Rousseau.

The guests were now in the salons and we had only to wait for my parents. People formed groups and conversed, and I told myself that when I was grown-up, beautiful, and admired, I too would make people wait for me.

Father came in with a very large packet, and I grumbled that I didn't want a present of any kind. I wanted Mama and nothing else. He put me in my place with a severe look, gave me a kiss, and told me that I was already a young lady, that I was eight years old, and that I had to behave myself like a great lady and stop grumbling like a badly brought-up girl. And he kissed me again and promised me that Mama would come to my birthday party, that she would be only a little late, and that we were not to wait for her for dinner. He pronounced this last sentence in a clear, loud voice so that all those present could hear. Everyone behaved as if nothing untoward had happened, but I noticed that their indifference was feigned and that they felt sorry for me.

My father gave me that enormous packet: "*De Maman!*" and I grabbed hold of it and left the room like a shot because the corners of my mouth were trembling and if I had said anything by way of explanation, my voice would have faltered. I ran upstairs to my chamber, threw the packet into a corner and, with my head under the pillow, I thought that if my mother wasn't coming, then I didn't want to see anyone at all.

After a while grandfather came in, made me sit on his knees, wiped away my tears, and held me tight. Then he himself took the packet and opened it. An enormous doll appeared on my lap, with blue-gray eyes like those of my mother. I thought that she had sent me a puppet to take her place for good. Once in the dining room, I placed the doll on my mother's chair and ordered the maid to pour wine in its glass and serve food on its plate.

After dinner I went into my mother's chamber; I wanted to paint the doll's face. I spread cream on its eyebrows until they disappeared completely, powdered its face, and drew high brows using black eyeliner, which gave it the expression of permanent and cold surprise that my mother so often wore. I straightened the hair of the wig and powdered it until it was white, and at the back of the neck I tied her hair up in a little net. I was happy with my creation. In the end I pinned her favorite brooch on the doll's breast, the half moon of diamonds on a background of sapphires, and on three of the doll's cloth fingers I placed the ring that bore the inscription MARÍA DEL PILAR CATEYANA DE SILVA, DUCHESS OF HUÉSCAR. Now I had my mama.

I have just taken a nap. I have reached the stage at which anything tires me, even memories. Consuelo, my chambermaid and confidante of many years, never stops giving orders and hopping about all over the place.

A long, long time ago, it was she who, with the expression of someone about to tell a secret, told me the story of a painter à la page in the highest of high society. "Especially among the ladies!" Consuelo smiled maliciously. "A fat little peasant from the back of beyond, from the Aragonese desert. With small, sunken eyes, a potato nose, and fingers like chunks of wood. The lady nobles do not want their portrait to be painted by anyone but him and they pay him their weight in gold, not so much for the portraits, which are excellent, to be certain, but rather for . . ." Consuelo whispered, always with the same ambiguous smile. "He is the lord of Madrid," she exclaimed. "There are so many children of his running through the city, apart from the ones he has with his wife. He has cured the infertility of more than one Madrid lady. But I think the only women who really attract him are the *majas* and the *manolas*. What's more, he's a regular of the dubious districts with the poor light in which the street girls wander. And our noble ladies cannot resist the temptation of tasting a man with a reputation such as his."

At that moment I made a violent gesture to shut up Consuelo so as not to hear any more gossip, but nonetheless a little worm of curiosity had begun to nibble away at my heart. No, I certainly wouldn't do as those silly noble ladies had done; I wouldn't let him paint my portrait. But what if I commissioned a portrait of my husband, playing the violin or the harpsichord? Don José Álvarez, Marquis of Villafranca, painted by mister . . . what did Consuelo say his name was? Gómez? No. Goya? Goyanes? My curiosity was getting the best of me, but I told myself that I wouldn't stoop to believe the tittle-tattle of the servants and I forgot about the whole business.

Get out, girls! Close the doors. I shall try and wash my face.

Where was I? Ah, yes, the doll: my mother's puppet. But it was truly my mother, it had to be, there was no other with me on the day of my birthday. I bathed before going to bed while the mama-puppet sat on a chair by my side. I dried myself and she followed me with her eyes. I put on a nightshirt and picked her up in my arms, very carefully so as not to tousle her hair. I even smelled her: it was she. Then I stretched out in bed, she sat on the mattress, and I rested my head in her lap, playing with her hair, which had become unfastened, playing with the brooch, the ring. Now my hand rested on her head. I went to sleep. Just for a little while, but happily, because Mama was keeping me company. I put her head on the pillow next to my own and tucked myself in. It was cold and the fireplace wasn't lit. I gave her a big hug. I covered myself with her arm. She dried my cheeks. Within her embrace the tears poured out of me like water from a fountain overflowing from rainfall. When I woke up, her arm was around my waist. I pressed myself against her and the brooch stuck my chest. I took hold of her hand and in my palm I felt the ring, with its inscription: CATEYANA DE SILVA. Then I saw that name by the light of the candle, written in reverse on my skin.

I took her in my arms so as to carry her into the bathroom. The servants were asleep. I filled the bath, let fall a few drops of perfume, and placed her in the water. It seemed to me that she was smiling voluptuously. *Mimamámemimamucho*, I sang while I took the slipper off my left foot. And splash! I submerged Mama into the water and then let her float to the surface. I removed my other slipper and with both feet in the bath I pressed on the cloth belly. The water was scented. I liked sitting with my feet in the water, and after a while, when I opened my eyes, Mama had dissolved. Her body had puffed up and then burst; the eyes and lips of the face were missing. The wig was floating next to my legs. Only the brooch and the ring were still whole.

I took my feet out of the bath, scented them with rose dust, and went to bed. Through the window I could vaguely make out the moon, and dawn was dyeing the sky pink, a sky as indifferent and empty as the day that was beginning.

It was very late in the morning when my mother woke me up, standing beside my bed with the dissolved doll in her hands. She knew . . . or did she? There was no way to read anything in those gray eyes of hers.

"It isn't right to treat gifts in such a way," she said, letting the doll drop to the floor, "Take this, at all events it forms part of what will eventually be your inheritance." On my bedside table she placed the ring that a few hours before I had placed on the doll's finger. "We shall see each other at dinner," she added from the threshold.

"Mama! Wait! I want to tell you that . . ." But the door had already closed.

She didn't come to dinner.

A little time after that, Father died. It was not as if I saw him very often, but suddenly he just wasn't there anymore. Then my stepfather died. I mean my mother's lover with whom, for a long while now, she had spent more time than with my father. Soon after, it was my grandfather's turn, in whose place I would rather have died myself. Then came the day of my wedding. Mine and that of my mother's, who was marrying again on that very day, beside me, in the same church. She even had to belittle me on my wedding day.

However, her new husband died soon, and she didn't take long to follow him. And then eventually, much later, my own husband died.

After my mother died, I got used to wearing the ring she had given me on my index finger. MARÍA DEL PILAR CATEYANA DE SILVA, DUCHESS OF HUÉSCAR. I turned the ring to the right and to the left. It was my ring of Gyges ring, a magic ring. I slept with whom I wanted to, but I always went to bed alone. Then I turned the ring which indicated who the next day's man would be. I couldn't bear anyone for very long, but I turned the ring and went on turning it.

Until Francisco turned up. Then I had the ring smoothed down so as to engrave a new name upon it: GOYA. Since, I have always worn the ring with the letters turned inward, toward the inside of the hand, so that when I close it Goya's name is imprinted on my palm.

"Consuelo, stop hunting around for spiders. They bring good luck! You were the one to show me, one day many years ago, that Goya, the royal painter, and de Godoy, the prime minister, shared a secret, didn't they?"

"The fact is, Your Highness, at that time . . ."

"If there's something I can't stand, it's cowardly excuses. That day you told me that Don Francisco Goya had all kinds of tangled love affairs, in houses of ill repute as well as the palaces of the nobility, and a permanent lover who, according to you, he shared with Manuel de Godoy—a village girl, vulgar but exciting, originally a *manola*, you assured me. Although she got everything she could out of the prime minister, she was in love, heart and soul, with the painter. That is exactly what you told me."

"Highness, I meant that the royal painter, already in the period before he met you, was the only man worthy of the name in Spain. I am certainly not one to judge, but it is undeniable that the painter Goya enjoyed such fame."

"He *was* the only man?"

"Is."

"Be careful. And who was the girl he clung to so?"

"It was the opposite: she clung to him. That would be Josefa de Tudó."

"Pepita! That snake! Do you know this for sure?"

"That is what they said."

"They said so many things, you gormless thing! I don't believe it. Francisco would never have fallen so low. Neither do I believe the rest of the gossip that was told behind his back. And now go, run! Your presence reminds of things that I do not wish to remember. And if anyone has to attend to me, let it be my *aya*; she is more restful. *Aya* María was both mother and grandmother to me, while I laughed at and ridiculed her endlessly. Go, girl, call for her."

◆

One day I was sitting in an armchair, curled up like a ball of wool, a kitten, just eight years old. I hid myself in the darkest corner, in my black dress with black lace, wrapped up in my black hair as if it were a blanket that hid me from the eyes of other children and from adults. The light of dozens of candles and the happy voices of the guests who filled the salon fell on me the way leaves fall in autumn, unstoppably. I didn't put up any resistance, but I made myself smaller and smaller. I burrowed into the depths of the armchair. I let more and more of these leaves made of light and voices fall on me; I imagined that they would bury me.

Someone touched my hair and brought me out of my dream world; to judge by her perfume, it was Aunt Ana. She took me by the hand and dragged me over to one of the circles of guests. I sat in a chair next to her.

"Aunt, how is it that suddenly people aren't there anymore?" She talked to me about heaven and the angels and the meeting up of twin souls, the same things my *aya* María told me, only that, unlike my duenna—where are you María, can you hear me?—my aunt expressed these thoughts with elegance, as befitted the select company.

"Yes, Aunt, but why did it have to be my father?"

Aunt Ana stroked my hand and turned toward the group sitting around her. She continued with the subject she had been discussing before my arrival had interrupted her. She was talking about the new flowers and trees she had seen in the royal gardens. I looked at the nobles and the ladies; some nodded their heads, yes, yes, while others shook their heads, incredulous. One of the nobles whistled from time to time and exclaimed

Caramba! I asked myself: What do they find so strange about a row of orange and lemon trees having been planted next to the royal palace and that dozens of orchids should have been brought from Japan? Yet it strikes them all as perfectly natural that someone should not be there anymore. They are there and my father isn't: That doesn't make anyone shake their heads and exclaim *Caramba?*

I watched the people who were standing and those who were walking about, and I felt a kind of emptiness that grew in me like a high tide, an emptiness so great that if it spilled over it would engulf all of Madrid and, what is more, all of Castile. I went to the window to see if the emptiness were still there, on the other side of the pane. Yes, it was certainly there all right. And in the middle of this emptiness was Miguelito, the laundry woman's son, helping the gardener to water the allotments. I took advantage of the moment when my aunt was playing the harpsichord to cross that emptiness and go over to Miguelito.

"It's great that you've come! Let's play hide-and-seek!" he said by way of greeting.

"Miguelito, how is it that suddenly someone just isn't there anymore?"

"What are you saying? I don't understand you."

"How is it that someone who has been here, like me and like you, someone who gave me a goodnight kiss from time to time, suddenly isn't there anymore and never will be ever again?"

"But you're there and so am I, so let's go play at hide-and-seek."

"You've work to do, Miguelito."

"I'll finish it later. You know what? We can go to the granary, take off our clothes, and swim together in a sea of corn."

I thought that Miguelito lived in a world of things that distract and tempt, a world in which birds sing and a child can play at hide-and-seek or fly a kite. All of that had disappeared from my world; not a trace was left. I was sorry that there were trees and a great dark blue sky around me. I felt as if these things were squandered on me, as if they were superfluous, things that someone should have saved the trouble of making. I walked past the cages of birds and animals.

"Miguelito, open up the cage of the roe deer for me!"

The roe deer stopped chewing and looked up at me with its sad, wet, unblinking eyes. One look from those eyes is enough for me to know that he understands me, I thought, that he shares everything with me. Little roe deer, why is someone who was always there suddenly not there anymore? And you, do you also live in a vacuum that engulfs and paralyzes you? How can you live in that cage? A few steps over there, a few steps over here, you can't even jump. My grandfather says that the most important thing of all is liberty. He doesn't tell me what to do; I have no obligations. Grandfather was reading about this type of education precisely when I was born. Rousseau's book *Emile* had just come out, as if the French philosopher had read my grandfather's own thoughts. He wanted me to be named Emília, but my parents decided they would name me after Santa Teresa de Jesús, who had stayed at our house when she was in Madrid. So they christened me María Teresa, but grandfather often calls me Emília. And he and Rousseau exchange letters laden with fire: Grandfather berates him for having relegated women to a kind of inferior being whose function is to serve men and for whom education and training are dangerous. Grandfather tries to persuade him that education and liberty are for all, for men and women both. He justifies this by using me as an example. He describes my freedom to do as I wish, to look at the sky and the tops of the trees, to be taught music and painting, to begin to learn through my grandfather the basic tenets of philosophy, and when it is over, in the afternoon to play in the garden with the children of the servants.

That is Grandfather's ideal. But there is something he doesn't know, roe deer, which is that here I feel like you in your cage. Do you want to come out, like I do? Come on, I'll help you escape. Miguelito, open the side door that goes onto the street. Shut up and open it! Now, little animal, off you go in search of freedom. Why do you drag your heels as if you didn't want it? You have to learn to run and jump, you don't even know how. Have your hooves become atrophied in the cage? You're free now! Run, go on, over there you'll find a meadow and a few trees!

I felt relieved. I imagined the roe deer discovering the beauty of nature. I went back to the soiree smiling because people didn't know my secret, that the roe deer had recovered its freedom and that, one day, I would follow it.

After a while, however, I saw Miguelito's face at the window, covered in panic. He was signaling for me to come out at once. I ran. The roe deer! It was lying in the middle of the lawn and behind it trailed a flow of blood. Its body and nose were covered in deep scratches. "It came back on its own, dragging itself with the last of its strength," Miguelito told me.

We took it to the cage. Miguelito poured water over the traces of blood so they wouldn't be found. I lay next to the wounded animal, which was panting and suffering in silence, and wiped the blood from its face. Is this liberty? I asked myself. Who did this to him? It could hardly have been another animal; it was probably the street children, probably our servants' boys and girls. The animal lay dying all night. And while the roe deer complained like an injured bird, I stroked the hair along its back and neck, and looked at its big, tender eyes, flooded with tears. All of the world and all of life was reflected there. And the world, which was mirrored in those sad, whiteless eyes, suddenly became full: more full than my world before the death of my father.

It was my most beautiful night. In the tear-filled eyes of the roe deer I found the strength of life once more: in those unfathomable eyes from which, little by little, life was fleeing.

I'm thirsty. Where did they leave my glass? Ah, yes, here it is, on the cushion. María, you who are the only understanding soul, dear old thing who will outlive me, pour me a little water, you who knows that I don't like drinking it from any other glass. How old was I when my grandfather gave it to me? He left it to me as a souvenir so that I should never be apart from him. I took it everywhere: Paris, Florence, Seville; even in Piedrahíta, I drank only from this glass. And that time, here in Madrid . . .

When I entered the salon, festively illuminated, all the guests were standing, waiting for me. The deep décolletage of my black dress was half hidden under the scarf with fire-red brocade: that of a *maja*, a village girl, a gypsy. In the salon, there was something that dazzled me more than the candelabras full of lit candles. When I had found my bearings, I was able to make out a shameless look, as if he had never seen a woman before, from head to toe, from feet to forehead. And there and then, I knew that those eyes were of the first man I had met in my life.

At that moment the man was talking to someone . . . maybe it was the Marquess of Villafranca, my mother-in-law. Yes, it must have been she. I remember the bright silver, her silvery dress and the ash color of her hair. She was asking him something, but he heard nothing. Because he was half deaf, but above all because he was obviously living in another world. I went about scattering greetings, looks, and smiles, and yet never stopped noticing that pair of sharp, small eyes, a little sunken in that fleshy face. All the looks with which I greeted my guests I offered mentally to the eyes of that man. Once in front of him, they told me his name. I didn't smile in the way I did when I was introduced to others. He too remained still and shadowy; I thought that he was as serious as if he was risking his life for something. I spent time with my guests, but never stopped feeling those two needles that had introduced themselves under my skin. And once again I went to stand in the circle that he was in. There was his wife, my husband, Doña Tadea Arias, the French ambassador, and I don't know who else. Doña Tadea Arias asked him whose portrait he was painting just then. He spun out the answer, his eyes fixed on me, his body turned directly toward where I was. He talked and talked and I knew that, apart from me, he didn't notice anybody else. And I? All of them put together were nothing but figures painted on a backdrop; he was the only living being. I felt as if I had been transformed into air and fire.

Abruptly, the French ambassador cut the tense cords that had begun to form between this man and me, which trembled with each breath we took. The ambassador asked me something. How impolite, I thought! And Francisco, which was the man's name, went over to the table on my left and—by coincidence? out of ignorance?—picked up my crystal glass, my grandfather's gift to me, raised it to his lips, filled his mouth with water, and without saying a single word, turned and left without so much as saying farewell. His wife, Josefa, looked at me as if apologizing for a third person whose behavior is incomprehensible to her, and I followed him rapidly to the door.

María, where did you put my glass? Hey, old woman, what's going on in your head? You're not dying like I am, so think for a bit. Woman, the one of cut glass, the one I took everywhere with me, to Seville and Sanlúcar, to Paris and Piedrahíta. Put a little water in it for me, come on! María, you old thing, older than Methuselah, do you remember how you told me off during the journey when I went to see Francisco for the first time? I laughed at your old woman's prejudices, and you took out your cross to show it to me, like a knight shows his sword to the enemy, like an inquisitor the Holy Scriptures to a heretic. The cross, your only lover, the cross that could never be unfaithful to you as could a flesh-and-blood man. The carriage advanced in leaps and bounds along the uneven pavement of the neighborhood in which Francisco lived, and I wanted to whack you over the head with that cross in order to stop the trembling which had gotten into me.

During the months that followed the reception at my house, not a week passed—but what am I saying? Not a day passed without me looking for the chambermaid to ask her if she didn't have a message for me from the only man in Spain. *"Je ne sais où me sauver,"* Madame de Sévigné, *ma soeur spirituelle*, she who was the sister of all women, had written a century before. I too had no idea where I could flee so as not to think about him.

He must have forgotten me. But the Duchess of Alba does not allow people to forget her. When she chooses a man, she makes him hers. And he ends up being hers, always. He stops belonging to himself in order to belong to her. When the Duchess of Alba feels an inclination toward someone, you can do whatever you wish to flee from her, but you will end up feeling such voluptuousness for her that you will never look at another woman again; you will end up the prisoner of a passion so great that all other women in the world come together into just one: the Duchess of Alba. María Teresa Cayetana de Alba is not a woman. She is fate itself.

You brought me to him, María, clutching your cross, but at once you were put at ease. Above the fireplace the painter had an image of little Pilar, Pilarica, as he called her. During my interview with him in his studio, I saw that little picture through a gap in the door and I told you in a whisper to ask the royal painter to hand it over to you. I didn't want my activities to be watched by the fire in the severe eyes of the Aragonese Virgin.

I didn't even look at the painter. I let my eyes wander over the jottings and pieces of paper full of sketches. The painter noticed the direction of my gaze and with a single movement of his elbow he swept away all the picturesque disorder that was on the table. Then, with a few kicks, he nudged the faces of those unbearable women I so often meet at the queen's soirees, and those of the foolish men who stick to me like the plague with all their tedium and mediocrity. As if aware of my sudden aversion, the painter stood in front of these pictures; he looked ashamed. Of his untidiness? Of the worthless people thanks to whom he made his money? I glanced at him. I started to tremble once more. In order to give myself time to get over it, I asked the painter to have a fire lit.

The royal painter, in his elegant suit, even if it was a little too tight a fit, contrasted strangely with the untidiness and the intimacy of his studio. He prepared the fire himself, saying that the servant used up too much wood. Oh, he was so tight fisted, that stout little man from Aragon! We still hadn't looked at each other.

A long cobweb stretched between two canvases, and there were more in the corners of the room. Next to the fireplace I discovered a half-written letter: Amigo Martín, Maldita sea, *hijo de tu madre*, what rubbish you write about my Aragonese relatives, you ass . . . This man is untidy, blasphemous, and what is more, doesn't have a full grasp of grammar, I thought. You could hear the crackling of the fire and the whispering of the damp wood where the flames started to lick it. The pieces of wood were like his arms; the pieces of wood were like his peasant's fingers. The greedy flames licked them; the flames sucked them.

The man was watching the fire. I raised my veil. He didn't stop watching the flames, but as he did so I had the feeling that he was looking straight at me, that in that fire he could see the slightest movement of my face.

"Don Francisco, he *venido* . . ." I said to interrupt his scrutiny. "I've come because . . ."

But the painter went out of the room without a word. After a short while, a servant entered with a tray laden with cheeses, little cakes, and a carafe of wine. The painter closed the door behind him. With one of the sleeves of his Sunday suit he cleaned the table, which was covered in colored stains, and offered me the repast.

"Help yourself, please."

He sat down in front of the fireplace. He still hadn't so much as looked at me.

"Don Francisco, I've come because . . ."

"Whatever your Highness says," he said, interrupting me as he moved his chair closer to the fireplace.

"I have come in order to ask you to paint me." He stayed seated, without moving.

"I want you to paint . . ."

The painter looked at the fire, as if he hadn't heard me. "I want you to paint my face."

"Madam, I do not do portraits of . . ."

Did he say dolls? I wasn't sure, because I had interrupted him.

"I am not asking you for a portrait, rather . . ."

"Now I am painting the portrait of the Marchioness of Pontejos," he said without turning round, "as well as a portrait of the family of the dukes of Osuna, and I have six more commissions."

Any closer and he would have fallen straight into the fireplace.

"Don Francisco, you have not understood me. I have come so that you can make up my face. Paint me, as you have never painted anyone so beautifully. I have to dine with the queen, and I wish her to die of envy."

Now he looked straight at me. His self-assuredness was cracking. I laughed and he became a little infected by my hesitant joy. At that moment he appeared to me as a totally inexpert lad.

Although a milky light was gushing through the window, he lit a few candles, let fall a few drops of wax on a zinc plate and pressed the candles to them. With this improvised candleholder he lit up one side of my face. I offered him the basket in which I carried my boxes of powders and paints. In silence he picked a color, mixed it with others, and drew a frame around my eyes. Like me, when I was little and used to paint my doll, I thought. What would he see when he paints me? The color of pomegranate with that of muscatel on the cheeks, the forehead, and the chin. Then he set about mixing ochre with a little silver and gold powder. He dipped the brush in it; he removed it. He ran his fingers full of color along my upper lips. Then his little finger, with a long nail, along the lower one. He saw me as an anonymous landscape. I felt his powerful fingers walking across my face, pausing at my eyes, my lips. And his breath so close . . . I couldn't even clench my teeth, or bite my lip, or move a single muscle. I drove my nails into the palms of my hands; that, he could not see. With one hand, the painter held my lips so that they stayed tense; with the other, he modeled their shape with the help of a brush. He did so conscientiously. He looked at me from a distance and then so close up that his eyelashes were almost touching my teeth. Then he began to mix a new color.

He took off his waistcoat. His shirt gave off a tart smell, like bitter almonds. I drove my nails further into the flesh of my palms. He mixed something up with the gusto of an alchemist, and a moment later he was leaning against me. I could do nothing else but close my eyes and let myself be carried away by the caress of the brush on my lips, as I had been, so long ago, by the caressing of the dying roe deer . . .

"There you are! What do you think of this silvery tone on the lips, the cheeks, the eyebrows?"

He held a hand-mirror up to me, but I looked at myself in the mirror of his face: it was there that I wanted to see myself, as he saw me. The only woman in the whole of Spain. I looked him straight in the eyes. He was the first to break the almost palpable tension, with his hoarse voice. I don't know what he said. My reflexes had gone. I turned to leave. He didn't accompany me. I went back to him, with questioning eyes. Instead of answering my look he took my hand and pressed it fleetingly, as if not daring to. A single gesture on my part would have been enough then for him to take me in his arms. But I made no gesture, just as dolls do not. I left his studio as if I were fleeing a fire.

Once in the street, I was unable to say a single word. I hid my face behind your shoulder, María, so that the passersby could not see it, so as to conserve within me the atmosphere of what I had just experienced. I don't know how long I was submerged in that delight. I lived the next few days as if I were under a bell jar that preserved me from the outside world the way a greenhouse preserves a rare flower.

Every day I went to sleep and woke up under this bell jar. I filled my days with soirees and receptions, banquets and literary teas, but I was living as a prisoner, like a fly that has been caught up in a cobweb and can't get out, the cobweb of his look and his breath, and the contact of his arms, which I still didn't know and nonetheless seemed to me to be ever present. I obliged my husband to organize more and more musical evenings. Don Francisco and his wife were usually invited, but my efforts when searching for that rough, shadowy face among those present were in vain . . .

In the same way today I search for it in vain next to my deathbed, among the faces that surround me so they can watch this life ebbing away from close quarters. To know what dying is, how everything comes to an end, it matters not. The busybodies of Madrid have spent enough time reveling in bullfights and society gossip, so now they have come to see another spectacle: the death of the Duchess of Alba. They would do better to pay attention to health and youth, and ignore the sick and dying. Or even to expel them from good society, as I hear they have started to do in France. I have always thought that is how things should be. And now? We are the sick, the dying, the pariahs, the banished. If I had known that I would have to die early, I would have lived in an entirely different fashion. María, tell the doorman not to let in Don Francisco should by any chance he decide to come!

Do you remember, María, how, much against your will, you brought him my personal invitation to an evening together just me and him? To Don Francisco: I will be waiting for you this evening at the Caracol Loco tavern, in Manolería, not far from my palace. María Teresa. Do you remember with what aversion you looked at me when the servants squeezed me into the dress of a *maja*, with its plunging neckline? When they did my hair with a little fringe, which I hardly ever wear and made me up with bright colors so that people wouldn't recognize me? In your hand you clutched your cross, which, as you know, has never been able to tame my will.

On the way to the Caracol you let me have one of your sermons, inspired by centuries of piety, although you knew that as far as I was concerned your God could make himself scarce, that I wanted a man, passion, and tenderness. Were you capable of imagining my desire, you who had been born to live as a spinster and deny life?

But that evening there was something you didn't know: that apart from Francisco, I had invited a pair of admirers of mine to the Caracol, two foolish little students. One was studying medicine and the other, theology, so you could imagine what kind of stuff they were made of. What was more, each was jealous of the

other and eager to find out on whom I would bestow my friend-
liness. As I say, silly little boys, but young, good-looking, with
beautiful, noble faces, qualities that stocky Paco from Aragon
could not hope to match. That is, he could not from his point of
view. From my own, well, you know the answer.

Surrounded by *majos* and *majas*, street merchants and humble craftspeople, I was sipping cheap, sour wine in the company
of the two students when Francisco appeared at the threshold. I
watched him out of the corner of my eye, through my black lace
veil which was lowered so that it only covered my eyes. He saw
me and was about to throw himself at me, but drew himself up
short when he saw the attractive young men on either side of
me. He stayed by the bar and ordered a jar of wine. Like the first
time, when he passed my crystal glass along his lips and took a
little of the water into his mouth so that when he had finished he
could leave without swallowing the liquid, so today he filled his
mouth with the wine that he passed over his tongue. He didn't
take his eyes off me; he didn't care for the wine.

I made out that I hadn't seen him, but the presence of the
man thrilled me so much that I began to dance, first with one
of the young men, and then with the other. While I danced I
pressed myself up against them, as I would have liked to press
myself up against the man who was leaning on the bar. My desire
grew. I thrust my breast against the young theologist, my waist
up against his belly, our legs became entwined, and the inside of
our thighs kept touching. We lost the feel of the rhythm. With
quick glances I saw the Adam's apple of the man at the bar move
as he drank the wine in fast little sips. Meanwhile, my theologist

had forgotten where he was and his hands passed over my body; his fingers drove into my skin through the thin cloth of the dress. Then I felt his nails and his teeth taking my skin. I melted under these caresses and closed my eyes to enjoy the presence of the man standing at the bar. I let go a sigh and almost fell. Never before had I felt what this painter, who was no longer at all young, made me feel at a distance.

Something broke on the tiled floor. The racket brought me back to my senses to make out the painter's back at the door, which he slammed shut, making more noise. I got rid of the young man and tread on the shards of pottery and the wine spilled on the floor as I went out into the street. I could see Francisco's curved back in the darkness and his head sunk in his jacket collar, as he turned the corner . . . and then I thought that I had lost him. Maybe forever.

It was not until much later that I found out.

María, draw back the curtain! The one covering the pictures! And stop complaining. Off with you, you and your cross. Wait behind the door. When I am ready to see the most hidden picture of them all, I will call you so that you may press the button. Come on, out with you! Don't let me hear you grumbling, you're distracting me!

The *maja* dressed. After a time, I discovered that when Francisco arrived home that night, without even changing his *majo* costume, he went straight to the studio. He took the largest canvas he had and started to paint . . . to paint a provocative woman, inciting beyond belief, dressed in such a way that the transparent veil makes her more naked than if she had been nude. Who was he painting, when he painted that woman? She isn't me, hers isn't my face. She is all the women that he has had in his life—in luxurious bedrooms and back rooms, in shady districts where you can smell the stink of the drains—and women he has desired without ever having them. A man possessed by desire, who releases himself by painting, but his eagerness only grows.

María, come in! I want to see the picture underneath. Don't grumble just press the button! Good, and now be off with you.

The *maja* nude. The man tears away the veils that enfold the desired body of the woman with the brush, so as to possess it. I know that he kept me at a distance, as I did with him. He possessed the woman who pursued him while he worked and while he slept. The body of the woman in the portrait does not correspond to the laws of anatomy that Francisco knew so well. She is an expression of a voluptuousness that knows no law. Francisco took over my body and then had little more to do than add a languid expression of love.

María, come, draw the curtain back again. Now I will leave you in peace. There is no need for you to show the cross to that poor painted girl!

Francisco had me. He had me in a way that for him was essential: he painted me. I think that never again, not even when he was pressing my body in his arms, did he love it so much as when he painted it. When his passion painted it.

María, come in. Add the following words to my testament: María Teresa Cayetana de Silva, thirteenth Duchess of

Alba, bequeaths her crystal glass to Don Francisco Goya, Royal Painter.

Have the notary sign it and seal it at once. And one other thing. I don't want Don Francisco to know of the state I am in. Do this in any way you wish, but the news must not reach his ears. When everything is over, go see him and tell him that I wanted him to design my mausoleum. There's more: it is my wish that, when deceased, he paint me in the same posture as the two *majas*, half-sitting, half-lying. Let it be his nostalgia that guides his hand, just as desire guided it when he painted the two *majas*.

Do I want to be celebrated? Legendary? Immortal? Even my beloved Madame du Châtelet, whom I have not had the pleasure of knowing personally, writes about the pleasure that fame brings. The love of glory as a source of pleasure. More or less she says: "There is no hero who wishes to distance himself completely from the applause of posterity, from which he expects more justice than from his contemporaries." This vague yearning that they talk about us when we are no longer there. . . .

I want it known that the Duchess of Alba was the model for the two *majas*. I want María Teresa Cayetana de Silva to live forever, as she emerged from the hands of Goya. I am sure that my beloved descendants will fight tooth and nail to deny it; I can even imagine them having me exhumed and bribing a few know-it-alls to certify according to all their knowledge that the proportions and pose of my poor bones do not match those of the painted woman. But they won't get away with it. And, even if they did get away with it, scientific treatises are always forgotten sooner or later, whereas art is alive and always will be. And I, the Duchess of Alba, will not die so that my passions and the love which consumed me may die with me, as happens in the case of other beautiful women, but so that they may live forever on canvases that I and only I was capable of inspiring.

Do you know what it is like to have a new lover every day? You can imagine that, can't you, you nun, hiding yourself behind that cross that I'd like to have you crucified on? It is so much work it leaves you exhausted, and what is more, it is tedious. Those two students I'd left standing the night of the Caracol Loco—I went back to look for them and I brought them to my house, remember? I raised a toast to Francisco with them. I drank to forget, for a new meeting, and yet again to forget. When they were drunk, I sent them on their way.

I had other students. The ones who excited me especially were the theologians because when I embraced them I imagined them dressed in black, unloading a sermon on morality from the pulpit. I had generals and common soldiers, writers, and musicians who were even more unbearable and egocentric, more *divos* than the literati, but, above all, I had a fair quantity of *majos*. To get rid of them, I made them believe I had a jealous husband. I had them leave through the window; I pretended I was helping them to escape, but I forced them to jump from the first floor and then set the dogs on them to make them run. How ridiculous they were when they jumped and yelled! What fun I had! But deep down the whole thing tired and bored me, and if it wasn't for the fact that I wanted to ridicule Queen María Luisa, I would have abandoned that particular form of amusement.

At that time María Luisa had that French lover who looked like an actor, or rather, an Italian opera singer. Wasn't he Italian, after all? I decided I would take the queen's concubine away from her. I went against the queen's characteristic bad taste as regarded music—Lully, how dreadful!—by arranging that Gluck and Haydn were played to and appreciated by Madrid, in the same way I managed to get Costillares, the bullfighter, accepted despite the general predilection for Romero—even though both of them were more obtuse than the bulls they killed—so it was that I managed to take the queen's lover away from her. At one dinner I made him sit next to me. To topple the royal lover from his pedestal I had only to rub his left thigh with my right leg, gently and not so gently, and to inform him after dinner of the well-known confidential fact that my husband did not fulfill all my needs. I took him to my chambers. All of this was nothing but cheap maneuvering, but really the queen's lover required little else. I left him so hungry for more that over the next few days he came like a whining dog wanting only that I would let him lick my hand alone, but I refused to receive him until he sent me a gift: a box of gold encrusted with diamonds, one of the gifts that the queen had given him.

Afterward I was able to do with him as I pleased, but I didn't once really sleep with him. To allow into me one who had drooled over the queen would have disgusted me. Meanwhile I gave the gold box to my hairdresser, the same one who also looked after the queen's coiffures, and I suggested that he use it to keep one of the rare pomades he used when arranging the royal hairs. It was thanks to this small amusement that the first attempt to burn down my palace in the Moncloa was made. The queen's retaliations were never very subtle.

But the days went by and Francisco didn't come. More than once I prepared to go and look for him myself, but afterward I was grateful to you, María, for refusing to bring him my messages and when on our way to see him, you ordered the coachman time and again to turn around and head for home. Meanwhile everything followed its usual course: the Duchess of Osuna came to visit me and I returned her visit, I took part in the *lever*, the elaborate mourning ceremony of the queen—the hypocrisy of the court has no limits!—and also in her teas, dinners, chocolate sessions, round tables, and walks. I listened to the king scratching at his violin, as well as to the Haydn quartets and sonatas that my husband played, my talented if henpecked spouse, that little-slipper husband whom I put on and removed with a kick as it struck my fancy. I appeared to listen to the queen's gossip about the Duchess of Osuna while knowing perfectly well that each and every one of them was exchanging gossip about me with great delight. I scoffed at them all because I had nothing better to do, and even laughing at them had long since become tedious to me.

Brother Basilio! My poor little one, my little hunchback! How old must that sanctimonious soul have been? Any figure between twenty and sixty. He was lame and stuttered; I would have devoured him with kisses. I loved him more than my dog and my monkey, more than María de la Luiz, my little black girl.

That day, it was summer in Piedrahíta, when we had gone out for a walk and he fell behind on his little donkey. How worried I was about him! Did you come with us that day, María? No, you were old already; you couldn't ride. You were at home praying, confess it! That day we went out and, once in the wood, my husband and I found ourselves alone. We waited and my Basilio didn't turn up; we also appeared to have lost the servants. I followed the path back and I saw Basilio, sunk in the mud in a hole. He was waving his crutch and with each move he made he sunk a little more. The other crutch was swimming in the mud, far from him. The man was barely able to move any longer, he was sunk in right up to the waist. And my servants all around him, haw haw haw! ha ha ha!, doubling up with laughter, to the point of tears. Instantly I made all of them go into the muddy hole to get him out! Consuelo, our cook, and then my confidante, told me that Basilio had seen a little calf that was drowning in the mud and not far away her mother who was mooing in the saddest of ways. Basilio went into the mud, pulled out the calf, and then the cow began to frighten him. Apparently she threatened to charge him with her horns. She took the calf from him, and then forced Basilio back into the muddy hole. Haw haw haw! Consuelo burst out laughing.

I slapped her so hard that she herself almost fell into the mud, and then I went from one servant to another, slapping them all and spitting in their faces. When my husband tried to calm me down, I became even more furious and he too was slapped on the cheek, in front of all the servants.

I summoned my carriage and had Basilio sit, and we went

back together to the palace. I myself disrobed the hunchback, bathed and dried him, rubbed him with scented oils, dressed him again, and all the time I didn't stop giving him little kisses. Once we were sitting on the sofa of the salon eating cakes washed down with muscatel, Basilio confided to me that my servants talked about me saying that he, the cripple Friar Basilio, was one of my lovers. That these scum spoke badly of me, the same people to whom I behaved like a friend and had wanted to bequeath my worldly goods to in my testament, made me indignant to the extent that I then made Basilio my lover. María, do you remember a night when I vomited without stopping, and when there was nothing more to spew? I vomited saliva mixed with blood?

I am getting senile, María. At that period I hadn't even met Francisco! As I come closer to death now, my sense of time falters. Or maybe I did know him then? Wasn't that when he painted that picture that seems playful at first glance, in which he depicts me as a bride and Basilio as a repulsive bridegroom who follows me tamely, poor thing? Francisco didn't know anything; gossip didn't interest him. And yet, he saw clearly everything that was going on inside of a person. Deaf as he was, he saw and understood everything.

How he tortured me, that man, doing everything the opposite way of what I wanted it to be. I, who entered a room and the musicians stopped playing! I could enter his house a hundred times and Francisco never stopped playing. That made me suffer, which amazed me. If I was in good health now, I would dispose of my life in another fashion. This slow death and the awareness that life is leaving me have taught me how to live. Too late!

It is too late for anything, even for Francisco. He, deaf as he is, is at the height of his powers and will still show the world how crapulous, libertine, dissipated, licentious, and debauched was the Duchess of Alba! Not only ungrateful, but perfidious. All that, but she was beautiful, charming, sublime. Make sure that nobody will forget it, Paco! Paint a portrait of *the* woman so that the generations to come will regret never having been able to have her! Because I am going. Paco, I know that we will never meet again, my old stocky, grumbling, so-often-unbearable Paco. The only person I will catch up with will be my husband. I will meet José some place in the underworld, in the kingdom of shadows. I don't want to be buried in his tomb to lie by his side for evermore ... No!

Please, María! Back you come to me with a bunch of flowers. Throw them into the garbage and stop bothering me, you wicked woman. So old, so ugly, and even you will outlive me! No, I don't want to know who has sent me this stinking mess. The devil take them all, all of them! I'm fed up, especially with you. Come on, María, little old thing, don't be offended by a few words from a dying woman, eh? Sit here with me. No, not on the bed, you disgusting old woman! Here, on this low chair.

Tell me, why did Francisco come to Piedrahíta, and not alone but in the company of his wife and children? What happened there? Yes, you're right, it was at the time of that extraordinary heat wave worthy of a tropical country. One day at a dance—we organized them every week, didn't we, on Tuesdays?—to which, in addition to the local minor nobility, we had invited some people from the village, I grew tired of dancing with the local faith-healers, and as for the nobles, well, you yourself know how little I cared for all those princes and dukes and marquesses! So I ended up sitting next to my husband. The whole time he followed me with those deer eyes of his, and I think he envied my vitality. He always envied it because he didn't know what an effort it was for me to get up every day, and if it wasn't for my obligatory attendance at the official *lever* I would probably never have been capable of getting up in the morning. But once I was up, I didn't want people to discover my aversion to life, so I put on the face of an enthusiastic little girl. But you knew how to look behind the mask, didn't you? I sat next to those deer eyes that I became used to seeing in the portrait that Francisco had painted of my husband, which we had hung in the salon, and I drank fresh lemonade.

"I want my own portrait, a portrait more beautiful than that of my mother, which was painted by Mengs. I want people never to forget it once they have seen it. I want a picture that makes me famous everywhere and forever."

"That portrait by Agustín Esteve . . ."

"Don't mention that name, *qué vergüenza, Don José*! Do you not know that in all Spain, Italy, and France, that is to say in all the world, there is only one painter capable of doing it? Do you yourself not have eyes to see your portrait hanging in the salon? Yes, José, what do you think is going to happen to you when you die? Who will remember your expression, your eyes? While your mother lives, with a bit of luck you will live on in her, with a little bit more luck, you will in me. But once we are dead, you will die completely and forever! Only in Goya's portrait will your deer eyes continue to move the viewer; only through his painting will the public of the future know that you admired Haydn, that you wrote to him as if he were your beloved, your adored one without whom you could not live, that you played the violin and the harpsichord like no one else in the entire country. All that can be read in your expression and in the shape of your hands, your fingers, the pose of your body, but much more in the picture than even in real life . . .

A week later, at the ball organized on the terrace of the Piedrahíta palace, I danced for the first time with Francisco.

He looked at me crudely. Although we danced separately, I felt that he was holding me firmly, that he was pressing me against him. I remember just one sensation: I am a piece of ice in the palm of a warm hand, I am melting, I am turning into liquid, into warmth, into boiling water, into steam, heat, fire . . .

"We shall have our first session, Don Francisco."

"Yes, tomorrow, if you wish."

"No, right now."

"But . . ."

I took him away with me under the fire of incredulous eyes. Everyone was gawking, not at what was happening, but at how it was happening.

I had Francisco sit in a low armchair in my chamber. Among the objects on the bedside table, he discovered my crystal glass; the other time he had filled it with wine and drank. He turned the glass in his fingers and watched the circles made by the wine as if I were not there.

"Don Francisco, do you know who Monsieur Le Nôtre was and what he asked of the pope?"

He shook his head.

"Le Nôtre was an architect of the last century who designed the gardens at Versailles. But that is not of importance either. What is, is that Monsieur Le Nôtre was received by the pope. I think it was Innocent XI, but that isn't important either. The most interesting thing about their meeting was what the architect asked of the pope. Do you know what it was? That instead of an indulgence, the pope grant him temptations. Don Francisco, what we should ask of God is passion, passion, and more passion."

He narrowed his eyes, he looked at me . . . Go away, María, and take your cross with you. What I am about to recall is not for your ears . . . While he poured himself more wine, I unfastened my bodice. He continued with his eyes half-closed, looking me up and down from behind his eyelashes, with a painter's eyes and the look of a man who knows how to appreciate what he sees.

"Does the lady Duchess wish me to paint her like this?"

I nodded.

"The décolletage should be smaller."

"Why?"

"This is not for . . ." he mumbled, caressing my breasts with his eyes.

"What are you saying, why?"

"No one should see this . . ." he grumbled in a low voice.

I felt that all of me had been reduced to my breasts. My face, my arms, my chamber; everything ceased to exist. There were only my heavy breasts, which the painter had absorbed in his memory so as later to give them to all the women in his paintings and engravings.

"Why, sir royal painter?" I asked him once more, with a touch of ironic disdain. Perhaps by ridiculing him, I wanted to hide the fact that not even nude could I dominate this man.

"For reasons of composition," he declared, finally.

I approached him until I felt his breath against the skin of my breasts and said to him: "Then arrange my décolletage in accordance with these reasons."

Was that how it happened? Or have I dreamt it? Perhaps I only wished that it had happened like this. Or perhaps it is only now that I know what I should have done. I never felt any shame when I disrobed in front of the students; their sense of decency amused me. But at that moment, was it not I who was standing confused in front of that man who seemed to me a little brutish? I only know that I leaned over displaying the full weight of my body in front of the painter, who was savoring me with his eyes. I took the glass from his fingers to take a sip and then . . .

"I am sorry, sir royal painter, but now I remember that I must attend to a visit."

Did he hear me? Or is it that he didn't want to understand? Did he know that it was a lie, that man who saw everything, before whom it was impossible to hide anything? That rough, brutal man . . . Rough and brutal? Really? Francisco was not like that, but I needed to think of Paco as rude and bestial.

"It would not be good if my visitor this night were to find me here with you," I repeated with words and gestures, so as to make sure that he understood.

What did I want? That he, the painter, would stay? My aim was to become the mistress and lady of this man.

Francisco glanced at me, full of hatred, and made a gesture as if he wanted to smash the crystal glass against the wall—like the jug against the tiles on the floor in the tavern—then controlled himself and left without saying anything.

Satisfied, I stopped thinking about the painter. At night I noted in my dairy: "I will not stop smuggling the French encyclopedists into Spain because no one can do anything against the Duchess of Alba, not even those of the Inquisition. In my bedroom I will hang nude portraits, banned in Spain, including the Venus of Velázquez and others that represent me myself. Let the grand inquisitor come to see them in person, to feast his eyes on them if he will! He can do no harm to the Duchess."

María, come here with your cross. You wouldn't want them to hang me up on it, would you? What did Don Francisco do after that ball on the terrace, María?

I remember that over the following weeks he didn't reply to the invitations to sessions with me. Exceptional shamelessness. He could not be seen anywhere. He did not turn up to the teas, the dinners, or the balls.

One day I was walking through the woods with the little black girl, the water spaniel, and the monkey. From a distance

I saw a man kneeling next to a huge oak. He was taking off the bark and examining it. I felt sure I had spotted Francisco, but as I had recently been spotting him in every man I saw, especially in the grooms and the men in the coach house, I wasn't sure. Then he embraced the trunk of the tree, as if he wanted to measure it. He remained like that for a while: a colossus, although not a very tall one, embracing another. Was it a coincidence that I liked to walk in those woods where he usually spent his time? I sent the little black girl back home with the dog and the monkey.

He turned around. We looked at each other without blinking. I walked a few paces closer to him, then he approached me. We were separated by the distance of a few thick trees, the branches of which barely touched each other. We looked at each other without moving. He took a few fast steps toward me, stopped, took me by the hand and set off walking again, dragging me behind him exactly as a father might do with a naughty little girl.

"Come on, there!" he grunted, menacingly.

He frightened and pleased me.

"Come on, come on!" he said and pushed me through the door into the little house he had his studio in.

In the cool, damp room there were a few canvases covered with pieces of cloth. Once again he looked me straight in the eyes, and smiled with a satisfaction full of malice. He surely read the terror in my face, the feeling that I had fallen into a trap and that, nonetheless, I felt all right there. The man laughed in an . . . animal-like way, I would say. Then, he really did make me afraid.

"Here!"

And with a violent gesture he tore off the cloth that covered one of the canvases. It represented an *aquelarre*, a witches' sabbath, presided over by an enormous phantasmagorical billy goat. The witches' faces were blurred. Only one had clear-cut features: I recognized my own face.

I was unable to control myself. My blood was boiling. I was eaten up by the desire to rip up the canvas with a knife, to destroy it with my bare hands, to spit on it. Furious, I glanced at the painter. He wasn't looking at me. In front of his work, he had forgotten me. Resplendent, he examined his picture, the masterpiece he had created. The fury and the terror ceased. But the joy, too. I looked at him again: this man was ignoring me, he was alone with his creation. Puzzled, I went over to another canvas, and, little by little so as not to disturb him, I uncovered it.

Two women, young and beautiful; a man with an expression of total surrender on his face hands a generous bunch of grapes to the dark one. The blonde one, with her gray eyes, watches him with tenderness. Envy and generosity come together in her face. The dark one feels honored: she knows that from now on the man's heart belongs to her. A little boy, a brown angel, takes a grape from the basket. It is Javier, Francisco's son. The blonde one is his wife, Josefa. The dark one is myself, rejuvenated, enhanced, good-looking. The man with the expression of surrender, who gives up his person together with the grapes, is Francisco.

The painter has forgiven me, then. He has managed to forget my madness the other night. How has he been able to do that?

Another canvas. A *majo*, covered by a cape, walks with a *maja*. From all directions, other men stick their heads out of the undergrowth to look voluptuously at the girl. She, however, has eyes only for her *majo*, and turns to him with a seductive expression; her body seems to dance instead of walk. But she has no need to make an effort in order to captivate her escort. Although his face is not visible, it is clear: his posture shows that he is smitten by the girl. The *maja* is myself, I recognize my smile, my behavior, and my posture, a little strange—no one knows that I have always had to hide a physical blemish. The *majo*, who seems violent, but underneath is a mass of tenderness, is him, Francisco. I recognize him under his cape.

What I had seen was quite enough for me. Yet, the painter was still enthralled by his own work. I slipped out as lightly as if I had grown wings.

The sessions started a few weeks later. My husband was usually present because he appreciated Francisco as an artist, loved him as a person, and got on well with him. Godoy, who had come to visit us, was also present on two occasions. If Rembrandt's *Venus* is an angel, as is that of Titian, then the woman in Francisco's picture is a demon. Each one of her hairs is a poisonous snake that twists convulsively. The expression on her face is imperious, the posture of her body despotic. The innocence of the white of her dress acts as a foil to her perfidious nature. Goya's picture of Venus is the portrait of a monster, of something that is even more inauspicious for being also beauty incarnate. But, only I know that Francisco saw me as I was: a woman lacking protection, so defenseless that she covers her nude body with the black mane of her hair, in an arrogant posture and a way of being that is ceremonious and provocative at the same time. He saw me as an abandoned woman who floats in a vacuum and has nothing to hold on to. Although nearly all Spain belongs to her, she has nothing.

María, María! Where has that damned old woman gone to? Consuelo, I want my *aya* here! What, where has she gone? How shameless of her! Consuelo, go and see her and ask her what happened after the summer at Piedrahíta, when the royal painter painted me dressed in white with a red sash. Run, my memory is slipping!

My husband was proud of that portrait. He organized soirees in which first he played the harpsichord, then invited everyone to dinner, and after coffee and liqueurs, as the culmination of the evening's entertainment, he gathered the guests in the salon to show them my portrait. On the opposite wall hung the portrait that Goya had painted of him, of Don José, Marquis of Villafranca. People cried out in their enthusiasm and, who was it that day? Osuna perhaps? Somebody said, amid the silence that fell after the exclamations: "What an ideal couple, the Duchess of Alba and the Marquis of Villafranca! How they resemble each other, what a match! It doesn't surprise me that they live in perfect harmony together."

In more than one face I saw a grimace of mockery.

I replied: "Now then, dearest friend! How could I compete with my husband? I have the face of a wild animal, though not as much as you do, my dearest, whereas Don José has the eyes of a deer, which are nothing if not the expression of his soul."

That is what I thought then of José, yes. Osuna had to shut up; José shone.

But I didn't think that when they engaged me to him at the age of eleven, and married me to him when I was thirteen. At that time I was standing in front of the altar next to Mama and her bridegroom. Any man there seemed to me to be more masculine than my bony scarecrow with his big brown eyes. Even Miguelito, the son of our laundrywoman, had bigger muscles. Oh, how I loved playing with him in the granary! We took off our clothes and then swam together in the grain. One day I told my grandfather about our games and he quoted me something so beautiful I've remembered it ever since. A philosopher, Diderot, I think, told him:

> L'habit de la nature, c'est la peau,
> plus on s'éloigne de ce vêtement
> plus on pèche contre le gout.

That is how I wrote it down and I took it seriously. I spent my wedding night with Miguelito in the granary. We swam nude among the corn, even though it was very cold. When my friends came to see me, I usually received them in the nude, following the advice of the French philosopher regarding good taste, and when the girls were frightened and about to flee, I made them a present of that wise sentence and added that I would dress myself with my hair, so as not to alarm them. At that time my hair reached down to my knees. But I never received Don José like that. Soon, he stopped coming to visit me and preferred to spend nights playing the piano and the harpsichord, the viola and the violin. Only after a long time did I receive him, almost fully dressed because I find men's bodies repulsive. I wanted a little child to play with, but he was unable to give me one. He wasn't even capable of doing that.

"Hey Consuelo, what does my *aya* say?"

"Milady, Doña María says that she is ashamed to answer your question."

"Wonderful, let her be ashamed, the pious thing. But did she give you an answer or didn't she?"

"Milady, she says that after you came back from Piedrahíta you became friends with Don Manuel de Godoy, the *Príncipe de la Paz*."

"Heavens, was it then? Yes, it's true. At that time I wanted to kill two birds with one stone, and the only thing I managed to achieve was to injure myself. Go, go, don't bother me now, girl."

Finally! How hard it is to get rid of these gossipmongers. It was at a soiree in my palace. I had very few candles lit. My husband played Haydn for the guests and he managed to make me sad. I realized that year after year my life was slipping away, years lived uselessly, without aim, without emotion. Nothing attracted me, nobody needed me. I sang *tonadillas*, I acted in plays, people applauded me, admired my beauty and my talent, but none of that meant anything to me. That evening Don José played, no, in fact it wasn't Haydn; he was playing something on the viola. I think it was Marin Marais, *Les Folies d'Espagne*. The same melody was repeated, grew like a wave, and then suddenly settled back again to rise quickly into a crescendo. Godoy stood behind my chair and whispered into my ear that never had any woman, that the affection he felt for me . . . that because of me he had neglected affairs of state . . . that I, that I, that I . . .

In short, the most common sort of praise. At the same time he tickled me in the most delicious fashion on the nape of my neck as he played with my necklace. My melancholy began to fade and I began to have the feeling that I was in heaven, full of music and of words and caresses.

The king and queen were seated in the first row according to protocol, and Godoy should have been seated next to María Luisa, as prime minister and her prime lover. But he had stood up to move away from her and approach the wall behind me. After a while the queen turned—the salon glittered with the brilliance of her jewels, so much so it seemed as if the candles had gone out—she saw everything. She went red with anger while I put on a listless expression so that my dear María Luisa should have no doubt about what was happening. Godoy became alarmed and wanted to go back to his seat, but I made him burn up inside with a furtive look that said now or never. He hesitated. I rose a little as if preparing to leave and immediately he nodded: yes, I'm ready. While waiting for me he went red as a prawn and his fingers ran over my skin with greater strength. He caressed my naked shoulders under my hair. My mother-in-law, dressed as ever in a ubiquitous pearl gray with platinum around her neck and silver in her hair, turned toward me to whisper that after the music we would dine with their majesties king and queen in a small group, but maybe I didn't hear her. The music was reaching its culmination, the wave grew. The music gave me strength. I got up, making a signal to Don Manuel. As he followed me, he reddened and paled by turn. I left a message for my husband saying I felt indisposed and that Don Manuel had been called away unexpectedly and needed to leave most urgently. So the intimate dinner with their majesties did not take place in order to avoid a somewhat uncomfortable situation in which two of the main heroes would be missing, the tenor and the soprano, and what was more, each from a different duo. The king, who never understood anything, didn't understand what was happening then either. I can imagine him perfectly, patting my husband on the back and saying how it was high time they played together, while Don José bit his lip—first from imagining the clumsy king in comparison to his refined fingers, which didn't play so much as produce magic, and second, when he realized the reason why his wife and the queen's lover were missing after the concert.

Once in my chambers, the spell that I had been under a moment before disappeared altogether, but I attended Godoy's amorous petition. The hope that I was hurting the queen with my action was a consolation to me. What was more, in some hidden corner of my soul I was feeding the illusion that Francisco, who had not come to any supper or musical evening at my little salon in the Moncloa, was a friend of Don Manuel. I had no reason to believe that Godoy was not discreet, and I hoped that this juicy piece of social news would reach Francisco's ear and if it didn't hurt him, that it would at least graze him. Graze him, the only man who did not respond to my challenges. The untamable man.

On the afternoon of the following day my chambermaid brought me an ochre-colored envelope which contained a letter.

Ma bien aimée,

Je vous supplie de souper avec moi ce soir après mon concert, vers minuit. For our intimate little supper I have ordered one of your favorite dishes to be prepared. If I could, I would have gone personally to fish oysters to serve them on your dish, and with them deposit a beautiful pearl on your knees. *Une perle qui ne pourrait en rien rivaliser avec vôtre beauté car vous êtes la plus ravissante des créatures.* We will have dinner in my little salon without servants; only you, adored one, and me. I hope that you will honor me with the pleasure of spending the day today looking forward to this charming *repas en tête à tête, notre petit souper intime que votre présence rendra inoubliable.*

José, votre époux qui vous adore
un peu plus chaque jour

We were sitting in the blue salon, lit by a single candelabra. The round table was covered in dishes full of exquisite food. Don José personally served the champagne. That evening I drank little, I was wary. Halfway through the dinner, what I had been afraid of happened.

"Adorable, let us make a toast now to my new projects, which from this evening on, I would like to share with you."

Why doesn't he speak clearly, why so much formality?

"To our journey, *ma chérie!*" And then he looked me straight in the eyes and said, slowly: "Venice and Vienna—I would like to present you à mon cher ami Joseph Haydn, to show you off a little, and to get to know his most recent works and play them for you, *mon âme*.

I concentrated on the oysters to keep my eyes lowered and so hide my perplexity. How could I go away on a journey just now, when any day I expected my strategy with Godoy to prove its worth? What would Francisco think? He would only come to one conclusion: that I had taken Godoy as my official lover and left him in the lurch. He would forget me; he would find a lover or get back together with his wife. And when I got back, no matter how much effort I made, reheated love would be more difficult to digest than a dish of stewed tripe left over from the day before. No, there was no way that I could leave now!

"Don José, my dear! Your invitation honors me. But I have a better idea. Let us put off our excursion to Vienna some six months. Let us wait for the snow to melt in barbarous central Europe and let the cold diminish. Let us organize, for now, a journey to our holdings in Andalusia. Let's go to the south, to springtime! Your delicate health would appreciate it."

To Seville, Cadiz, or to Sanlúcar de Barrameda, where I could invite Francisco, perhaps with the excuse of a new portrait. Or I could find him a commission myself!

"No, Teresa, *cariño mio*. My decision has been made. It will be Vienna and that is it. Let us talk of it no longer."

He wanted to take me away from my world, why doubt it? Perhaps he was jealous of Godoy? That would surprise me. His sensitivity regarding human relationships would surely tell him that a puppet such as Godoy, crude and superficial, could only really please a person as ordinary as the queen. Perhaps he had guessed something about Francisco? No, because nothing had happened. Or had he noticed the depth of my affections for that painter who was already mature, and had realized that it had nothing to do with my usual coquettishness?

"I would love to satisfy your desires, *mon cher époux*, even though, given the state of your health, a journey of this nature *signifie una grave impudence*. However, it is not possible. Soon it will be carnival time and for Mardi Gras I am holding a masquerade ball in the Moncloa. The invitations have already gone to press, apart from the fact that I have already invited many people personally. For this occasion, the dressmakers have prepared a costume for me of a kind that has never been seen before in Spain. It is almost finished. *Je suis désolée, mon cher, mais il m'est absolument impossible de quitter l'Espagne maintenant.* And now, forgive me, but I must go, my head feels heavy. Have them prepare an infusion, *una tisane de verveine*. À propos, I advise you, dear José, to pay attention to what I say. Go to Seville where spring has just begun, as you haven't been feeling very well lately. I will come and see you there often, *parole d'honneur*. We will repeat *ces petits soupers intimes*. It will be wonderful."

Once in my room, I undressed without the assistance of the chambermaid. I drank the infusion in front of the mirror and thought that I would not go to Vienna, not even at the risk of a serious disagreement with my husband and his mother.

✦

Consuelo! Have them prepare me *una tisane de verveine*. Serve it in the sixteenth-century Japanese tea set, yes, the white one with a touch of pink.

José, in the end, went to Seville. He was ill. I stayed in Madrid because it was ball season. Carnival was coming up.

The masquerade ball! I wore a dress which even the most daring of the *maja*s would never have worn. But for carnival, everything is permitted! The dress was designed in such a way that Francisco, if he came to the ball, could only recognize me from the décolletage. I danced with many young men, and also with Godoy, who couldn't take his eyes off my décolletage and didn't stop pushing me into a corner, like a common village bumpkin! I freed myself from his grasp by reaching out for another glass of champagne. And another, and more. I didn't want to dance with just anyone; I was looking for stocky men. I observed one of them. It might be him. I kissed him, another, and another. I kissed all of them for a long time. How to know a man: by his kiss. We danced. A new roundish man took me from the arms of a young man. I had drunk too much champagne, my head was spinning. The dancer supported me, then he left the crowd with me, holding me firmly by the waist so that I didn't fall. Once in the corridor, I stumbled on my dress and my dancing partner pressed me against him, but I bent over like a stalk holding a too-heavy flower. My partner had an unusual custom: he didn't stop looking me in the eyes. Only the eyes, not like Godoy. I didn't understand a thing, but I felt lighthearted. Suddenly Godoy, of all people, discovered me and pulled me out of the arms of the short, strong man to take me away. But I kept on feeling the arms of the unknown man around my body.

No, don't put it on the bedside table, girl. Leave it for me here, on the low table, that's right. Thank you, Consuelo, I don't need you anymore.

The following morning the maid brought the hot chocolate to my bed, together with an envelope that was larger than usual. I found a drawing inside, without any letter or note: a woman in a mask, dressed like a *maja*, and in front of her a man leans forward and looks into her eyes; around them is a group of masked men, drawn to look repulsive. And a title that read: *Nadie se conoce*. The title meant that people don't recognize each other, but also that they don't even know themselves. An ambiguous title. And what do these repulsive men, these monsters, standing around, mean?

In the evening a new envelope arrived of the same size with another drawing: a very beautiful woman with naked breasts was half-sitting, half-lying across a man's knees. Her head, with eyes half-open, was bent down like a broken ear of corn. The man is wringing his hands and wailing, his desperation limitless. Title: *Tántalo*. Tantalus, the king whom the gods punished by surrounding him with paradisical fruits, which when he tried to pick them, moved away. Temptation is offered and then immediately denied. There is no doubt: the man is him, the features of the face are his. The woman, who lies across his knees, showing her marvelous breast, is me. It is my face, my figure, my hair. And now I realize that the posture of the body in the drawing is the same as that of the clothed *maja* and the nude *maja*.

Two drawings.

Francisco the courtesan, who reproaches his lady for not recognizing him.

Francisco Tantalus, who desires the tempting fruits that are forbidden to him.

"María, bring me my husband's letters. I keep them in the alcove."

"But all the correspondence which Your Highness received from the Marquis of Villafranca is in the bottom drawer of the bedside table!"

"Is it? Well then, give me the letters. Just the last packet. Yes, they are from him. Let's see, one of the last, chosen at random."

Seville, April 1796

My dearest,

Your Madame de Sévigné wrote to her absent daughter: *"Il faut se consoler en vous écrivant."* I identify completely with these words; writing to you is my only consolation, my only joy.

This time I am unable to write anything new to you, but just what I always write: that I miss you, that I see you in all women, in all young and beautiful women. But I do not want my words to influence you in any way. I know perfectly well that you have been through the period of dances and carnival and that you, as always, have been the most admired woman in Spain. I trust that you take pleasure from this, my love. I really do not want you to change anything because of my letters full of longing. I wish this for you from the bottom of my heart, I give you my word of honor. I only ask of you that, even if occasionally, you write me a few lines or a few words and nothing more, just so that I know you remember me sometimes. Is this a selfish request? Yes it is. Is it blackmail? Yes, it is. Do forgive me, my darling.

For me you are a dream, always very brief but intense enough to stay in my memory and keep me alive. I like to imagine where you are and what you are doing, and I would visit the places where you are with more eagerness than I would the seven wonders of the world. But I am ill, weak, and unable to support a journey to Madrid. What I most desire in all the world is forbidden to me. But what I have lived with you, I keep inside me, and I shall have to make do with that.

It might interest you to know that now I am playing something new. That is to say, new for me. The piece in itself was written a good ten years ago. It is *The Last Seven Words of Christ* by Haydn. It is a commission from the canon of Cadiz cathedral; it was he who gave me this wonderful score. What I prefer most is "The Fourth Word" *largo* in F minor, "Father, father, why have you abandoned me?" impregnated with the most absolute desperation. They are seven minutes of tragedy, tragedy conceived as *adagio, la tragédie maintenue adagio,* that is to say, a real tragedy. Will you allow me to play it for you some day, my love? Would you like to know what it is that I am living? I am sure you would and I am grateful to you. I know that you have always liked my way of playing music. I am well aware that I am not a suitable man for you. You require someone stronger, more masculine, and yet you also have a sharp sense of what art is. I trust that you shall find him and wish this for you from the bottom of my heart.

Beloved, I prefer not to reread what I have just written. I am afraid that I would also destroy this letter, as I have others during the last two weeks. I do not like my style; I do not know how to express myself in a few brief words, as you do. I would know how to say what I feel with music, and what I would know how to do is caress you with a hand that holds no pen or bow. What is to be done with me? Nothing, I will die soon. Let it be a rapid process! But before I go I would like to embrace you still and see myself in your green eyes. I have to tell you that I feel very sad. I haven't felt like this for years. Yesterday I played Haydn's "The Second Word"—*grave cantabile*, which starts with desperation and agony, and reaches hope and recovered health—and found that I was shedding tears that flowed down my cheeks to the neck of my shirt. If you come and see me, as you promised on the day of our supper, I would like to go, just the two of us, for a few days to a place where nothing would distract me from you. I would place you in such a way that you would fill my entire horizon, so that there were nothing in the world except for you.

Have fun my little one, while I remember you from here.

I kiss your hands and forehead.

Your José

Thank you, María, you can take away all the open sheets of paper now. Take Don José's letters to the alcove and put them away carefully, so that none are lost. Burn them after my death, keep the ashes in an urn, and place the urn in my coffin. I won't die? Come on, you mad old woman, deceive the scatterbrained if they let you! Well, go away and let no one enter, understood?

When was it that I first read that letter from my husband? Yes, one day after returning from the theater and dinner. It was in the early morning. I felt like going to bed, and I didn't really understand what my husband was saying to me. I didn't understand why suddenly he had become so sentimental and loving. That year the theater season was exceptionally amusing. I myself often sang the *tonadilla* and the audience's hands practically fell off, they applauded so much. And above all, La Trina, the most celebrated actress in Spain, came to Madrid from Barcelona. Her husband didn't want to let her go, and had requisitioned all her costumes. But even so she came, and I had a set of dresses made for her according to the latest Paris fashions, even more splendid and lavish than those I wore myself. During her visit to our capital, I kept her under my protective wing and could not go to Seville to see Don José. In obedience to my wishes, Goya, the royal painter, painted La Tirana: a divine portrait of a divine woman.

One morning, I had a dream. I was a little girl and was playing with a roe deer who began to die right in my hands. I felt absolutely impotent. I dreamed of its eyes, like two halves of a brown globe, full of tears, eyes that knew everything because the animal was dying.

That day, I ordered the servants to prepare everything necessary so that I could go to Seville. The July heat was exhausting. My friends asked me to think again, saying that it was not a good time to journey to the south, and promised me more amusement with La Tirana and summer nights full of fandango.

I left with the minimum luggage necessary and a few servants. The others were to follow me, bringing the rest of the things with them. I made the coachman gallop through all of Castile. The eyes of the dying roe deer pursued me; I could not stop seeing them in front of me. I did not want to lose so much as a night spent in an inn. We changed horses frequently; my coachmen took turns, and we ran and ran post-haste. Before we got to Cordoba we were recommended to take a detour to avoid bandits. I didn't want to know anything about any detour; the bandits did not frighten me. I promised a double salary to the coachman. We hurtled down the straightest road through a starless night, lit only by a pair of luminous eyes that shone with the last of their brightness. They glittered in the darkness, I am sure of it.

Seville. The palace of the Duke and Duchess of Alba. Reproachful looks. Eyes which placed the guilt on my shoulders. I knew it; I had arrived too late. Surrounded by a cloud of dust from the road I ran to the chambers where José lived. His mother stood in my way, looking at me with disdain, with incriminating hostility. I pushed myself past her to continue on my way.

José was lying in bed, his face and hands a greenish color, an olive shade. I could barely recognize that skeletonlike face with the eyes sunken into dark holes. Very carefully, I stroked the back of his hand. I still did not understand how there could be something so icy in the torrid heat of a Seville July. The face too was a piece of ice. Only the chest retained a little heat, the last remains of life.

"José, my love!" I whispered, desperate. "José, my Jose, say something to me!"

José's eyes were half-open. I wanted to see those roe deer eyes, but his look was glassy. His eyes were not looking at me: they stared, immobile, at the wall opposite. I sat on his bed and curled up. I placed myself in such a way that the faded light in his eyes rested on me. What a cold and impersonal look! Icy as his hands and forehead, icy as perdition and ruin, the end, and death. Those eyes horrified me, those eyes that were turned toward me and did not see me. I got up. Was that really him, that cold, unknown, strange object? What had the tender warmth of his letters turned into, the delicate life of his hands, that had engendered so much beauty in music, the solitary beat of his heart that I—oh, how I regretted it!—had not wanted to accompany.

"José, my love!" I threw myself on him. "You can't do this to me, José! You can't do this to me, no!"

Exhausted, I sat on the bed again. My head felt empty. My eyes rested on something that was on the bedside table. A letter.

It was from Joseph Haydn. My letter was not there. How could it have been, if I hadn't written any to him? But in the end, what could I have told him? *Les petites bagatelles de la vie des salons?* Haydn's letter began: "*Mon tres cher ami José*" and informed him that he was working on his oratorio *La Création*. He hoped that this would be his masterpiece and enclosed a few pages of the score so that José should give his view. My José had been judging the work of the greatest of living composers!

"José," I shook his body, light as that of a little boy. At that moment I had the feeling that it wasn't my husband who had died but my son, a boy to whom I had never paid enough attention, a child for whom I had never wanted to sacrifice anything, in the same way that my mother never paid attention to me.

"José! I am with you, I am here. I have come just as I promised you! You wanted to go with me someplace to be alone together. Let us go then now, let us go!"

The body, like a rag doll, fell back on the pillow. I thought of my first doll, which I transformed into my mother, how it floated of its own accord in the bath while one piece of cloth after another emerged from its belly. I thought of my father in his coffin, of my grandfather, my aunt, my stepfather, my mother. Why did everyone abandon me? At that moment I understood why my grandfather had married me off so young. He sensed that everyone would abandon me and had looked for someone who would protect me. He could have found no man better than José, I am sure of it. José, who admired me at a distance and in his generosity, wished me to have my amusements. How I would like to be with him now, to hear him play the harpsichord and the piano—one was an instrument of the past, the other an instrument of the future, he used to say. We would have gone together to visit Joseph Haydn. José would have been proud of me, and I would have been proud of his talent. But nothing was possible any longer. The time you have not lived is dead forevermore.

Some time earlier, in the period when my roe deer died, my life became full. It was able to become full because until then it had been empty. It was in the eyes of the tender animal, full of tears, that I learned to see the world in vivid colors. Now, when José's deer eyes closed, life became empty once more and the world, empty of meaning. And now I was alone. An orphan, abandoned. All living beings were against me.

"José you can't do this to me!"

"Madame!" The icy voice of José's mother, up until then my only ally, interrupted my lament. "Madame, your mourning clothes are ready. It is time that you changed and prepared yourself to receive the condolences of visitors."

The next day I had another dream. I remember it quite clearly. It was the day that they took the coffin to Monasterio de Jerónimos de San Isidro del Campo. No one went up to the deceased; the decomposition had started and, in the Andalusian July heat, was simply dreadful. I wished to melt into that smell, to impregnate myself with it. The Marquess of Villafranca said to me, in an icy voice I had never heard her use before, "You are a true witch, and you provoke horror." She herself looked like a dead woman; her face and hair and skin had taken on an ashen hue. She did not want to live after the death of her son. That is love. Yes, that day I knew what love was. I, a witch.

That night, I had a curious dream. The roe deer of my childhood came to see me. It dragged itself up to me with the last of its strength. It was full of scratches, with one mortal wound next to the other. I was absolutely astonished: I suddenly realized that it was I who had caused those wounds. I embraced it and helped it, but it died in my arms. Miguelito got ready to bury it; the animal had its eyes wide open and in those globes full of tenderness I read an accusation.

"Miguel, I don't want you to bury my roe deer!" I shouted.

But the boy continued as if he had not heard me.

"Miguel, no!" I wanted to yell, but I couldn't. My voice could not leave my throat.

I cut off my legs, put them into a sack, and set about burying them. And then the other parts of my body. Miguelito looked at me questioningly, while caressing the animal's head.

"Miguel, if you go on, I will bury all of myself!" I said in a hoarse voice.

Miguelito smiled and went on burying the roe deer, while I cut off one part of my body after another, and, wrapping them in sackcloth, I buried them. When only the neck and the head were left, I looked around and in the nearest mountains I saw all kinds of people. No, in fact they weren't people but rather human mouths that laughed like crazy people with a noisy echo. When they stopped laughing, each of those figures beat its wings and took off. The sky darkened. The monsters flew toward me, and wanted to peck at me with their curved beaks. Suddenly I grew a pair of wings, and from the neck down I turned into a bird. I tried to fly away to escape the pecking, but my attempts to get off the ground were useless. I was stuck to it as if I had grown roots as well as wings.

I woke up bathed in sweat.

María, María! Have Consuelo come here, so that she can set my pillow straight. No, I don't want you to do it. What have we got that woman for? Have her bring clean sheets. I hope she's put dried thyme on them so they smell like a summer meadow. And have her change my nightgown. I want to put on the lilac one with ivory-colored lace. Have her fix my hair and put wild flowers, daisies, forget-me-nots in it, whatever is on hand. And you, meanwhile, uncover the harpsichord and call José Antonio. He's there. Good. And I want Piti to sing. You can invite a few people to the concert, not many. I don't want crowds of people in here. Just before the concert—come on, come on, everybody in! And once the concert is over, move, come on, out, quick! No useless chatter. Shake your head should anyone ask me about my health or if I feel better, or say that I look a lot better. Otherwise, I shall throw something at them, and at you too. Draw the curtains of my bed so that I may listen and not see anyone. I want *Ariadna a Naxos*, by Haydn, to be played and sung. Is that clear?

After José's death, I played different pieces by Haydn most of all. I myself sung many of the arias. Music offered me some consolation. Then I also discovered the score of Monteverdi's *Il lamento d'Arianna*. Every day I sang, or gave orders to have sung, the aria "Lasciate me morire" from that piece, which awoke in me a strange and sad voluptuousness. In fact, I suffocated my bad feelings in music, just as poor José had done. Are not all us mortals the same as one another? From Monteverdi I passed on to Haydn's *Ariadna*, much more realistic. After so many weeks of singing it, I could have organized a concert to sing it without having to be ashamed of my performance. And in the end I sang only the last song of the series, the most cheerful. How could I forget it?

Hurt me no more, pain of my heart,
I have not the strength to suffer;
may the mourning time be far from me,
I do not wish my heart to beat so.

Approach now, daughter of the sea,
may love come with you to seek pleasure
the graces will also come with you
the dance shall delight the sure of foot.

Like this at all times will I be able
to spend a pleasing time and will not mourn;
sadness will be with me no longer
and the grieved heart shall breathe.

I sang and while singing I felt like living again. I decided that I would abandon Seville, where the entire palace was in mourning and where they had kidnapped José's memory so that nothing was left over for me. I took my carriage, a few servants, and, almost without luggage, I fled. Like a thief! I laughed on the way. I left a few letters behind and nothing else. One I sent urgently to Madrid:

Francisco,
I await you in one of my Andalusian estates, in the Palacio del Rocío near the town of Sanlúcar de Barrameda. At once! Do not allow your coachmen to stop cracking the whip for a moment!

María Teresa

Thank you, Consuelo. Clean clothes make one feel like new. Wait, one more thing. Tell María that I don't want them to play *Ariadna a Naxos*. I would prefer someone to play Vivaldi's *La tempesta di mare* for me. Why? You ask too many questions, girl.

Why, indeed? Well, because I'm not in the mood to listen to Haydn. I want to think about other things. I ran away from Seville at tremendous speed, and my newfound freedom added to my feeling of vertigo. On the way I stopped wherever struck my fancy. Arcos de la Frontera, El Puerto de Santa María, San Fernando, Cadiz—ports in which I walked under the dusty palm trees; amid the crowds of maids and sailors I began to dream once more. I had dresses made for me, many, many dresses, and in the evening while walking I flirted with the officers, but especially with the common sailors. Life came . . . and it was unstoppable. As unstoppable as death when it must come. The sailors looked at me out of the corners of their eyes, straight at me, and I smiled. I am seventeen years old and I am starting to learn what life is, I thought.

One day I had tea with one of them. I had ordered cakes and drinks in abundance and, when it was time to pay, the sailor had to leave his uniform in the café as collateral. He didn't have enough money on him, poor thing! How I laughed watching him get out of there as fast as his legs could carry him in his under-clothing and nothing else! The next day, I invited him to come to my palace at Cadiz, where I was in the service of the Duchess of Alba, so I had told him. He came, and the servants brought him to me. I sat on the podium, covered in gold and fine lace, surrounded by maids and lackeys. The sailor, very much afraid, recognized me and wanted to leave, so frightened was he of the Duchess of Alba. The whole thing made me curl up laughing. I had a special tea prepared for two. We had tea together, and then I accompanied the little lad out to the street and, in one of the dark corridors I pressed myself against him with the full weight of my body so that he could see that the Duchess of Alba was not mean. He left perplexed, red in the face, and confused. And in that moment I decided the time had come to continue the journey again, this time directly to the final destination.

Our dog came out to greet me. What was his name? Gluck, per-haps? No, Gluck didn't jump. It was Sirio. He recognized me, after so much time! He barked and jumped just as he did when he was a puppy. I noticed that from out of the pine wood a huge moon was rising, of an intense yellow, almost red, and I thought that the dog would feel upset at night because the full moon has influence over the sea and animals, on women and artists. And I now saw the Palacio del Rocío, a white palace with Moorish windows, a few servants in front of it, and someone who was coming to receive me walking at a slow pace. A disheveled head on a strong body, fitted into a suit that was too tight . . . My Paco! I didn't think he would come. Francisco was waiting for me. I had lost one man and gained another. One life had finished, another was beginning. It has always been like that, and it was now. Paco! I cried mentally, while he, all confused, kissed my hand.

The bath was already prepared for me. I sank into the scented water and made a mental drawing of what I would do afterwards and how he would behave. I lay there with my body relaxed and thought about Francisco, who now seemed to me to have gotten older, to be stout and ugly, a man who was frankly not attractive at all. But he radiated a closeness that was so great . . . as if he was one of mine, perhaps more than any other person. My Paco, ugly and fat! I looked at my body and jumped out of the bath.

We went for a walk in the Coto de la Doña Ana. First we went into the mountainous part, covered in pines. I wore a comfortable outfit, of the kind the village girls wear, and Francisco a suit, which squeezed him like a corset. I didn't feel at all tired after the journey. We walked fast, we almost ran as if pursued by a herd of elephants.

"I would like to offer you my most sincere condolences for the death of the Marquis of Villafranca."

"Thank you."

He observed me, with a questioning look. A doubt. "Was it terrible, his death?"

"I appreciate your having thought about it. But life, is that not terrible too?" I replied.

A doubt was trembling, clearly visible in those green eyes. A suspicion.

"More than death?"

"What is death in comparison with an incomplete life?" I answered him with a question. The suspicion in his eyes had turned into an incrimination.

"Is there anyone whose life is not incomplete, in the end?"

"You yourself," I answered, tersely. An accusatory look sprung up in his eyes like the spire of a cathedral.

"What makes you think that?"

"You have a reason for living," I said with conviction.

"As do you, your duenna, and your deceased husband."

"You paint."

"I paint? Hmm. I try to earn my daily bread, as do most men, in fact."

"You are an artist."

"You do not know how many things I have to take in silence from aristocrats like yourself in order to earn my living with what I like doing."

"You, take anything in silence? With your character? I don't believe it."

After a moment's pause I insisted: "You are an artist, you have a mission."

"What do you mean, I have a mission? I am an artisan, and I do my job in the best way I can."

"You are not an artisan. Artisans do not interest me. You are an artist."

"In the end, perhaps you too are an artist, an artist of life."

"What does an artist of life mean?"

"To live off what we have in the here and now," he said, slowing down.

From time to time he kicked the little pine cones that covered the ground of the wood.

"I pursue something absolute, that is to say, undefined. The closer I get to it, the faster it runs away from me. As I want to have everything, I will never have anything."

The suspicion in his eyes had given way to a reflective look. I longed for him to tell me something about life. He had to tell me, he was fifteen, twenty years older than I! But he talked about painting. For him life was painting.

"There are no rules in painting," he said, "and the oppression or the servile obligation of having young people study or go all in the same direction is a great impediment for them and for all those who profess this difficult art, which is diviner than any other given that it signifies what God has created."

The moon had already travelled far enough to be directly over our heads. I felt that it shone for us alone. Now we were walking slowly over the sand of the Guadalquivir. I took off my shoes. The painter fell silent and I listened to the music that was weeping in some distant place. It was a flute. I pointed it out to the painter. He didn't hear it. I sighed. He was so involved in his own reflections that he didn't even notice that his new shoes were sinking into the sand. In silence, I pointed at the moon. The man leaned back so as to contemplate the sky.

"What profound and impenetrable mystery is hidden in the imitation of divine nature, without which nothing is good, and not only in painting!"

I listened to the enthusiastic tone of his voice and the flute that accompanied it. I thought once more of Madame du Châtelet and her reflections on happiness. Truly rich and noble people who have been used to comfort all their lives do not know how to savor happiness and even less, how to find it. On the other hand these . . . these men and women from the villages, the *majos* and *majas*, know happiness. Why, indeed, do I look at Francisco as if he was an uncultured donkey? Paco, a coarse and brutal man? No, it is I who wishes to see him like this. If I saw him as a refined intellectual, the magic would disappear. I would begin to find him dull.

"I see nothing more than bodies and forms which are illuminated, and bodies and forms that are not," he went on, looking at the cypress and pines, which shone as if someone had poured a basin full of mercury over them.

"Dimensions that move forward and dimensions that fall back; reliefs and depths. My sight never discovers lines or details. I do not count the hairs on the beard of the passerby or the number of buttons on his suit, and my brush must not see any better than I do."

"That is true, but why do you tell me this right now, Don Francisco?"

"I tell you that nature is the only master of a painter and any other artist. Unlike nature, the candid masters see details in the whole and their details are always false and conventional. Nature is the only drawing master ..."

He did not know how to tell me what I wanted to hear. Why did he insist on not seeing me as a woman? In that enchanted moment, his monologue on art seemed to be sterile. Why, art was nothing in comparison to what we were living! I had the feeling that he was younger than I. Perhaps I would grow tired of him very soon. Nonetheless, I envied the fact that he had something to live for.

He spoke to me of Aragon, of the desert of stones in which he had grown up. He described the white nuances of the Aragonese sky to me and I found myself, instead of in a pine wood flooded by moonlight, in thirsty, stony terrain whipped by wind and forever implacable.

"Whenever I feel distressed," he said, "which is something that happens to me fairly often, I feel like an animal that is sinking into that Aragonese sand and wants to save itself, but does nothing except sink ever deeper. It pants, but the sand spills up over and drowns him."

"You feel like an animal?"

"Like a dog."

We walked for a while in silence. I wanted to tell him about the roe deer of my childhood and of the dreams in which it reappears. But when I looked at him, I ran once more into a wall of suspicion. I said nothing.

"The death of a person close to us makes us more human," I

said, instead of telling my story. But, did I really say it or do I just think I did? Yes, at the time I was silent. It was he who spoke.

"The death of a person close to us makes death intimate . . . It surprises us how we can live with so many deaths all around us."

I wanted to protest, but he looked at me in such a way as to indicate that I had no right to talk of such things.

"Don Francisco, why have you come here?"

"If only I knew!"

"You don't know?"

"No."

I touched his hand.

"I am happy that you don't know."

Suddenly I felt like a hot air balloon from which ten bags of sand have been thrown and which goes up and up. To better concentrate on my thoughts, I asked him about his painting. He began to talk about it at length; I put my hand under his arm. He probably didn't notice. Words and more words poured out of him.

"What a scandal it is to despise nature in comparison to the Greek statues, if the comparison is done by one who knows neither one thing nor the other. What form of statue can there be that was not copied from divine nature? No matter how excellent a professor he is who has made the copy, will he cease shouting that one is the work of god and the other of our miserable hands?"

I wasn't listening to him with any particular interest, and if I asked him a question from time to time, it was to make conversation.

"Don Francisco, why don't you seek inspiration in the Greek masters? Did they not create beauty?"

"I shall explain this at once to Your Highness."

"My name is María Teresa."

"Madam, he who wishes to distance himself from nature . . ."

We were returning along the bank of the Guadalquivir. No, I didn't want to distance myself from nature. I felt the muscles of his arms; I heard the melody of his words and the sounds of the flute.

The moon moved into the other half of the sky. Now it was shining like an old silver trinket. It pushed against my back and made me walk with a light step. Francisco sank into the wet sand of the riverbank.

The moon had set earlier. The servants were already asleep. I took him into the kitchen; he preferred a modest ambience, given that as a good Aragonese peasant, elegance and sumptuousness, dazzled him. We found some wine of an extremely dark red color, olives, and cheese. Francisco was hungry and I served him more and more wine. He made jokes, laughed. Now it was he who wasn't listening to me. When he drank, he heard even less than he usually did. I also savored that rustic wine with a smattering of oak wood in its taste. Time came to a halt.

Suddenly, I noticed that the kitchen began to fill with a pinkish light. After blowing out the candle I went out into the garden and bathed in the first light of the sun, which still hadn't come out. Francisco followed me with the carafe of wine and a glass. I sat on the swing that hung from the branches of two enormous eucalyptus trees. He swung me, so strongly that the trees shuddered and my skirt flew up over my head. He sat on the lawn and watched me; from time to time he took a sip. Now, finally, he was looking at me like a man. Avidly. He sat and contemplated me, in ecstasy. But then the painter in him woke up and his look took on an edge that was more analytic, aesthetic, and dreamy. I threw one shoe at him and then the other; he caught them in midair, waking up from his dreaminess. I jumped to the ground to run back to the house with him behind me. I went up the stairs, we chased each other through the corridors. Then I entered the alcove of my bedroom and sat on the sofa. He lay down there, resting his head in my lap.

"I am completely drunk!"

I caressed his disheveled hair with the palm of my hand.

"What are you going to do with a drunk?" he shouted.

I put fingers over his lips so that he fell silent. He still wanted to say something. He didn't stop laughing, but I didn't take my hand away. I pressed against his lips with my fingers. I released the pressure as he calmed down. Suddenly I felt something wet in my palm: it was his lips which were taking me, all of me. At length, avidly. Insatiably.

When, after a long time, I opened my eyes, my bedroom was full of sunlight.

"Drunks have to sleep. Come on, get out! Sleep off your hangover!"

I pushed him into the corridor, drunk as he was, and not just with wine. I locked the door. That unexpected happiness did not allow me to sleep anymore.

There was no sign of him all day. He didn't turn up for dinner.

I went to bed, but could not get to sleep. I tried to make out all the sounds I could hear. I lit the candle.

Then the door opened. I pretended to sleep. I know that he observed me for quite a while. Then, delicately, he took off my summer nightgown, and looked at me once more. I felt him kissing my feet; he started at the toes. He did so slowly, like a drunk eager for more wine. Interminably, as he had done with the palm of my hand the day before. I dug my nails into the bed. He took a long time to reach up from my feet to my lips.

Every day in the evening we went to look at the sunset on the coast of Sanlúcar. I dressed like a *maja*; Francisco wore peasant's trousers, a shirt and a waistcoat, and always brought along a sketching block and a pencil. He drew the fishermen and the *majas* who flirted with them, children with their mothers, people's faces. He was beautiful when he drew, and happy. I let myself be charmed, looking at him framed in the last rays of the sun which dyed his hair an orange color, and watching the people from the village who, in the twilight, looked like orchids. I enjoyed the present moment, looking forward to the evening, the night, the awakening. I didn't think about what would happen afterward, the future had ceased to exist. I didn't want to spoil those moments thinking about the meaning of my life and about what I could give people and the world. In this way, I was able to be happy. The awareness that I was filling the man drawing beside me with happiness was enough for me. There is no other happiness, I knew it, I know.

After the sun had set, we walked along the harbor, out of the town, in silence, absorbed in the nature around us that was preparing to sleep, and we listened to the tranquility. Amid the silence and the hot, dark air, we were visited by desire. Oh, that southern air, salty and sweet at the same time, which at nighttime still holds the perfume of the sun and decomposing fish and seaweed! That air would revive me, even now when death surrounds me. In that air I would be cured, yes, but only if he were there, if everything could be as it was then.

One day, in the evening, Francisco complained about the mugginess. I told him that women do not suffer so much: the light and transparent cloths that we wear uncover us and let the air run along our skin. Francisco, in his obtuseness, didn't understand anything, so I stepped ahead of him and, with my back to him, I hitched up my skirt and petticoats to show him my nakedness which the air could caress. I stayed like that for a while; after a moment, I turned my head and gave him a fleeting, teasing glance. He was as still as if he had been turned to stone, and looked at me as if stunned. And when he had recovered a little I understood that he was trying to engrave that image in his memory. Only after a little while did he start to chase me. He took me in a wild, fast way, and was eager to go back home already. Once there, he went straight to his improvised studio.

After a long time, he went down to the kitchen, served himself a large glass of wine, and cut himself a piece of cheese.

Another day, I was sitting, nude, next to the fountain in the park of the palace and pouring water over myself. It was siesta time and everybody was resting. I thought I was alone and, intoxicated by the sun, the air, and Sanlúcar's shining white sky, I sat with my legs open and played with the water, my body, my hair. Suddenly something moved in the undergrowth and I saw Francisco's disheveled head.

"Susanna in the bath," I laughed.

"Susanna and the old men," he answered.

"Who is the other old man?"

"I am both one and the other," he replied, devouring the image with his painter's eyes. He took me up in his arms and carried me to the grass amid the pines. But he left soon so as to place on paper the image that he had kept inside him. Meanwhile I woke up my chambermaid so that she could clean away the thorns that had gotten stuck to my back.

The days went by. We went horseback riding; through the rays of low morning suns, we headed for the little chapel of Nuestra Señora del Rocío. On other days we reached the bright white villages splashed with women in black—Almonte, Sanlúcar, Coria del Río. Each time, we came back home full of beautiful impressions. Francisco grew fond of making expeditions to the lagoon of Santa Ollala and decided to paint it. He placed me in front of one of the streams that run into it. I soon grew impatient standing still. I preferred to ride, to walk, or to have tea on the sand while he drew with his fingers. I inscribed the words SÓLO GOYA there. From time to time I went back to renew the inscription after the wind had erased it. Francisco saw it and included it in a picture in which there is a tree with silky branches, a sandy stream near the lagoon. On the sandy bank, however, there is a human figure. The Muslims fear the representation of the human figure. For that reason, in their paintings the human element is missing. And, like them, I also believed, superstitiously, that if Francisco placed me in his picture, something would go wrong.

María, don't spy on me from behind the door. Come in and tell me if you remember the milky light of Sanlúcar in which, at twilight, particles of golden dust glided. You don't remember? How is that possible? You're a silly old thing. You remember all my headaches, my pain and suffering, my jealousy and my dissatisfaction, and yet happiness has fled from your memories? Nobody is interested in happy love affairs. And the same thing happens to you as to the rest: when lovers overcome all obstacles, they are no longer good to play. The performance is over. Go away, go away, you silly old thing.

We didn't want to know anything about the world, but the world had decided that it would not leave us in peace. Francisco received letters with commissions from his customers. He answered them, putting everything off for an indefinite period of time. I received messages from the court, in which they called for me to present myself there urgently. My mother-in-law, the Marquess of Villafranca, wrote me especially strict letters. I had to return so as to observe the period of mourning prescribed by etiquette, she told me. I ordered my lady-in-waiting to answer these letters, saying that I was not well and would be indisposed for some time. One day in early December, Francisco received a letter from Madrid, from his wife. She complained that she had not seen her husband for a long time, that their youngest daughter had fallen ill, and that she was all alone with all the children. Would she have to find herself in that situation over Christmas too? She asked her husband to come home as soon as possible.

I did not abandon Francisco when my husband was dying. Now, Francisco ought to have done the same as I did then, less than a year ago. But he got his baggage ready to depart urgently for Madrid.

"Francisco, if you leave me now, you will never see me again," I told him.

He mumbled something about the responsibility he felt for his family and continued getting his things ready.

"Very well. This is what you want. Today you have seen me for the last time."

I locked myself in my chambers. In the morning I got up before dawn. I was sure that, in the end, Francisco would be incapable of leaving, that he would stay with me, for me. It didn't happen like that. He had already left, the evening of the previous day.

Never will I forgive him for leaving that day. I understand him: by leaving, he hoped to turn himself into the master of the situation, to enslave me completely. And I allowed him to do it. I, who had been brought up in an atmosphere of liberty, equality, and fraternity, with the spirit of freedom, just as Rousseau had wanted it for men. Francisco's image pursued me wherever

I went. I imagined him with his wife, whom he never stopped loving and whom he appreciated more than any other person.

Although my *aya* María wanted to convince me not to, I could not do otherwise; immediately I sent him a letter:

Come back at once. I am gravely ill.

María Teresa

I myself gave the letter to the messenger so that he made a superhuman effort and flew like the wind, to catch up with Francisco on the way and make him come back.

It was all in vain. He didn't come back. No, I will never forgive him that. That Christmas a lukewarm, pleasant sun made the days cheerful, but I saw in front of me just the cold darkness. I didn't leave the house. The aristocrats and the wealthy bourgeoisie of Cadiz and Seville came to see me often enough, but I didn't receive anybody.

In the end I found out that the Goyas had lost their youngest daughter, Pilar. Deep down I felt that Paco deserved it. If I was suffering . . .

One day he appeared. It was the Feast of the Epiphany. He burst, breathless, into my chamber, collapsed into my arms, dug his nails into my back.

"Have you remembered me?"

I nodded, sadly.

"Me, too . . . always."

Coming from that taciturn man, these three words represented a full-fledged declaration of love. He had never told me that he loved me. I believe he didn't want to desecrate his feelings with words.

"You are not ill anymore?"

"Not anymore."

"I never believed you were. Thank you, Teresa."

It was the first time that he had addressed me in that fashion. The weak person needs the confirmation of words. And I was the weak person, in the moment.

We lived as we had before. He painted me. Now I posed for him with pleasure. He included me in the picture with the stream, the lagoon, and the wood, and the air full of silvery cobwebs, which could only be breathed here in the Coto de la Doña Ana. He painted me dressed as a *maja*, with a black dress, a black mantilla, a black veil. On canvas, I look sad. Even though I smiled like before, I didn't feel lighthearted anymore. And he painted what he saw inside me. In the picture I wear my two rings, one with my name, the other with the name of Goya. I point out the sand and the words that I inscribed there: SOLO GOYA. If in my first portrait, when I wore the white dress with the red sash, Francisco painted me as a cold, haughty, and arrogant woman, like a demon wearing a charming dress the color of innocence, in this picture I am a black angel. And a sad *maja*.

I felt as if they had poured three sacks of sand from the banks of the Guadalquivir into my insides. Francisco painted; he stood upright in front of the canvas, under the blazing spring sun, half-naked, even at midday; streams of sweat ran down his back and chest, more because of the effort he was making than because of the temperature. He was painting; he needed nothing else. He knew what he was and what he wanted to do, whereas I was sinking into a sea of uncertainty. In the morning I destroyed what I had built up during the previous evening. I did silly things that afterward I was ashamed of. I made up for them with difficulty, and then ended up doing them again. I moved in a vicious cycle. No, my portrait brought me no blessings. The Muslims are right: to depict the human image brings bad luck.

Between the painter and I there was a shadow. I did not forgive Francisco. Why did I have to forgive him if forgiveness is a sign of one's own weakness, if forgiveness is giving in? And he . . . Again I noticed the old recrimination in his eyes. One night he said to me: "You are a witch."

The same word, the same charge used by the mother of my husband on the day he was buried.

"Why?" I whispered in the darkness.

"You put a spell on my daughter. My little Pilar is dead. Just as you did with your husband. And now with me. What am I doing here?"

"I don't understand you."

"What am I doing here? Now that I have completed your portrait, I paint little. I simply stare, eat, and drink more than I should, and pay no attention to my obligations."

"You can go, if you wish."

He embraced me in the darkness.

"Don't tell me that. You know that I cannot."

"But you wish to, do you not?"

"Yes. But I will not do it."

"You will."

"I cannot, I tell you. I cannot."

"You will see all right."

"Perhaps, who knows."

I now felt as if all of me had turned into black marble. For quite a while I was unable to recover: I trembled, I had shivers, I don't know if I was suffering from a love that was never to be, or if I was starting to relish a new victory.

"I am suffering, Teresa. Can you not see it?"

"But why?" I asked in a low voice.

"I cannot go on living like this. I need some form of security."

"Do you not have me?"

"No, it isn't that."

"Are we lacking something, perhaps?"

"I do not feel well."

"But why?" I whispered again in the night.

"I need some form of security."

"Like what?"

"If we live together, we ought to marry."

I burst out laughing, a strident laugh, full of victory.

"Evil witch!" he spat in the darkness.

He took me in a violent fashion, as if he wanted to punish me. I heard a few sobs. Then he went quickly to his bedroom.

He was mine.

Really? No, with that man such a thing was not possible. He wants to go, after all! He himself has admitted it.

He wants to go? Very well, he shall go then, I thought. But first he will experience certain things. The Duchess of Alba does not let herself be tortured so easily. The duchess is a woman who, when she enters a salon, stops the music. And the man who can torture her without being punished for it has not yet been born.

I sat down at my desk and wrote a letter to Manuel Godoy, prime minister and lover of the queen, asking him to leave everything and to come and see me at once, to keep absolutely quiet about the existence of this letter, and not to be surprised at anything he might see when he arrives.

"María, come here. Closer, talking aloud tires me. That's right, come closer. The concert was no good. Didn't you hear how out of tune they were? It is as if since the death of Don José music has fallen into a decline. Nothing can be listened to. Do you know what I want now? I want Juan and Manuela to dance a fandango for me. A very fiery fandango. Listen, María, do you remember the Coto de la Doña Ana? And our Palacio del Rocío?"

"Yes, and the magnificent portrait of Your Highness, which the royal painter did at that time. I still don't understand why milady didn't take it."

"What? The picture or the man?"

"I am talking about the picture, milady."

"Why have you gone all red? My good woman! Why did I not take it? That is my business, María. What I really regret is not having kept that man."

"There are few men like the royal painter. Apart from the fact that he believes in demons and witches and paints winged monsters. But on the other hand, he carries an image of Saint Pilar around with him everywhere. But for you, my dearest

María Teresa, it is better to forget about him. If it is a man with a large family, as I have always told you. No, do not cry, child! Oh, I didn't want to make you sad, my little one."

"I am not crying. Let's see, María. When Don Manuel came, how long had it been since Francisco was with us?"

"Ooh, it would be better for Your Highness not to recall that episode. I don't know; I don't want to think about it. It was not long afterward, a matter of weeks."

It was the month of February. Spring was in the air. Through the open windows you could hear the cries of the birds that always rest at the Coto de la Doña Ana on their way to warmer climates and on their way back. We were having lunch, Francisco, Godoy, that boastful, good-looking man, and myself. After Godoy's arrival I accepted visits from Francisco only very occasionally, and less and less frequently. He made some dreadful scenes, he yelled and bellowed and took me as if I were a cheap harlot.

We ate *fruits de mer* and fish, each dish with special silver cutlery. That peasant Francisco didn't know how to handle them very well; I mocked him for it and Godoy joined in. Paco was sweating. I conversed with Godoy in French. We spoke fast. Aragonese Paco didn't understand us and huge drops of sweat rolled down his forehead. Afterward, Godoy and I began to talk in low voices, so that the half-deaf painter couldn't manage to make out anything more than isolated words, sounds, laughter. Finally I arranged a journey by carriage to the coast, just he and I and then spoke loud enough so that Francisco could make out what was going on. The blood rushed to his face, but he kept control of himself.

"I think I am in the way here," he said in a hoarse voice and got up.

I let out an especially joyful laugh while patting Godoy's hand, so that he too, laughed.

"You don't know how to do anything other than leave, Don Francisco. Where are you going? To cry on your wife's shoulder?" I mocked him.

I was triumphant, and afraid. Francisco had already staggered out the door.

After a while María came in to tell me that the royal painter felt ill. I stopped eating dessert and rushed to Francisco's room.

I walked across his studio. Another portrait, a large bust of me, just started was cut to pieces, and another had been cut through by a dagger. The painter had collapsed onto the bed, white as a sheet, his lips bitten until they bled. I kissed him. I cleaned the blood away with kisses, as I had done, a long time ago, with the roe deer. He didn't so much as move. I shook him gently.

"Paco, my love, forgive me," I whispered.

The man didn't move.

"Paco, Paco, my love, do you hear me?" I exclaimed in a panic.

The man opened his eyes, and gave me an ugly look. When he saw my expression, he softened a little. He wanted to say something, but the words wouldn't come.

"Paco, say something, my love . . ."

He looked at my lips.

"I hear nothing," he said in a hoarse voice, "only the echo of the tide in my head."

"My love, what can I do for you?"

He read the question on my lips. With the last of his forces he said with a grating voice: "Don't go out for a ride with that conceited oaf. Stay with me."

"Francisco, the Duchess of Alba never changes her plans. You didn't change yours either, before Christmas. But what does this matter? What matters is that I am with you!"

"I can't hear you. I'm as deaf as a post. But I know what you are telling me. I will never hear you again; all I have left is this dreadful tide," he said, hoarse. He covered his ears with his hands and turned face down.

"Paco, my love, you will always be mine, only mine," I whispered desperately, even though the man who was lying down could not hear me.

I had María come in so that she could take care of him.

I went with Godoy to see the sunset by the sea, but I was restless and came back quickly.

I ran up to Francisco's chambers. His portrait, cut into slithers, stared at me. The drawing album and the portrait of the black *maja* had disappeared. As had Francisco. Instead of him I found a self-portrait. He had done it with ink and brush. I know of no other painting so full of disgrace and unhappiness as this one. The curls of Francisco's hair, the chin covered with the hair of his beard, the face of a destroyed man. And what eyes! It was as if they were looking straight into hell itself, as if they saw a dance of monsters such as those he often saw everywhere. Or, what is worse, as if he were looking at any empty space that cannot be filled in any possible way. In that look there is all the horror that a man is capable of feeling. And something in it that was addressed to me. The face of a destroyed man.

"María! Where is Goya?"

"The royal painter left an hour ago."

"For Madrid? A messenger, fast!"

"Perhaps for Seville, or possibly for Cadiz. Or for Madrid, who knows? The royal painter was not feeling at all well. I think he is seriously ill. But no human effort could have kept him here."

"María, I'll make you pay for this. You should have stopped him no matter what! Wicked thing! Monster!"

"Your Highness knows perfectly well that no one can do anything against the will of the royal painter."

"Harpie! You are the cause of my disgrace!"

That same evening I got rid of that conceited fool Godoy. The next morning I went to Madrid. I didn't find Francisco there and nobody could give me any news of him.

I wanted to wait, but time for me had ceased to exist.

A little later I went to Italy to make time reappear.

While abroad, I decided to start a new life again. It was the most reasonable thing to do. When I came back to Madrid I went to live in my little palace in the Moncloa, where I had yet to reside ever. I was determined not to let myself be plagued by memories. To be free, independent, like before! I bought new furniture so as to get rid of the old. I changed the paintings on the walls. I had new dresses made up for me. In the mornings I, who had adored tea and coffee, stayed in bed until late having chocolate and lady fingers, and looked out the window at the clouds chasing each other. Midday, the obligatory *lever*.

In the afternoon, conversations to which I invited new people, young poets, painters, philosophers. I received piles of banned books from Paris, which I read aloud at these sessions. Nothing could happen to the Duchess of Alba, even though a hundred wretched consciences might decide to denounce her to the Inquisition.

And one day Goya's name came up. Without wanting to, I paid attention. They said that the painter had just made a new series of etchings and that it was something never seen before in Madrid, in Spain, or in all Europe. Each of the etchings was blasphemous in its own way. General interest in them continued to grow, said my fellow conversationalists. Madrid spoke of nothing else but these etchings, which showed the perfidy of women, the corruption of priests, and the ridiculousness of those in power. In vain I tried to change the subject; nobody was interested in anything else. The past appeared to me, drawn in vivid colors. There was no way I could escape it. I could not free myself from it, I saw that clearly.

I shut myself up in my palace with a few servants and no one else. I told everyone not to come looking for me because I felt indisposed and needed rest.

It was winter. I stayed in bed all morning. At midday I made an effort to get up, but didn't have enough energy to so much as do my hair. Little by little I even stopped washing myself. I sat in the salon with a book on my knee, which I was unable to read. I focused on a space on the wall. I could spend hours and hours doing that. But I didn't know how the hours passed. I only know that all of a sudden it started to get dark and night fell. I had the feeling that as soon as it was daytime, the evening and the shadows were already on their way. It was as if I were barely alive in an endless night. I couldn't get up, I weighed so much. In the evening they brought me dinner, which I either left without touching or ate little without hunger, just to give me something to do. I went to bed early, and in the darkness, I counted the seconds as they passed. And so my days were spent. Sometimes I saw visions: the monstrous owls and billy goats of Francisco's pictures pecked at me and tore me open with their horns. The nights left me exhausted and I didn't get up until after midday. On other days I had the horse saddled up so as to find forget-fulness in the speed of the ride. I found it, certainly, for half an hour, an hour at most, but as soon as I stopped the owls of the nightmare came in flocks, herds of chimerical asses and goats besieged me, bleating and howling.

One day, as usual, I was sitting in bed with my arms by my side and looking at nothing in particular. I thought of a few words that Madame de Sévigné had written over a hundred years ago: "*Je dois à votre absence le plaisir de sentir la durée de ma vie en toute sa longueur.*" How absurd! I thought. The French are comical, they even glean *plaisir* from melancholy and sadness. Nonetheless I would like to be French so as to know how to turn pain into beauty. To your absence, Francisco, I owe the pleasure of feeling the length of my life to its full extent. Magnificent!

I asked the maid to bring me the book and, once I had found the sentence, I let my eyes wander a few lines down: "*Pour moi je*

vois le temps courir avec horreur et m'apporter en passant l'affreuse
vieillesse, les incomodités et enfin la mort."

I couldn't go on reading. The pages fell to the floor, the
draught chased after them. It does not matter, I thought. Nothing matters. I had to take off my stockings before going to bed,
and I couldn't. I managed to take off the left one, but had no
energy left to remove the right one: a sad, unbeautiful Pierrot.

"María! Come here and sit next to me. No, I don't want to scold
you, I just want to get to the bottom of something. Come on, sit
down. And now tell me how things really went that time when
. . . But first you have to give me your word of honor that you will
tell me the truth and nothing but the truth. Do you remember
my long illness, when I didn't even leave the house? Good. Did
you say something to Don Francisco or was it he who . . ."

"Your Highness, I would never have dared to speak of it,
but as you wish me to . . . Your Highness surely does not realize
that . . ."

"Leave the highnesses out of it and get to the point. You are
a walking headache."

"Milady, your condition was very serious. Spiritually, I mean.
I went to see the royal painter and told him about the state you
were in. Goya did not hesitate for a moment. Immediately he sat
down and wrote you a letter. He told me that it was an invitation
for you to come and see his latest work. He told me that he was
very proud of it and that it was the best thing he had created up
until that moment. He was concerned about your health. I was

pleased about that. I knew that a man like him wouldn't let me down because he carried the Saint Pilar of Saragossa with him wherever he went."

"María, when talking about himself, Francisco would never, but never, have used the verb 'create.' You know that I have an aversion to that type of grandiloquence. What else? And the *majas*?"

"Your Highness, pardon milady, I have told you all that I know. If, at the time in question, I hid from you that fact that I had gone to see the royal painter on my own initiative, it was because I sensed that my visit would have irritated. If I did it, it was only and exclusively for the good of milady."

"'Only and exclusively for the good of . . .' Come off it, you clown. I asked you what you knew of the *majas*?"

"I did not know anything about them. The royal painter told me only that I was not to deliver the letter to you until the day afterward. An order that I obeyed."

"Ooh! Oh! Getting something out of you is . . . Thank you and go!"

Where to look for freedom and independence? Among people, I didn't find it, nor in solitude and silence. I insisted on living in my isolation. I grew heavier and heavier inside. The fog around me grew thicker. I was living a long night.

On the morning of a rainy day they brought a huge packet to the house: they were pictures. How strange, I thought. It has been a long time since I commissioned any. I had them unwrapped, and waited with indifference. Then they opened the door; they brought them into my room and I saw two of them. They represented two magnificent *majas*. The dressed one seemed even more provocative and naked than the undressed one. Beautiful women, masterpieces. A whole series of questions immediately sprung to mind: Where could I hang them? Who had sent them to me? What did it mean? Was it a joke? Or a mistake? All of a sudden I knew the answer: they were not two *majas*, but one—a woman who included all the other women in the world and everything tempting, dangerous, and seductive that the feminine sex had; the woman was me and Francisco had painted her, had painted me. It was his hand! It was a declaration!

I had the pictures hung in my bedroom. I observed my reclining body with Francisco's eyes and felt the excitement he did.

And one day afterward, I walked over to his studio. I had the keys. I went without having said anything to him; I hoped the painter wasn't there. But at the same time it is true that some hidden part of me was looking forward to the idea that the painter had spent the night painting and that I would still find him there.

I turned the key. He wasn't there. So I was able to look at the engravings in my own time; I saw they were all over the place, out of order. Each image bore a title, inscribed at the foot of the picture. *Volaverunt*. A woman—transformed into a witch, in whom everyone can recognize the Duchess of Alba, beyond a doubt—flies over the bodies of her lovers to a sabbath of witches and wizards. *Todos caerán*: the same duchess, painted as a bird of prey with a woman's head and breast, tempts bird-men to approach her; Goya's face, when he was young and adult, can be recognized in more than one bird-man. After their inevitable fall, the woman plucks the feathers off her victims as if they were chickens. The woman, the duchess. *El sueño de la mentira y la inconstancia*: while Francisco looks lovingly and imploringly at his beloved, she takes his hand and embraces it. The woman, here too, is without doubt the Duchess of Alba. The woman turns into a double and her other half receives letters, looks, and messages from other men. *¡No hay quien nos desate!*: a man uses all his energy to free himself from his beloved who holds him in her grip, like the chimera of a nightmare. The man is he, the painter. And more and more etchings, all of treacherous women, sometimes depicted as cheap prostitutes, other times as brides or rich ladies who are for sale. And, what is more, all kinds of enchantresses and witches, all with the beautiful face and exuberant figure of the duchess. And then asses and chimera, monsters and priests. And the queen. Yes, the queen too, ridiculous and deserving of pity.

This, then, is the new masterpiece that all Madrid is talking about, I thought. *Caprichos*, a series that is unprecedented, so they say. It is the testimony of the emotional suffering of the artist, they say. Of the hell of love that Goya has lived through. Everyone says this, and maybe everyone is right. But they do not know one thing: that this series of engravings is above all an act of vengeance. Goya transformed the Duchess of Alba— the most beautiful, the most admired and the most celebrated of the noble ladies of Spain, the woman for whom, whenever she entered a salon, the music would stop—into a crude, ordinary libertine, into a dissolute woman deserving of disdain. Yes, Paco. You have in your hands a weapon, which is more dangerous than any of the arms that the second most powerful woman in Spain has at her disposal.

The days that followed were marked by visions of the etchings. I wanted to meet up with the painter. I would not say that I knew his work, I decided. If he shows it to me, he will see nothing but an expression of the most absolute indifference. Why do I wish to see the man who has humiliated me, I asked myself? Because he is more powerful, stronger than I? I love him because he is stronger and has me at his mercy.

I went back to his studio.

For the last time. How many times have I pronounced these words as a threat? I used to think of them as words like any others, insignificant, featherweight. I played with them as a child plays with her doll, like a lady with her fan. Only on that one occasion, when I said them in front of him, did these words become the chimera of a nightmare, a monster with bat's wings and donkey's ears, with a beak and claws designed to inflict punishment, and when it has finally abandoned its horrible task, flies off with a heavy heart, as if reluctantly leaving a trail of incense and sulfur.

For the last time . . . There was just one candle lit. The light avoided the corners, the walls dripped with humidity and darkness. I thought that I had come in vain. The emptiness without his presence frightened me at first, but then left me feeling relieved. I had made the journey to his house on foot at a hurried pace, stopping every now and again, determined each time not to go one step further. I had gotten rid of my carriage because I couldn't simply sit there without doing anything, just shouting at the driver to go faster and thinking, heaven help me, let him run over whomever in the happy crowd might be blocking our path. The happiness of others struck me as unbearable, out of place, and I jumped from the carriage so as to go ahead on foot. I was desperate.

I reached his house without feeling the pain in my feet. Of course, Venetian slippers covered in emeralds are not made for trotting through the badly paved streets of Madrid. I climbed up to the third story with my skirt raised up above my knees. I cared not if the neighbors saw me. Desperation and anguish made me run as if I were fleeing from a gaggle of cackling geese.

Darkness reigned in the spacious room of stone and the little flame of the candle lit up only the small space immediately around it. Wherever you looked there were half-painted canvases, like white monsters, full of folds and wrinkles. Little by little I grew accustomed to the shadows, and amid all the folders, paints, and pots, I found a carafe of wine and poured myself a little. In the candlelight, the Manzanilla looked like honey in its glass. At that moment I smelled the familiar odor of bitter almonds and heard the creak of a bench from which a man was rising drowsily. In the shadows, the barely visible figure tied up his shirt and trousers. Before entering the circle of light from the candle, I smelled his odor as he shifted in his sleep. So he was there! I was overcome by a feeling of relief, just as his absence had been a relief to me a moment ago. So powerfully could he move me! Suddenly something whispered to me that I should punish him for making me suffer in this way, that I should show him who I was. He didn't give me time to do anything but took hold of me with his large hands that sunk into my back like claws. We were standing, sitting, lying, sitting again, he with his claws forever dug into my face, in a sweet violence that made me feel lost. And when I came to again, he was bending over me, nursing the wounds that the long race through the streets of Madrid had left on my feet, licking off the blood as a mother bear does with her cubs.

For the last time . . . These words came back, they grew between us, a monstrous bat that beat its wings blindly against the walls. Was it he who spoke them? No, I myself released the monster from its cage. The need to punish the man in the unlaced shirt was uppermost in me. But the bat flew out of the room of stone; it followed me when I went down the stairs, when I was fleeing. Fleeing? And the man with the creased shirt stood at the threshold of the door. His wide shoulders slumped, his hair, twisted like a nest of snakes, hung lifeless. I turned around, perhaps to tell him something, perhaps—yes, that was it!—to take back those words, to withdraw them, to cancel them out, but he had already closed the door after saying, with indifference: Go, and don't catch cold.

✦

"María! Where are you? Come, old thing, and answer me a question, you who are not only my duenna, but also my confidante and lady-in-waiting. Tell me, am I vindictive?"

"How can you think such a . . ."

"Shut up! No, speak, but be brief: Am I vindictive?"

"What a question, milady! Surely not, but as you have asked me, I must think on it. Give me a week."

"I have not got a week to give you, María. I have barely got a few more days. So?"

"Let us see, milady. With all the goodness of your heart . . . I apologize, these words may displease you. Well then, with some people you are capable of being vindictive."

"Am I, now?"

"And I think that the person you most hurt when you do this is yourself."

"María, I am the second noble lady of Spain, and as very few people take the queen seriously, I am the first lady of the empire. Apart from that, you know perfectly well that I am one of those women who, when they enter a space, the music stops. I do not avenge myself, I punish."

"Highness, punishment or revenge, what difference do the words make? The pity is that neither one nor the other serves any purpose."

"But in love . . ."

"Love is a gift."

"A gift?"

" . . . that is given to very few people. What wouldn't I have done so that it was given to me, and like me there are so many,

many women and probably men too . . . Of what importance is it that when a woman walks into a place, the music stops? Above all, it is a question of not wasting the gift."

"You understand nothing. You are getting off the subject. Go."

Who could ever take this old woman with her cross seriously? I prefer to be alone.

The empty days went on. Gray, useless, lacking in meaning, lacking in content. Time ceased to exist. Only from time to time it struck me all of a sudden that everything might have turned out differently. First I got rid of such thoughts; I didn't want them to get to the end, to reach a conclusion. Nonetheless these were the only moments that, thanks to the pain, made me feel I was alive. So I began to call for those thoughts, and they came, little by little, lazily . . .

Punishment and revenge, pride and vanity—to a woman of the kind that when she enters a salon, the music stops . . . So love is a gift? And life? How not to waste it? Life. Revenge. Music. A gift. Punishment. Revenge. I couldn't go on. I knew it was too late. Everything could have turned out differently, but it was late. These words made me panic, as the chimera and the monsters of a nightmare did to Francisco. I began to frequent society dinners once more, to forget the winged monsters. I know that in that period the queen wrote to Godoy in a letter "*La de Alba está hecha una piltrafa.*" He himself told me.

The illness I am suffering from is not natural, I know that. They have poisoned me. Who? The queen, without a doubt.

What muggy heat comes in here, even through the lowered blinds and the solid walls! What a cloying smell from my body, which is already beginning to decompose. Like Don José, once he was dead. I didn't imagine then that this smell was to be my destiny. If only I could get away from this heat! I have a fever.

María, I'm thirsty. No, I don't what a pear. I want water in my crystal glass, you know that. It isn't there? Of course. You are right!

The crystal glass . . .

No, no it wasn't the last time.

Yesterday morning . . .

"My love, look at me! For the last time! Open your eyes to see me looking at you. So that you can see I am yours."

He kissed my forehead.

"You are my joy and my perdition," he whispered into my ear. "I carry you engraved within me, always."

He kissed my cheek.

"I will always have you before me, only you, all the women I paint will be you. Open your eyes to me for the last time, my love!"

He kissed my eyes.

In the end, María had to drag him out the door.

I didn't open my eyes. I pretended I was asleep. The last punishment, the last revenge.

Your morning words, spoken in a low voice, with tenderness . . . Were they a dream, or a vision?

The crystal glass has disappeared from my bedside table.

María Teresa del Pilar Cayetana de Silva, Duchess of Alba, died in 1802 at the age of forty. Francisco de Goya, sixteen years older than she, outlived her by another twenty-six years. He designed the tomb of the duchess. In the drawing, the good spirits and the angels raise up the deceased; the duchess is in the same position as the dressed and naked *majas*.

During the rest of his life, Goya had among his possessions the duchess's crystal glass, an object the owner had always kept with her whenever she travelled. And, during the rest of his life, the painter remained faithful in his work to a certain type of woman. With very few exceptions, all his women are María Teresa, Duchess of Alba.

THE GARNET NECKLACE

"'A dangerous woman.' That's how the Vienna prefecture described her in their report: 'Dangerous. A flirt. A bad mother.' That's literally what they put in their police report. It goes on:'She indulges in literary activity and is a firm defender of the Czech national cause; she mixes with influential people, not only in Bohemia but also in Moravia and Northern Hungary. The police should keep an eye on her, albeit discreetly.' Here's another item, also concerning Madam Božena Němcová. Listen to this, Fräulein Zaleski:'The friendships she cultivates make her highly suspicious; she should be obliged to return to Prague. I beg of you to see that this is done.' Do you see what I mean, Fräulein Zaleski? I have just been quoting from a coded telegram from the chief of the prefecture of the Civil and Military Administration of Northern Hungary. Do take off your coat, there's a hanger over there. Please be seated."

"Thank you. What do you wish me to do?"

"Have you found out the current address of the person we are tailing?"

"I've been trying to find—"

"Fräulein Zaleski, please don't give me any talk about 'trying'! You have pledged yourself to work for the secret service of the Prague Prefecture. Are you aware of the importance of your mission?"

"Herr von Päumann, the authoress Božena Němcová currently resides in Slovakia, excuse me, I mean Northern Hungary, in a mountain village called Brezno. She visits various hamlets scattered at the feet of Dumbier Mountain."

"With whom does she stay?"

"The Slovakian poet Samo Chalupka. He and his wife have taken her in."

"What does she do?"

"She studies the local scene, collects Slovakian folktales, and writes them."

"How do you know that?"

"She told me so in a letter. At this stage she has complete confidence in me. Her husband tells me that in every letter she writes to him, she sends me her warm regards and asks after my health, which is rather poor, as you know."

"Your health is none of my concern. You had better tell me what this writer's husband, Josef Němec, told you about her in privacy."

"Němec wrote to her that since she can allow herself the luxury of dedicating herself to literature and strolling through the countryside with a bunch of poets, it would be nice if she could send him some money to pay the rent. She wrote back and told him how to obtain some funds. She was furious, however, that her husband had thought that she should swindle her patron, Count Kolowrat-Krakovsky."

"What else?"

"Němcová went on to tell her husband that as she has been ill for years, she would stay and continue to live in the country, and that she would never get better if she returned to their miserable Prague surroundings."

"A few days ago, General Kempen, chief of the Imperial Prefecture, told me that Němcová's journey to Northern Hungary would have cost more than the allowance she receives from Count Kolowrat-Krakovsky. By this, he was insinuating that some sort of organization financed the endeavor and that her move was, without a doubt, politically motivated."

"Herr von Päumann, heaven knows I have no wish to defend her, but I am convinced that this is just a cultural trip."

"Please be silent! General Kempen has spoken openly about this as a nationalist, pan-Slav undertaking, and has severely reprimanded me for issuing a three-month passport to the author."

"It is not for me to question that judgement, sir."

"What other information do you have as regards the suspect, Fräulein? Please do not waste my time."

"She calls herself an emancipated woman with liberal opinions, and a dedicated nationalist, both intellectually and politically. What is more, Němcová supports the unity of all Slav peoples. Yes, she is certainly involved in revolutionary politics, but I have not been able to discover much in this regard, because the arrival of her husband from Hungary, where he was held prisoner, put an end to any such investigation on my part. It is quite impossible to talk to her husband about Němcová's politics. Indeed, it's quite impossible to talk to him about anything."

The woman, still young, accompanied the doctor to her bedroom. His eyes were shy but glinting, and gave the room a once-over.

"I'm just a medical student, but I hope that—"

"Everyone has had to learn sometime, even Purkyně."

She smiled. She knew that a medical student working on his degree was legally allowed to work as a doctor, and decided that that was how she would address him.

"Yes, even Purkyně, you're quite right. I'm fairly well acquainted with Central European medical methods and procedures. I've also travelled in the Orient, where I learned many things."

She knew of the Orient only through a few of the tales from *A Thousand and One Nights*. She wasn't at all sure if that was the kind of Orient he was referring to. Who knew why she imagined Bengal lights, the smell of sulfur, and a man playing a penetratingly loud flute in the middle of the brightness. She saw that the people around him were enraptured and watched him with crazed eyes while they all danced to the rhythm of the shrill, tremulous flute.

"Would you mind if I opened the curtains? In order to examine you, I need as much light as possible."

She didn't care for that very much. Why was she so averse

to light? she asked herself. She wasn't one of those women who were in the habit of kidding themselves and she told herself that the medical student was much younger than she, by eight or ten years at the very least. Light knew no mercy, she thought, and would lay bare all her wrinkles, even the least pronounced ones, and the ones she hid under her clothes, the worst ones. But there was nothing else to be done. She stood, touched the curtain, and watched the smooth movement of the rings on the curtain rod as the day was revealed.

The young man also got up and brusquely opened the other half of the curtain. The day burst violently into the room. He was surprised for a moment by the view of the Vltava River and the Smíchov Mountains on its far side. He stretched his arms lazily in the golden light of the afternoon. Like a leopard, like one of the Orientals, she thought.

"Show me your tongue, please."

He studied it carefully and jotted something down in a notebook.

"Don't blink."

She looked up at the ceiling. The doctor's breath smelled of coffee.

"Make a fist. Stay still."

The woman heard blood pulse. Whose was it? Hers or his? It was banging away like a fire bell. Does a doctor really need whole minutes, which feel like hours, to find her heart rate? He stared at her with penetrating eyes.

"Kindly take off your blouse," he said.

As if on purpose, the buttons refused to leave their buttonholes. He looked at her with imperturbable calm. Only one left to go, at waist level. Her vest, too? Remember he's a doctor!

She had never felt as demure as when the young man listened to her lungs. He's a doctor, she told herself time and again. His mustache tickled. In that instant the whole world was in that mustache. She lost interest in everything but the movement of that gentle paintbrush against her body. He's a doctor! Nonetheless, the mixture of modesty and sweet pain didn't go away.

While she buttoned herself up, he never so much as looked at her.

The doctor left. But during the day she felt the gentle touch of his mustache against the different parts of her body. In the evening, when she sat under the yellow lampshade with a cup of tea in one hand and a book open on her knees, she had the feeling that a Bengal light burned in the room, and that something moved in the corner.

"This is the dossier on Betty Niemetz, an Austro-Hungarian subject who uses the pseudonym Božena Němcová. In your report, you have written the following: 'It is quite impossible to talk to her husband about the political activities in which Mrs. Němcová is involved.' Do you wish to add anything? At this point I would like to remind you, Fräulein Zaleski, that you entered the secret service voluntarily, and that if we pay you, we do not do so in exchange for nothing."

"Once I managed to get her talking about women who'd become famous during revolutions. Because I have made myself out to be a revolutionary, Božena felt comfortable confessing all of her most secret thoughts. She told me the following. I shall read it to you: 'As far as politics are concerned, women will achieve more than men, and I mean women from all social classes, from the proletarian to the most culturally refined. Because who could be more sensitive to the misery around her, be it material or intellectual, than a woman? She is the one who bears children, and so she is the one who foresees the future.' She then added, 'Who would dare to persecute or punish a woman? Especially a brilliant, cultured woman who has influenced so many people?'"

"Mrs. Němcová is making a big mistake by considering us to be so benevolent. What else does she say with regards to the state of affairs for women today?"

"I managed to look at her notes. I know where she keeps them hidden and was even able to take them home to make copies. At one point, she says, 'We women have a heart of wax; any image which interests us is easily impressed upon it. Nonetheless, everything strikes me as being cold and pale and barren, and now having written this, I feel as if I had ice water running through my veins. When I look at myself, I feel an urge to cry, yet I know that within me burn the most violent passions. Sometimes I want to open my arms and hug the whole world to my breast, but I know it's far too late for such idealism—'"

"Such useless moaning, so typical of women, is of no interest to me, Fräulein Zaleski. Concentrate on the information that I ask of you. We will only pay you for your work if it turns out to be useful to us."

"Pardon me, I thought—"

"What relationship does this emancipated woman have with her husband, and with men in general?"

"Mr. and Mrs. Němec have completely different characters. He is tough, soldierly—"

"What I require is proofs in writing if possible."

"Of course. Here, for example, she writes to her husband: 'It often happens that when I go out for a stroll on my own, I feel very lonely and wish you were with me, but I have learned to do without many things and this, too, is one of them. On the other hand, I think that if you were here, everything would be as before, we wouldn't get on, and then I would relish being my own woman again.' Would you like me to go on?"

"Go ahead."

"Very well. 'Few women have had so much respect for the institution of marriage as I had, but I soon lost my faith in it. How could I have done otherwise? All I see around me are lies, adultery, gilded servitude, obligations, that is to say, vulgarity. I had very much longed to be loved. I needed love as a flower needs the morning dew, but I have only found overbearing men who wanted to become my masters. This cooled my passion, and bitterness and rancour took its place. They took my body, but my desires flew off far away. I don't know where.'"

"Fräulein Zaleski, isn't this all rather farcical? Němcová is a writer and she knows how to deceive people with words."

"As I told you, I have delved into her heart. With me she is sincere, which is why I know her well. In these notes she has given voice to her soul. Shall I go on?"

"All right. But please do spare me expressions such as 'delved into her heart' and 'given voice to her soul.'

"I beg your pardon, sir. She writes: 'My children are my only joy yet their instinctive love does not satisfy me.'"

"Look, skip these sentimental outpourings and read only those passages that could be significant to our investigation."

"Very well. What about this excerpt: 'I have become a fervent adherent to the national cause, believing that it would satisfy my yearning. But no. It is true that over time this cause has become a firm conviction and the achievement to which I have dedicated great efforts, but . . . I have known the world, I have learned that there is no such thing as perfection in the world. The longings of my own heart have often disappointed me. What I thought to be gold turned out, in the end, to be nothing but mud.'"

"*Gut*, Fräulein. But in these notes of hers is there anything that might be of interest to the police? Our next visitor is now in the waiting room."

"This strikes me as of interest: 'What I long for is love, a true love, not for one single person, but rather for everybody, for all humanity, a love that asks for nothing in return, a love that would improve me, that would bring me closer to truth. This is my objective. This gives me strength. What would I be without this love? Yet the world will not flatter me for this; the world would see me damned for that which I consider to be my finest and most beautiful quality; that which is natural is held to be sinful. Those who do not run with the herd to the feeding trough are crucified; sooner or later they become martyrs. But it is better to be a martyr than a good-for-nothing who doesn't even know why she's alive."

"Before we finish, Fräulein Zaleski, is there anything this dangerous, emancipated woman has written that represents a threat to our Austrian fatherland?"

"I believe so . . . just a moment . . . yes, here. She writes the following to her husband: 'What I really desire for both you and me is to do with pleasure everything that has to be done with pleasure, and not simply because we are obliged to do it. Goethe says, *Wat ist Pflicht?* What is an obligation? An obligation is that which one imposes on oneself as a duty. But one can't do everything to order! Men ought to forget their conviction that they are the masters and to treat the women they respect as if they were their lovers. They should show their feelings more and behave with less vulgarity.' Do you not think these are most dangerous opinions, sir?"

"You will have to carry out a far more detailed investigation into this woman. Write me a report on Němcová's entire life. We need to know who has been such a bad influence on her, which other people we need to go after. I want a thoroughly detailed biography of Mrs. Němcová. Is that clear, Fräulein Zaleski? Keep in touch with her. Don't let her out of your sight for a second. Auf Wiedersehen, Fräulein."

Unnerved, she slept fitfully that night. Her dreams were flooded with the purple of a Bengal light, snake charmers, rat catchers, and legendary paladins with the heads of dragons under their arms, appeared then vanished. She woke up feeling hot, until she got undressed so as to feel the pleasure of the sheets against her naked body.

The following day she would begin the medical treatment. She got up early in the morning to write. The words didn't flow from her pen; she was distracted and allowed herself to be carried away by the confusion of images that each disappeared as soon as it appeared before her eyes. Then she decided she'd do some shopping. What a strange shape the bread has today, like a river stone, as if you have only to wet it for it to shine. And while the druggist filled a paper cone with a pound of sugar, she watched the fine sand and felt like sinking deep into that sweet white dune.

"No, don't send in the next one, not yet. I'll tell you when, Fritz. Inform this visitor that the prefect is busy carrying out some unexpected, important tasks."

I had realized that to get Němcová, we needed a female informer. I told this to my superior, Kempen, but at the time he couldn't make his mind up whether to do so. But he changed his attitude when I explained the matter to him in detail.

To the attention of the head of the Vienna Prefecture, Johann Kempen, from the head of the Prague Prefecture, Anton von Päumann.

Subject: Vítězka Paul, informer

December 31, 1954

Your Excellency,

As women since time immemorial have had a considerable influence in political matters, I consider it a serious failure on the part of the Secret Service of the Prague Prefecture not to have an informer reporting on the circles of Czech woman intellectuals, especially those of Amerling, Staňková, Zapová, etc. When you, Excellency, ordered me to keep an eye on the writer Božena Němcová, it seemed to me clearer than ever that an informer was needed. I have managed to find a person I consider suitable. Vítězka Paul is the daughter of the chemist František Paul, who works as an informer for our service under the code name of Fidel. Vítězka Paul studied at Mrs. Amerling's school and now works as a teacher; she has made a few less-than-impressive stabs at writing, has connections with the aforementioned ladies, and could make the necessary contacts. In the years 1848 and 1849, she herself was a militant Czech nationalist, but a series of misfortunes—the death of her mother, her father's long years in prison, her concerns for the welfare of her numerous siblings—have acted as a considerable brake on her enthusiasm, to the extent that she has now agreed to serve the Austro-Hungarian government.

No, I most definitely had not made a mistake. We urgently needed a female informer, and this one was no fool. It is true that she has allowed herself to be swayed by the woman who we have her investigating. Clearly, she envies her subject. That suits us just fine. Vítězka Paul, which is to say Fraülein Zaleski, cultivates certain literary ambitions, but has no talent for them herself. She is one of those ladies who scribble verses along the lines of *"Aus meinen grossen Schmerzen mach' ich die kleine Lieder."* She lacks any defined personality, not only because "out of her little pain she makes little songs," but also because she is too unsure of herself and doesn't know what it is she wants. She has eccentric friends, and above all that crank František Skuhravý who fills her head with his Oriental nonsense. But let us allow the girl to dream, because dreams are all she will ever have. She must be twenty-something, but seems older; seems, indeed, prematurely old, worn out, gaunt, curve backed, with bags under her eyes. She is not at all attractive, poor creature. I would bet anything that she also has tuberculosis. Better for us that she does! She will need money for her treatment and so she will work with greater zeal. Mr. Sacher-Masoch, who was prefect of Prague before me, complained more than once of the difficulty of obtaining an informer who could penetrate right to the heart of the conspiracies against the state. That was, until he found the father of this Vítězka, František Paul, who had been sentenced to years and years in prison for speaking out passionately as a Czech nationalist during the 1848 revolution. When he came home, he found that his wife had been buried, his house was in ruins, and he had five children to feed. It didn't take him long to get in touch with us. When he did, Sacher-Masoch licked his lips and said, "His close ties with the Czech Nationalist Party—which, by the way, regards him as a great martyr for their cause—will make him invaluable as an informer." Soon his eldest daughter was here too, asking for a job with our secret service. We'll get that Czech nationalism out of their heads, even if we have to beat it out of them! This is how Vítězka Paul has become Antonia Zaleski the spy.

In his last letter, sent by special courier to Vienna, Herr Kempen tells me to search Němcová's house as soon as possible in order to investigate her writing and correspondence in particular. Very well, that is what we shall do. Němcová is a dangerous nationalist, as well as a feminist and . . . Is she really so dangerous? Is it possible that her writings could be a threat to our empire? "The world will not flatter you for this; the world will see you damned for that which you consider to be your finest and most beautiful quality; that which is natural is held to be sinful. He who does not run with the herd to the feeding trough, is crucified. Sooner or later he becomes a martyr. But it is better to be a martyr than a good-for-nothing who doesn't even know why he's alive." Or that quote from Goethe, which I didn't know. "*Wat ist Pflicht?*" What is an obligation? An obligation is that which one imposes on oneself as a duty." Exactly. I have made this quote my own. My obligation is that which I impose on myself. Němcová says that one cannot be ordered to do absolutely anything. I, on the contrary, am convinced that absolutely any order may be filled, as long as one is convinced one is serving a just cause. And I am certainly convinced of the importance of my cause.

The enemies of Austria-Hungary never rest and one must

be forever on the alert. Society is full of conspirators. The other day at a reception, the former ambassador of France told me that the Austro-Hungarian government makes the same mistake as similar regimes by thinking that revolutions are prepared by groups of secret conspirators. He said, "Revolutions emerge from unbearable social conditions, but you, my friend, like the rest of the Austro-Hungarian police, have shut your eyes to this obvious fact!" It is rather the French who have shut their eyes to the network of conspiracy that is being woven across our empire! As a police representative, I am the best defense against the conspirators: with a good nexus of informers, control over the mail, and other such tactics, I will create a state of permanent fear within society. I will be unpredictable, mysterious. Taken to extremes, this strategy will make the people tremble. Yes, I wish to keep the Czechs in a state of terror. May they tremble before making any decisions on their own. In Austria-Hungary we have no need of a few geniuses, but rather of a mass of happy subjects.

In other words, there can be no compromise. I shall write a letter to Herr Kempen about this woman writer.

Božena Němcová belongs to certain circles of so-called 'emancipated' women. She is an educated, well-informed person. At all events, she is an outstanding personality, capable of exercising considerable influence.

A rather special woman, this Němcová. Why is she complicating things for herself? She has now started to publish her novel, *The Grandmother*, in monthly installments. I forgot to ask Fraülein Zaleski about the book and above all, about the coded political programs and revolutionary messages that might be found within. I'll have her brought here at once.

The student of medicine came in with a heavy suitcase and headed for the patient's room with eyes fixed to the floor. From the suitcase, he took out various glass cups, cylinders, small bottles, needles and scissors . . . A thousand years' worth of knowledge transformed into objects, she thought. As if he'd overheard her thoughts, he glanced at her, a slight smile on his lips, and asked her to undress and lie down on the sofa that they now used as an examining table. Meanwhile, he went on blowing into his flasks in order to clean them, before placing them on the chair next to the bed.

"Please lie face down."

He undid her corset, leaving her back exposed. He rubbed the palms of his hands together; sssssssh . . . and the fragrance of a beech forest filled the room. He started to massage her back with his palms, fingers, fists, the backs of his hands, and his forearms. The touch of his hands was firm and tender at the same time, and produced tickles, then caresses that stretched out over her skin and penetrated beneath the epidermis, deep into her body. He then proceeded to take the glass cups, one by one, and she felt the circular objects cover her back, sticking to it like suckers.

He took the cups off her body. A new smell of wood filled the air, probably pine, this time, and his palms spread that perfume over her skin, up to her shoulders, then down, until he was putting pressure on her waist, then he continued on to her buttocks and thighs.

He laced up her corset.

"Turn over, please. And try to relax."

Eyes fixed on the ceiling, she made an effort to slacken her tensed muscles and make herself comfortable. The doctor, or rather the trainee, placed a chair behind her head and sat down. Having rubbed his fingers with an oil that smelled like a jungle after the passing of a monsoon, he rubbed her nostrils and, like some mad painter, used the tips of his fingers to draw all kinds of doodles and scrawls on her cheeks, chin and forehead.

Now his fingers slid down her neck, over her collarbone, to her shoulders. They followed the shape of the bone from which the ribs emerge. Through her silk underclothes, they traced the outer circle of her breasts. Then, briefly, he put pressure on the breasts themselves. Half dead from the shock, she couldn't so much as ask herself if this formed part of the treatment.

But the upper part of her body was already wrapped in a blanket, and the doctor's fingers were now playing with her belly. They prodded its muscles, and, in a way that revealed they were experienced, put pressure there where the belly ends. At that moment she felt a wave of desire that spread rapidly to the tips of her fingers and the ends of her hair, and showed no sign of going away. The patient lay there with her eyes firmly closed, half maddened. The doctor's soothing voice simply intensified her feeling of pleasure.

"I'll be giving you this treatment every day for a week. What I'm doing is touching certain nerve endings in order to give your body energy, strength so that it will be able to cure itself."

Then he picked up several folded paper envelopes, tied with different colored ribbons. He gave her instructions regarding the medicines she had to prepare for herself using the herbs in the envelopes which she had to drink in the form of infusions, and place on her body as poultices, especially on her chest, stomach, and kidneys.

"After this week," he added, "I will let you rest for ten days. We will then go ahead with a further week of intensive treatment. At that point we'll take stock of the situation. Perhaps you will already be feeling better and will not require any further care from me."

As he spoke, he put his objects back into his case. Only now and again did he run his eyes over the face, neck, and shoulders of his patient, as if involuntarily, like a shy child. She suddenly felt that he wasn't a doctor at all, but rather a little boy who in his innocence had caused some irreparable harm but was unaware of it and continued to go on happily.

"You may get dressed. See you tomorrow!"

These words, spoken from the half-shadow of the hall, cut through her dreaminess like a sword through a bridal veil. She wanted to run after him to make him stay, but she was half-naked. The sound of the front door as it banged shut went through her like an icy gust of wind.

✦

That good-looking young man, with his broad shoulders and butterfly waist, has been visiting the Němecs' apartment since Božena came back to Prague, in order to cure her. They say he is a real doctor. If he isn't one, who cares, he's so attractive. The kind of man I would describe as Oriental, at least that's how I imagine Oriental people to look from the descriptions of František Skuhravý. Yesterday I dreamed of that young doctor. I was Božena and he came to cure me. But what was I thinking of just now? Oh, yes: if he's a doctor, maybe he could show me some kind of exercise for my back, which I just can't keep as straight as I should. I have the feeling that everybody laughs at it. Yes, people, even when they're being serious, are forever staring at me, their mouths like open drawers.

My woman friends make fun of me too. When they told me that František had left me, they laughed. I will always remember their wide-open mouths, so happy were they that František got engaged to another woman. Never again will František share with me his enthusiasm for the ideas, colors, and perfumes of the Orient, never again will he tell me I look like an Indian girl. Later I saw them together at the theater. The golden hair of his fiancée had so stunned me that I preferred to look at her fan. I do believe it was painted by Hellich himself. At that very moment the brilliance of her engagement ring stung my eyes. When they went to take their seats, my woman friends laughed their heads off.

But now it's me who's laughing. I'm the one who's got this woman writer—the one everyone's talking about—whom everyone reads—by the scruff of the neck. All by myself, I can liquidate her, invalidate her, neutralize her, how and when I wish. Afterward, I will show everybody who the real writer is and what writing is really about. I wouldn't bore my readers with legends and folktales the way Božena does, nor would I write stories about workers and peasants. I'm going to write about the kind of life I myself would like to live, which is like the one Božena has had for herself. She has her husband and her children, she publishes one book after another, people read her and worship her, and on top of all that she has dozens of male admirers, maybe even dozens of lovers! They adore her. Božena writes to one of them in a letter: "What you have written to me, about having a right to feel proud because people honor and respect me, you yourself cannot have really believed this even when you wrote it, and now I myself can do nothing but smile as I read it."

That's how she replies to her lover's praises, playing at being a foolish little girl, the goody two-shoes, and delicate flower, to whom success means nothing. And the things she writes next! "A sincere heart, the endeavor to achieve perfection, the striving to help my people to the utmost limit of my capability—these are the only things at which I am superior to normal women, who do no good in the world."

I will tell the police exactly what I know of you: that you are an illegitimate child, that the people you think of as your parents are not your real ones; that you married an imperial civil servant on purpose to cling to as you pave your way to Vienna, but in Prague, among Czech patriots, you also want to stand out, which is why you won't stop boring the pants off us with your verses and stories and pretty words about the unity of the

Slav peoples. In my police report, I will also include the fact that when only newly wedded you couldn't bear to be with your husband, that you went in search of male friends and lovers, always in such a way that they helped your literary career; that you used the same criteria when choosing your female friends, who always had to be wealthy girls from good families, like Johanna and Sophie; that your friends are influential, well-known, and respected people, people such as Čelakovský, Purkyně, Erben, and Havlíček; and how you flirted your head off with all of them so they would contribute flattering reviews of your writing in the newspapers. I will not forget to add that you are a heartless mother, your children do not get enough to eat, while you just go on writing, even though you know that if you write you will hurt your family because the imperial police are after you. But above all, I will tell them that you have a lover. I do not know for certain, nor do I care. The police, and eventually society in general, will know that you are a fallen woman. From then on, no one will give you a helping hand, no one! What more is there to be said? I will fill in the details myself. I have a rich imagination and my dreams are in full bloom. Yes, you are a depraved woman who pursues relationships outside wedlock.

But no matter how much this may be the case, if, in the future, people remember ideas from this time, they will be yours. For they are easy to listen to. When you say: "What I long for is love, a true love, but not for one single person, but rather for everybody, for all humanity, a love that asks nothing in return, a love that would improve me, that would bring me closer to truth," that sounds pretty, very much so, and when seen in an album of memorabilia, next to your phrase "it is better to be a martyr than a good-for-nothing who doesn't even know why she's alive," people will be stunned and they'll believe it as if it were gospel. They will always read your work, both today and ten years from now and probably a hundred years later as well, they will read your writing and marvel at your ideas and your style, and they will remember your physical appearance. It is far more romantic for a woman writer to be beautiful than disagreeable to look at, even though the latter might have written volume after volume and suffered more.

And what will become of me? What will remain after me? A few reports written for the police, with which I will simply help turn you into a martyr, whereas I will always be a parasite for the coming generations, a shameless woman gnawed by envy. You will always be the superior one, even though you will die of hunger, even though everyone will abandon you.

It does not matter! If a parasite is what I must be, I might as well be a genuine one!

Božena Němcová is the illegitimate daughter of Duchess Katerina von Sagan. As to the identity of the aforementioned person's father, we have only rumors to go on."

No, no I can't go on like this if I don't want them to think I'm full of envy. First I will have to get everything straight in my own head and will then enforce upon all my thoughts a style and form that will suit the police. But do I really believe the Duchess von Sagan is Božena's mother?

The other day, when she was flat broke, I gave Božena a little loose change so that she could buy milk for her children. I
needed to search her apartment. In the cupboard I discovered
an engraving with this curious inscription: "The artist dedicates
this print to his daughter." The artist was none other than the
Spanish painter Francisco Goya. Perhaps a future historian or
relative will try to prove that Božena is Goya's daughter, to add a
little extra charm to her history.

What is the relationship between Božena and the duchess?
She told me how, in the park of Ratibořice castle, where she
grew up, from time to time a beautiful Amazon woman would
emerge from the trees and vanish in an instant: the duchess, out
riding with her admirers. I am sure that more than one of the
wonderful princesses and good witches in Božena's stories have
been based on this duchess.

Now they have summoned me to the prefecture. What a pity
I can't finish what I'm writing. What does that bore von Päumann want from me this time?

On the second day she realized she had to rein in her feelings
and, when welcoming the doctor in and when bidding him farewell, she gave him her hand in a gesture that could only be interpreted as forthright and friendly.

In the evening, when thinking everything over, she jotted in
her notebook: "What powerful and unfathomable charm, I ask
myself, can be hidden within a person who with a simple look,
a simple handshake, can strip me of all strength, whose tone of

voice can make me flutter like a reed in the wind? Why does the heart remain calm when a friend presses my hand, while the handshake of another man injects fire into my veins? Today I have experienced the power of such magic."

No matter what the cost, the prefect wants to uncover the conspiracy that he believes Božena is hatching, or at least, participating in. Von Päumann doesn't strike me as feeble minded, but a conspiracy? Božena, a conspirator? For the lousy handful of pennies they pay me now I have to invent a detective novel, preferably one with a mysterious murder in it. Oh, I'm getting fed up with old man von Päumann.

Right away, Herr von Päumann. Let me catch my breath, I tired myself out climbing the prefecture stairs. All right, let us begin. Forgive this cough of mine, you see, I . . . The other day I visited Božena at her home near Emmaus church and it was raining a little. The lamplighter was lighting the blue flames of the streetlamps and on the far side of the Vltava numerous yellow lights flickered like dozens of illuminated cat eyes. Not all cat eyes flicker though, do they? You don't know either? Excuse me, I am dithering on so. The Němec family was sitting in the kitchen, which they also use as a dining room and lounge. They had just finished dinner. Božena's husband was reading the newspaper and puffing on his pipe, comfortably ensconced in a chair; her daughter was playing Schubert's *Impromptus* on the piano (an old upright piano which the previous tenant had left behind); and the boys were looking for certain places on a map of the world. Božena was sitting at the table with her back to the others, her head bent a little to the left, and she was writing. Now and again, she turned to the boys to tell them where to find such and such a place on the map. It was one of those evenings that conjure up an idyllic image of an old, old world that has now ceased to exist.

"I was sitting on the sofa, reading the manuscript of Božena's latest short story. Suddenly I noticed that Němec puffed on his pipe ever faster and more violently. I watched him out of the corner of my eye; he held up his newspaper not with calm hands but with clenched fists. He was hiding behind the *Daily Prague*, but I thought I could see how his pale face concealed an inner fury. His daughter, Dora, was playing something by Haydn, then fumbled and had to start again. I glanced sideways at her; she was biting her lower lip, hard, looking first at her father with fear and then at her mother with eyes of silk, as if she wished to protect her. The boys plied their mother with questions about Duchess von Sagan; Karel was to go to Germany, to the castle of the duchess, as a gardener's apprentice. Božena answered them impatiently, because they kept on interrupting her work. In the end, she recommended they put such questions to their father, who could tell them not only where the Sagan family estate was, but also all the different places in Hungary where he'd worked during his years of forced exile. The brothers turned to their father and looked at him timidly; one shrugged his shoulders, the other signalled that they should drop the matter. They went silent. The newspaper in Němec's hands trembled visibly. Dora lost her concentration altogether and stopped playing. Her mother sat up, glanced at the wall, and began to put her books and papers in order. She stood up. One of the boys went to her and the other followed like a shadow. I realized that there was no point in staying and got ready to leave. Němec's slippers were so worn out that his bare feet must have been touching the floor.

"Whack! I nearly fell over. What a blow! By the time I'd recovered, Němec had left, slamming the door. The first bang had been a slam of his fist on the table where Božena sat tidying up her notes. Still frightened, I looked at the others. Dora appeared relieved, the boys smiled. Božena got up and headed out of the room. I followed her."

"So Mrs. Němcová's marriage is an unhappy one is it not, Fraülein Zaleski?"

"I have simply described her married life. That conclusion is your own, Herr von Päumann."

During the next curative session, the doctor seemed cold and reserved. She thought he was afraid that someone might interrupt their session, her husband or the children. Everybody had been warned not to enter the apartment so as not to interrupt the cure. But it dawned on her that the doctor's expression was one of fear, of concern. The doctor opened the curtains with a brusque movement, as he'd done on their first day. A milky light filled the room and she had the feeling she was sitting on a block of ice, in nothing but her underwear, drifting off toward the unknown. She tried to make the cold go away, putting all her energy into inventing questions for the doctor about the purpose of his instruments, about the countries he'd visited, but he answered only in a brief, clipped fashion. He left some of her questions unanswered.

"When that outburst was over, Herr von Päumann, Božena and I sat together in the half-shadow of her room. It was cold. But that smell of decomposing leaves, or of undergrowth after the rain, mmmm! Božena sighed with relief. She let herself go, and complained about her publisher, Mr. Pospíšil, a greedy man, a real stuffed shirt, who had released Božena's novel, *The Grandmother*, in installments instead of turning it into an attractive book; and the fee he paid her, she said, was so little she couldn't even buy winter clothes for the children. To change the subject and get the information I wanted out of her, I asked which of her jewels were the most beautiful.

"She opened a small box. Against the sky blue velvet, a pair of long earrings glimmered—Božena's wedding present from Duchess von Sagan. Then Božena removed the inner layer to reveal the bottom section, in which lay a smaller box made of wood. When she opened it, a necklace glittered before my eyes: five rows of garnet stones, linked by a silver coin with the portraits of the Emperor Josef and the Empress Marie Therese. Božena told me that in the little apartment in Ratibořice far from Prague where she lived with her parents, brothers, and sisters, they were accompanied for a few years by their grand-mother. This elderly lady possessed just a single dress for all the days of the week and one other for Sundays. Her only treasure was a painted trunk. Betty—this was Božena's name back then, Betty; she did not adopt Božena, her *nom de plume*, until she arrived in Prague many years later—liked to look at the trunk with the red flowers painted on it. Her grandmother kept papers and dried medicinal herbs in it, and right at the bottom was this little wooden box, and inside this, a garnet necklace.

"'Grandmother, why don't you ever put this necklace on?' Betty asked.

"'I wore it while Jiří, your grandfather, was alive. Do you like it? Well then, do you know what, little girl? When I die, the garnet necklace will be yours. Yes, I want you, my eldest granddaughter, to wear it. My garnet stones will protect you from all sorts of evil. If you ever get rid of it, you'll regret it. Remember, pretty one, if you want to make something of your life, always make sure you keep these garnet stones.'

"Božena remembered it clearly. She said that once at Christ-mas she didn't have anything to give her children to eat, and was obliged to pawn a gold chain and a ring in order to buy a few apples, eggs to make a sponge cake, walnuts, and a little tea. But she would never part with her grandmother's necklace, no mat-ter what.

"Božena confessed to me then that as a young girl she used to laugh at her grandmother's hopelessly old-fashioned clothes, her opinions, and her habit of speaking pure Czech, without a trace of German in it. Her grandmother taught her the names of the trees and plants in Czech, told her folktales. Betty asked her grandmother to tell her these stories at bedtime. The more often Betty heard a tale, the more she would like it."

Her next medical treatment continued to be as cold and mechanical as that of the day before. Although the palms of his hands woke up previously unknown desires in her, while his fingers made her delirious with pleasure, the doctor's expression remained abstracted, distant. He touched her belly and she wanted to look him in the eye. She half-opened her eyes: he wasn't looking at her. As his fingers stroked her body, his eyes focused on something far away, searching for the white light of day, staring at the far side of the river.

Fräulein Zaleski, do you know anything about . . . No! I'm not talking about the novel *The Grandmother*. You've written us a whole epic poem about this grandmother of hers and I'm fed up with that subject. Do me the favor of not interrupting me from now on. All right? I believe I've been too patient with you. Do you know Václav Frič personally?"

"*Nein*, Herr von Päumann, not personally."

"What do you mean, no! That is a great mistake! Frič is one of the worst enemies of our monarchy, of the Austro-Hungarian Empire and of our institutions. He is one of the great revolutionaries who set off the 1848 revolution! Němcová invites him to her home almost every day."

"Yes, Herr von Päumann! At Božena Němcová's I read some of his writings, all of them full of revolutionary fervor."

"This man has been released from prison and has had the impertinence to start up a magazine to which the most ardent revolutionary leaders of the Czech movement are supposed to contribute. What do you know about this?"

"I have been able to find out that, indeed, Němcová is preparing her contribution to this publication. Frič and his group are all good friends of hers. She told me once that she shares her frugal teas with them and laughed, saying that, while they converse, she darns their worn-out underwear."

"Prague society cannot accept such insolence."

"Mrs Božena is so shameless that the bad things people say are of no importance to her."

"What about her husband?"

"I don't know."

"Find out if that impudent man Frič is a frequent visitor even when Mrs. Božena is not at home. He may be plotting something with her husband. Auf Wiedersehen, Fräulein."

"Herr von Päumann . . ."

"*Bitte?* Do you have some information for me?"

"I have started to work on . . ."

"On what?"

"You once broached the subject of Božena's lovers. So I . . . I've started to work on . . ."

"Then by all means get on with it. But please do leave right now, for heaven's sake!"

✦

"Do you know," the doctor said unexpectedly in a changed voice, as he put his medical instruments in his case and she buttoned up her blouse. "You once asked me about my travels. Deep down, I don't really believe in travel as a way of discovering things. A certain someone has written words that show I am not mistaken: 'You can know the whole world without leaving your own home. This is why the wise man knows without having travelled, understands without having seen.' Do you follow me?"

"Perfectly. What is more, I am in complete agreement. In the evening, when I sit down under the yellow light of this oil lamp, there appear worlds I have never seen. Then I do no more than describe that which I imagine, and from this, novels, stories and, above all, folktales are born. People ask me how I know those immense seas, those cliffs, and sweet fruits from the garden of delights. I cannot answer them because I have not seen these things; or rather I have, but here, in my room. It is under this oil lamp that the branches of the most unusual-looking trees sway and let fall multicolored flowers."

"Yes, I understand you. The wise man whose words I have just quoted, also said: 'If you wish to possess the whole world, own nothing. If you are always busy, you will not take pleasure in the world.'"

"I feel that way, too. I own only the things you see around me, those books on the shelf, the table, and the oil lamp, and I take most pleasure in the world when I am inventing it." She broke off, and then added: "Who was the wise man that wrote those magnificent sentences, or rather those marvellous verses?"

"Legend has it that he was a librarian, whose name in his

mother tongue means 'old master.' At the end of his life, he reached the conclusion that mankind was a lost cause. So he took his yak—"

"Yak? Is that an animal?"

"Yes, it's a kind of mountain bison. And with it he headed off into the wild and savage world of nature, where reason and logic reign. At the peak of a mountain gorge he decided to record his thoughts on a piece of paper. He lived roughly five centuries before Christ."

"What about you? Why are you not a philosopher; why are you a doctor?"

"For me, both callings are identical. As a philosopher I would help people; as a doctor I can do so in a more direct fashion. I believe that the more one gives to others, the more one acquires personally. I find this to be the case every day."

I was received by Božena's husband. He looked downcast, as was his wont, but when he saw me turn the corner of the staircase, his face expressed the absolute repugnance of someone who has just woken up to find an insect on the pillow. Reluctantly, he invited me in, and without offering me a seat, sat down himself on an old, gutted armchair and lit his pipe. He puffed away in silence and looked at the white wall, just as if I weren't there. I didn't even take off my coat; it was so chilly I could have caught my death of cold.

Božena wasn't in; her husband was ignoring me; only from time to time did he turn to look at the window from which you could see the building's interior balconies. I went over to the window and saw a man outside. He spotted me and waved. Then I recognized him: he was Božena's new friend, or I should say, her doctor. I answered his wave with a nod of the head. Němec, noticing this, leapt over to the window, elbowed me out of the way, looked down, and banged on the window frame so hard he made the glass shake. He was red faced and frightened me. I slipped away to the outside staircase and I leaned on the wall to catch my breath. When I was back home I realized the back of the dark brown coat I'd been wearing was completely covered in white from leaning on the wall.

I will send Herr von Päumann the notes I have written here. Let him make what he will of it. What does he expect me to write if there are plenty of days when nothing happens? I am halfway through the text that will destroy Božena. Now I must write her biography. Von Päumann has been going on to me about it. It's as if his life depended on it.

Yes, I shall destroy Božena. Materially, she is so badly off that things couldn't get much worse for her. I will ensure that she loses what is left of her reputation. I remember what she said of my lost friend, František: "What is left of an enemy may come back to life, as happens with the remnants of diseases and fires. Which is why they must be exterminated altogether. One must never ignore an enemy, no matter how weak he might be. He can be dangerous at any given moment, like a spark in a haystack."

Yes, I'd been wearing my dark brown coat with its back all covered in white. Božena lives precariously; she is even poorer than I am. Her husband's madness has led her to this point. Is it worth having a husband like Božena's? Whose solitude is more desolate: mine, living among five younger siblings who need to be fed; or hers, living in the company of someone with whom she has nothing in common?

The wind at the edge of the Vltava sweeps away the fallen leaves. But what is this young woman doing at the riverbank if she went out to buy a few bread rolls and half a dozen eggs for supper? When she realized her mistake, she laughed and started to walk, but in the opposite direction of home. She skipped like a little girl who can't walk past a geometrical shape on the pavement without jumping over the corresponding paving stone. She was moving in the same direction as the river's current, jumping and skipping like a frog, and after one especially long jump, her feet took off from the pavement. Without touching the ground, the woman glided, her feet grazing the fence along the river, until she was flying over the trees and could see everything that was happening on the first floors of all the houses. Before her appeared a green ravine in which sat an ancient sage with a thin white beard, jotting down his thoughts. She flew over the roofs of the houses, between the chimneys. She looked down into the twisted streets; the sage was sitting there in the shade. Then she, a svelte black figure with her hair blowing, stretched out a hand toward him, who put aside his pen, reached his hand out to her . . . and now the two of them were gliding together over the red roofs, between the spires of the chapel and church towers. As they flew above the bell towers and headed for Charles Bridge, she smoothed down her lace petticoats and her wide, pleated skirt, which the wind kept blowing upward, and the ancient sage kept his left hand on his beard, which flew and fluttered like a silver veil.

How to begin the biography of Božena, then called Betty? What do writers do when blank pages stare at them, immaculate, mocking, whispering, between grimaces: "You'll manage it . . . or maybe you won't!" I will start by describing a specific fact, for example, that it was autumn and the apples were ripe.

It was the beginning of autumn. A sixteen-year-old girl was sitting in front of her house, eating one apple after another, picking them straight from the tree. Her eyes never ceased wandering over the castle garden, where trees and bushes burned with yellow and red flames. The girl's name was Betty. She was combing a doll, whose name was Wilhelmine, like the duchess who spent her summers at the castle. Betty imagined the doll was a princess, the most beautiful one in the world, who would one day be rescued by a prince from the dragon that was keeping her in thrall. The doll-princess was she herself; this miracle she dreamed of was supposed to happen to her. Suddenly, she heard footsteps. A tall, swarthy, uniformed man with big ears was approaching her at a military pace. She quickly hid the doll behind her back. The man tried to smile, but it came out as a grimace.

"Hello, little girl!" he said, or rather shouted, in a hoarse voice.

Which little girl was he referring to? The man went on.

"Don't hide the doll; show it to me!"

That was when Betty got really frightened and ran off. She ran as fast as her legs could carry her until she got to a friend's house. In the evening when she returned home, her mother told her that the arrogant, noisy man had come to ask for Betty's hand in marriage, even though he was the same age as her mother. They had looked all over the park for her so that she could meet her future husband. Where had she been?

"At Pepinka's house. Mama, I saw that man. I don't want him for a husband."

"Nonsense, Betty! You have to want him, because I like him. He's highly eligible."

"I don't want him and that's that."

"Betty, we're packed like sardines here, eight people in a small flat. Don't you understand?"

"I want to earn my own money. I'll work as a maid or a cook."

"Have I made such an effort to turn you into Fräulein Betty, just for that? No, little lady. You will marry Officer Josef Němec."

"Mama, I would much rather be a laundrywoman like you!"

"You will be Josef Němec's wife. End of story."

"No Mama, please, no! Anything, but not that! Please, I beg of you, please!"

"Don't beg, it won't get you anywhere. I have thought everything out. And you know perfectly well that I never go back on my word. Now, go to bed."

◆

On the morning of September the twelfth, four carriages with uniformed coachmen belonging to Duchess von Sagan waited in front of Betty's house. A swarm of curious bystanders surrounded all this aristocratic splendor as they tried to guess the color of the bride's dress, how the maids of honor would be dressed, who would stand as the witnesses for the bride and who for the bridegroom. The witnesses were already climbing the staircase from the basement apartment and behind them walked the bridesmaids, Helena and Josefa, in pink dresses, with their escorts. Betty's father, the elegant Josef Pankl, climbed the staircase and turned to see Betty, his Betty, whom he had tried to liberate from the bridegroom, but could not override his wife. Betty walked slowly, making an effort and lowering her veil to conceal her tear-stained face. She stoped at each step; at the top of the staircase she turned, as if wanting to go back home. Her mother grabbed her by the arm and lead her to one of the carriages.

The bystanders gossiped about it all; some said the bride, in her sky-blue dress and white veil, looked like an angel, while others repeated that blue was not a suitable color for a bride. One woman, who noticed the aversion to the bridegroom stamped on the bride's face, concluded the debate with an old superstition: "A blue dress will never bring happiness to a marriage."

These words were passed on in a trice. Everybody was now convinced of this truth, which sounded like nothing so much as a curse.

The carriage Betty was sitting in moved forward on the path lined with plane trees; she knew it like the back of her hand.

She felt weary, having spent almost the entire night and the early morning crying. She would never have believed herself capable of crying for such a long time. She looked out at the scenery; now, in such changed circumstances, deep in a kind of desperation previously unknown to her, the familiar spots seemed strange to her. Some trees have begun to go yellow, which made her think of the crown of green branches that, according to custom, she had crafted with the help of her friend Josefa. As she made it, she said farewell to those ideals that she had been weaving together for seventeen years. Once the crown was ready, she threw it into the waters of the Úpa, together with her hopes. Now at this moment, she had just one tiny hope left: that some kind of miracle would take place that could separate her from the future, from that terrible time to be, lived by the side of the man to whom she had been allocated, from the future that she saw as an endless grey and windy November day.

They were now approaching the church. When walking from school to home she always used to think that this cheerful church looked splendid, with its steeple that had a huge onion on its top. Betty loved to look at the clock hung under the belfry, how its golden hands shone even on overcast days, and she liked to imagine that the saint in front of the church was making that gesture with his arm to say, "Goodbye for now, girl, see you tomorrow!" Now it was just the opposite: everything struck her as alien and hostile. The church was full of people who had come to the wedding, spreading out along the pews like a grey avalanche. She was aware only of two side altarpieces, baroque ones, their candles lit, and the altar that reached to the ceiling. She was afraid. That altar covered in ridiculous ornamentation, with two equally absurd puffy-cheeked cherubs that filled her with horror, as if in place of two playful angels the Pope of Rome himself was there, ready to cut off her head. Why the pope? She didn't really know, in her anguish she could only see the stern papal mitre, a scream and the end. They led her over to the priest. For the first time in her life, she panicked. She lost track of everything that happened afterward . . .

Later, she was sitting at a table on the terrace of the White Lion restaurant next to that man. She couldn't eat; she lowered her head down to hide the tears that fell, against her will, like heavy raindrops onto her plate. She glanced sideways at him. He didn't look happy either. Poor Josef. Poor Josef, she would repeat to herself throughout the night.

The following day, the dahlia festival was held in the spacious room next to the restaurant. Some fifty growers exhibited their creations, magnificent dahlias of many different colors. There was a banquet, and prizes were given for the most beautiful flower, after which there was a ball. When the music began to play and the bridegroom offered her his arm, Betty started to dance in a vehement fashion—she led that man in the dance so that people should not notice that Josef, her husband, was someone also deserving of compassion. That it was not only she who was unhappy with him, but that he, too, would be unhappy with her. Betty, seemingly happy as a lark, spent the whole night dancing. She realized the extent to which she was exciting all the men present and to the joy of her uninhibited male partners, threw herself into each dance as if at least for that night she wanted to forget what was coming. When the time came for the Queen of the Festival to be elected, Betty was chosen.

She said goodbye to her parents as if she never wanted the farewell to end. Everybody else was turning to leave, only she stayed on until her mother gripped her arm and said firmly: "You have to go, daughter, you are no longer mine!"

She was looking through the window to see if the young doctor was on his way when a group of officers quarrelling in the street reminded her of her husband. On the evening when she came home flying—yes, she flew all the way into the main room, having left the ancient sage sitting on Petřín Mountain—her husband's expression soon had her putting her feet down on the hard floor of the kitchen. She knew only too well what would follow: recriminations, shouts, fist banging, door banging. By this stage, she was almost indifferent to such scenes; the only thing that mattered to her at that moment was to keep intact the magic that filled her to the brim, that urged her to take flight once again. Her husband, his arms folded and a ferocious expression on his face, had placed himself firmly in front of the window. To get in my way, she thought with a smile.

She went into her bedroom, closed the door, and turned the key in the lock. On the other side somebody started to bang on the wood of the door, but she took no notice; her room was immersed in the orange of a Bengal light, in which the long dying tones of that curious flute could be heard. She made a few movements, as if to dance to its rhythm, and when that shrill instrument went silent, she sat down at her table. She thought about the white-bearded old man, and how right he was that you can know the world without stepping out of your front door. She wrote down: "When I don't have reality, let dreams make me happy! How many times have I satisfied my longing for the sea in dreams? How many times have I dreamed of joyful landscapes? Dreams have brought me people I love whom I will never see again; in dreams, I can live as I wish and be happy. Why complain about them being only dreams if these feelings will be with me for the rest of the day! I am grateful, deeply grateful for this kind of dream." She wrote these words down in a notebook, but in fact she knew they were addressed to a specific person, somebody with whom she never ceased to converse in her mind. She wrote more and more, until six o'clock in the morning. She produced folktales because they allowed her to write about a certain type of happy love affair which can only be found in such stories.

Today she looks through the window to see if her doctor has arrived, but on the street she can see nothing but a few uncouth officers whacking at maids' skirts and untying their aprons. Today, oddly enough, even this she finds amusing and thinks about a story or novella that could be set in this kind of environment. She goes off to jot down a few notes. Later she returns to the window so as not to miss the sight of him coming to her home. What must he look like when walking along the street? People probably look at him.

They weren't looking at him. On the street, nobody took any notice of the moustachioed man who swung his cane with confidence as he walked. She, on the other hand, upon seeing him, thought that Neptune himself had made a hole in the dark grey sky, or rather several holes, so that the rays of the sun, like countless torches, could project their light on that broad-shouldered man with a cane.

"Let's not waste time, Fräulein Zaleski. You visited Mrs. Němcová after she returned to Prague from Northern Hungary."

"More than once, Herr von Päumann."

"What comments did she make about her deportation to Northern Hungary?"

"She told me that when she arrived at Banská Bystrica, the city's prefect, whose name was Zólom, told her that he had received an order from his superiors to the effect that she should return home at once. She answered: 'Dear me, whatever must I have done for them to be so afraid of me!' She was very sorry not to be able to finish her literary tasks in Slovakia."

"Northern Hungary."

"I'm sorry, I meant Northern Hungary. That evening on her way from Northern Hungary, after having reached Bratislava and gone to the house of some acquaintances to spend the night, the police went to fetch her. She had to go with the officers at once. At four in the morning, they put her on the first train back to Prague."

"All of this confirms our own information. What else were you able to discover?"

"After coming back, I visited Mrs. Němcová several times . . ."

"You already told us that, also in writing. I have it here: 'I visited Mrs. Němcová more than once . . .'"

"Forgive me. I imagine you will be interested in her relationship with the Czech writer, journalist, and revolutionary Karel Havlíček, who was deported to the Tyrol."

"We are certainly most interested in that!"

"'The last time I saw her, Němcová declared that she had to go and see Havlíček's wife because she hadn't visited her for a long time."

"I will make a note of that. You may go, I will summon you here again soon."

What Němcová cannot possibly know is that Julie Havlíček is seriously ill. Tuberculosis, like that pathetic informer of ours. Mrs. Havlíček will die before her twenty-seventh birthday. And she will not see her husband again. Havlíček, that arrogant journalist who, despite our efforts, we could never get on our side. I don't want to wish anyone any harm, but fate will pay him back for all the damage he has caused our empire.

We have managed to silence many of the ringleaders of the 1848 revolution. We removed Palacký from the ranks of our scientists, we obliged Rieger to emigrate abroad, we forced some, such as Tomek and several others, to come to our side. But Havlíček is a tough nut to crack. We banned his newspaper but he went on publishing it clandestinely until we were obliged to deport him to some remote corner, in this case the Tyrol.

Oh, this Czech nationalist movement is so absurd! We have managed to paint it into a corner. Only this Havlíček remains! Now that we have reduced him to powerlessness in the Tyrol, the Czechs have converted him into a symbol of all their suppressed attempts to keep going. Yes, Havlíček, you'll get what's coming to you. I'll make sure of that personally! Just as we shall knock the stuffing out of that miserable witch Němcová!

He came in. She melted in the shine of his smile. Then she lay face down, her muscles happily relaxed, lots of glass cups suctioned to her back. He went to the kitchen and brought out a steaming towel. When removing the glass cups he dropped the towel onto her back. The patient almost screamed, the burning fabric scalded her back so, but she imagined herself looking like a screaming pig and controlled herself. Afterward, he spread the burning towel over her entire back, pressing it down in various places: the nape, the waist, the thighs. Now the towel was warming her up agreeably.

"Turn onto your back."

Betty Pankl signed the marriage certificate in her childlike, ornamental handwriting. Then her husband took the queen of the dahlia dance off to his prosaic, brutal, military world.

Červený Kostelec—a city both small and poor. A world of

disappointment, misery, and suffering. Her husband's coarse manners were better suited to the barracks. Betty got to know his habits well, without ever getting used to them. She never quite managed to tolerate Němec's personality. From the start, fights broke out between husband and wife, leading to violent scenes: her husband was jealous of Betty's admirers at society balls, he would haul her off mid-dance and at home he gave vent to anger befitting a military man. People said that one time he wanted to shoot his wife and that some day he might really do it.

Later came the journeys, those journeys that left Betty half-dead from exhaustion, those transfers from somewhere to somewhere else in Bohemia or Moravia. In this way, the Austro-Hungarian monarchy made Němec pay for his active participation in the Czech national movement. From Červený Kostelec they had to move to Josefov, and when Betty was seven months pregnant, they set off on a long journey along dusty, uneven roads to Litomyšl. From there they went to Polná, then back from the east to a place far in the west, to Domažlice, and then to Všeruby, a mountain village, and then all of a sudden off to the east again, to Nymburk, and when that was over they headed north, to Liberec. Over this period, Betty had four children, became chronically ill, met Czech patriots, and burned all the literary drafts that she had written in the German language.

Above all, when her husband was transferred to Prague, she got a chance to spend a long time in the city. She decided that it was there where she would put down roots. Not long after her twenty-third birthday she felt healthy enough to take part in social and cultural life. Prague made a deep impression on her. This young woman never missed a ball, or any operatic or theatrical performance, or any excursion or meeting organized by Czech writers.

It was Sunday, a lukewarm March day. Betty put on a new spring dress and a straw hat with a ribbon. I like to imagine that the ribbon was green, so it would match the color of her eyes. Writers, artists, students, and their girlfriends met up among the rocks and woods of Šárka. Spring was already in the air, even though the branches of the trees were still bare. She had always liked that time of year just before the arrival of spring; she called it the era of hope. The groups of friends headed toward the castle submerged in the Star Forest. Nebesky, the poet whose pseudonym was Celestial, approached Betty, whom he'd met a few days earlier on Sofia Island. In Šárka, the poet admired the wild-looking rocks; Betty looked at the emergent grass. The young poet picked a bunch of violets with which he decorated his friend's hat. He talked to her about German philosophy and other things, but the main theme of the monologue was the role he believed the Czech nation would one day play. Celestial made an effort to impress her, this beauty from the provinces, and she listened to him attentively, but with reserve. The poet held forth more and more because he found this young woman had unusual intelligence and powers of understanding. On their way back, they reached Saint Margaret's Chapel, where they broke away from the group to continue their walk to Strahov. Prague was at their feet, the dark blue ribbon of the Vltava dividing it in two. From up above, the river looked like a winding stream that crossed a few narrow walkways. Above the couple's heads, the stars blinked and winked. Both felt that this moment was as unusual as it was unrepeatable.

Even now, a decade later, Božena still remembers that sudden sense of connection. She told me that the world opened out before her: her intoxicated mind immersed itself in the shadows of the universe and flew around its lights; in that labyrinth of the infinite there appeared before her a small but brightly lit place. As if ashamed of the grandiloquent words she was about to use, she whispered them into my ear: "my country." Then and there she promised her new friends that at home she would write a poem about the ideas they had discussed. She wrote it down immediately when she got back, in the silence of the night. The title was: "To Czech women," and she signed it: Božena Němcová. This is how Betty, who had expressed herself in German, turned overnight into Božena, a writer in the Czech language.

The poem, that Celestial reworked as best he could, soon appeared in the magazine *Flowers*, it was followed by other poems and in a short time the name Božena Němcová penetrated the consciousness of the Czech literati.

Then came the summer. Celestial went off on a holiday in the woods around Kokořín castle. Božena went to see him there. For one of their walks around that romantic castle, she wore the garnet necklace that her grandmother had bequeathed her, and told its story to her friend. Celestial wanted to have it as a token of her love for him. You gave him everything, Božena, you gave yourself to him unreservedly, despite the terrible scenes your husband made at home. And Celestial lorded over you, but he never managed to obtain your grandmother's garnet necklace.

In the fall, Celestial left to work in Vienna. Božena sickened with sorrow. She was cared for by the doctor Čejka, one of her countless admirers. He brought her books on ancient Greece and spoke tenderly to her. He hoped that by reading the Iliad and the Odyssey, she would become interested in classical culture—that is to say, in him—and would distance herself from romantic literature—that is to say, from Celestial. Both men, Celestial in Vienna and Čejka in Prague, competed with each other by writing verses that spoke of you, Božena, and of their jealousy. Prague society had fun at your expenses. Since then you have never ceased to offer yourself up as a subject for gossip, for anecdotes recounted at the dinner parties of certain artistic circles in Prague. That has never bothered you one bit. But, for some reason, it saddens me.

You were forever curing yourself of lovesickness as if it were a contagious disease. Later, once the worst was over, you started to write. First poems, then folktales. When it comes down to it, everything you have written up to now has been fairy tales. In your novels and stories you write about the things you had dreamed of as a girl. Long ago, your grandmother told you all those Czech folktales that have happy endings, and you, ingenuous as you are, thought that life was like that too. Even now you still believe in dragons, witches, and Prince Charming, admit it! You've been looking for Prince Charming in the kind of men who more resemble dragons. You know this perfectly well, yet you go on searching, you dunce, you keep on trusting, so naively!

But . . . your quest for ideal love will be the end of you. I promise you that. I, Vítězka, whom none of you have ever taken into consideration, promise you that.

The doctor massaged her more attentively than ever. In fact, were his fingers moving above the surface of the corset or beneath it? Where did the doctor end and the man begin?

In the evening, she rejected her husband's advances. She couldn't stand him. Her head was full of the young doctor. She asked herself what good could come of it, unable as she was to allow herself any false hope. Even if he had taken a serious interest in her, how long could it last? Soon he would find a girl his own age, and Božena would be the one who suffered. Having thought it over for a while, she told herself: I will turn it all into literature. I will celebrate him through my stories and novels, that would be the greatest thing I could offer him. In this respect, no other woman can ever outdo me. But I will not let myself be deprived of reality. Let whatever has to happen, happen. I will experience it to the fullest, even if it costs me my life.

"Your medical treatment has a sweetness to it," she told the doctor the following day. "Your methods are as gentle as the caress of a bird's wing. In general, doctors tend to like the sight of blood. At the drop of a hat they bleed you or reach for their scalpels."

"Yes, my methods are rather refined."

"Everything can be cured with refined methods?"

"Curing somebody is like fighting against an enemy. If you

can't make headway with a subtle, painless method, you attack head on."

"Why are you treating me? You are caring for me, a poor woman, free of charge. What do you get out of it?"

"A doctor's mission is to help people. Our mutual friends told me that you, an admired and respected writer—I will not use the word 'famous' because it is not in my vocabulary—are being persecuted by society at large and perhaps even by the secret police. A moment ago, I said that refined people will defeat the vulgar ones. This is a truth difficult to deny, but it is just as difficult to make it fit into real life. I try to do just that: I am always on the side of the persecuted."

"You're treating me for free because you think I'm well-known, even though I am not well-regarded by most people."

"Be careful with the business of fame: remember that the tallest trees are the ones that are felled."

"Or perhaps you are treating me because I'm a Czech writer who defends everything that is ours, everything Czech, and tries to instill meaning in it all."

"What interests me is the universe, not national questions. Although there is no doubt that you are right."

"What do you mean, I'm right? What is truth?"

"Paradoxical, always."

"What does that mean?"

"That you have to bend. If you don't want to be broken, bend."

"How can I bend when I have a goal? I feel that I should become a kind of educator. Or a writer who teaches."

"An educator, a master? I would only accept the second meaning of the latter word: a good person is the master of a bad one."

"I have set myself a goal, namely, to conquer ignorance."

"You, conquer? What is victory? The most appropriate way of celebrating a victory is by organizing a funeral service, a sensible person would say."

"Come down to my level. Although there is much I do not know, I know much more than most: I know Czech history, the Czech language, Czech culture. What I want to do, what I need to do, is share this knowledge of mine with other people, so that they may follow me if they wish."

"Have more humility! Nobody knows anything, you included."

He grabbed his cane and hat, and took a long look at her from the doorway, saying, "Recognize that too, dear friend, and you will be happy."

She leaned back on the window frame and watched him leave. He didn't swing his cane; the points of his mustache no longer pointed all the way up. Neptune did not illuminate him with torches. On the contrary, the light emanated from him, she thought.

"Fräulein Zaleski, we do not have enough information on the activity of the writer Němcová during the revolutionary upsets of 1848. Unfortunately, during that period we had not yet started to intercept correspondence. We have asked you for a minute description of this writer's activity then. I do not need to add that this material is of the utmost importance to us. Do you have it?"

"In 1848, when Němcová was twenty-eight years old, her husband was transferred to Všeruby, a small mountain village on the border between Bohemia and Bavaria. The Němec family was billeted at the home of the pharmacist. The people in that area tended to speak the German language and prefer German culture. Once in the village, Němcová dedicated herself—as she had done wherever she moved—to bringing Czech culture to these people, to popularizing Czech culture, to spreading the use of the Czech language. She ordered Czech books from Prague booksellers, paid for them with her own money, and then set up a kind of mobile library and bookshop."

"Have you any proof the writer was involved in these activities?"

"Of course. I have a copy of a letter of hers addressed to Pospíšil, a Prague publisher, dated April 17 1848: 'Last year, during my stay in Prague, you and I decided that I could run a bookshop aimed at educating these country people. The people here know almost nothing about the world. I consider it most important, as would anybody concerned with the well-being of their nation, that country folk be better informed. For the time being, the only way to educate people is through reading. Which is why I have set all my hopes on the idea of a mobile library and bookshop, an enterprise that would prove to be of great value to ignorant people.'

"How did this enterprise fare?"

"As was to be expected, Němcová lost a lot of money with it. Not only that, but also the inhabitants of that geographical area, who had at first been indifferent toward the Němec couple, became openly hostile. This is natural enough: Němcová woke them up from their lethargy and somnolence. Should you require proof in writing, here is a note of hers dating from that period: 'They've shown their true colors, these people from the villages and the town of Domažlice. My husband and I cannot so much as step out into the street, because they have threatened to beat us and throw us out by brute force. This churlishness instead of gratitude for our sincere concern for them.'"

"Could it be said that this writer launched a campaign of political agitation?"

"Yes, what she was doing was mobilizing the poor against the rich."

"Have you proof of that?"

"Yes, a letter of hers dating from March 1848: 'How human misery upsets me! Oh, Lotty, you have no idea of the poverty suffered by humble people. Believe me when I say that a wealthy man's dog would not eat what the poor have to eat every day. How much money is wasted, how many fortunes are lost to gambling, or spent on clothes and other trifles, while all the time there are people who are dying of hunger! What justice, what Christian love! When I see all of this, I feel like walking among the poor to show them where to search for justice.' That is literally what she says."

"And what was Němcová's realtionship then with the Catholic church, one of the mainstays of our empire?"

"Our writer published a few markedly anticlerical articles. On May 24 1849, she wrote in Prague's *Afternoon Post*, about an event in the district of Klatovy. The title of the article was 'A Little Story about the Religious Beliefs of Jesuits.' In it, she detailed how the Jesuits visited some dying people with a miraculous cross on which the crucified figure shook his head and moved his eyes. When they had left, a citizen of Klatovy got hold of the cross and saw that it was put together with wire: when one wire end was pulled, the crucified figure moved his head and eyes."

"Thank you, Fräulein Zaleski. I am most pleased with your work today. Write a report about these educated ladies who are friends of Němcová: what they do and what they are like, what their relationship is with the writer and vice versa. We will see each other again shortly, Fräulein."

She went out onto the street and had the sensation again that the wind was lifting her and taking her over the city, over the river. "Dear friend," echoed his voice in her ears. She was flying fast, gaining height. Today she was heading for the steeple of Saint Vito's Cathedral. "More humility . . ." Everything was whirling around in her brain. She looked down and in front of the cathedral she saw a beggar. She descended in order to approach him with a few coins in her hand, all that she had. But that's not a beggar! she realized. The old sage was half-kneeling, hands joined under the wide sleeves of the worn kimono he wore. He looked at her as she came zigzagging down toward him, but he did not see her.

Like the last time, she reached out to the old man, to take hold of him and bring him flying into the air, up to the furthest heights of happiness. He looked beyond her, through her, to where he had been before he was born and to where he would return after death.

Seeing him so concentrated, she left him there and took flight once more. Her hair was loose and she wanted to share the happiness she felt with the castles of clouds and the networks of sunbeams, with each and every ribbon of smoke from the chimneys.

Then she flew in the direction of her room. She sat at her table and started to write a folktale. The title she chose was: "The Willow Tree and the Maiden."

A dangerous woman, whichever way you look at her. She thinks logically, like a man. Everything she does has something to do with forwarding the cause of women's emancipation. She has reached the conclusion that customs and social prejudices should not stand in the way of women and defends their equality vis-à-vis men. She is convinced of it, and as if that weren't bad enough, she even puts it in writing. She must be destroyed. Not in a violent or underhanded way. In that case, the Czechs would have a martyr, like their beloved Havlíček, whom we have imprisoned far from Prague and who continues his attacks against us even so. Fräulein Zaleski is taking her task as an informer to heart. I do believe that the envy and jealousy that she feels toward this other woman are greater by far than any admiration she might feel. She leaves no stone unturned in search of material that can do her harm, and I wouldn't be surprised if she weren't preparing some kind of surprise for us, some revelation that we have not asked her for, simply out of spite. I would swear that she is probing into the most private corners of Němcová's life in order to sabotage her. I imagine that Zaleski wouldn't balk at the need to invent something, or at the pleasure of inventing it, even if it comes to her in a dream; she, all of whose amorous advances must surely have been spurned.

For years we have been humiliating Němcová's husband and we will go on doing so. Mrs. Němcová, we will make a beggar of you. We will let you die of hunger. Alone, friendless, you will be an example so that people will fear all suspects under police surveillance, as if they had the plague.

After a few hours of writing, she looked out of the window and saw the day's first light. The most appropriate way of celebrating a victory is by organizing a funeral service, she thought again. She crossed out the title "The Willow Tree and the Maiden" and in its place wrote "Victoria." *Yes, it has be Victoria, Victory,* she told herself, and went on writing:

> *A man and his wife had been living together for quite a time already, when one night, Vítek woke up. A full moon was lighting up the fields as if it were day. With indescribable pleasure he watched his wife as she slept peacefully, and bent forward gently to kiss the black curls that twisted their way*

down the length of her body, over the pillow and the white sheets. He looked at the sleeper's beautiful face, when suddenly startled, he moved closer: it seemed to him that this beautiful woman was no longer breathing. He placed a hand over her heart: it wasn't beating. Her hand was cold, his beloved lay lifeless, like a flower fallen from an apple tree. Desperate, Vítek jumped out of bed and called his mother-in-law for help. "Do not fret, my son," she answered him, "because there can be no good reason for your fright."

Together they entered the bedroom. Lo and behold, Victoria had revived and, surprised by the commotion, asked what the matter was. Full of joy, Vítek took her in his arms and told her about his shock. "Listen, Vítek, and I'll tell you about my dreams: on clear moonlit nights I dream I hear the tempting voice of the willow tree calling me. I open the window, the willow tree bends in my direction, and I cannot help but throw myself into its arms. But then it is no longer just a willow, but a great lady, a noble lady who leads me through her palace toward a resplendent golden throne. As far as the eye can see, there stretches a magnificent, perfumed garden. Everything is alive, blooming. The trees, the flowers, bend toward each other like lovers, telling each other secret legends in silvery voices, and I understand their language. Then from the rivers and the fountains, from the cliffs and the mountains arise nymphs dressed in white. They dance amorously, sing and laugh, and invite me to join them. I understand what they say; I hasten to revel in their embraces; I too sing and dance and have such fun with them. The queen, this eternally young and splendorous queen, is delighted with her daughters. When I have to leave my friends, I can still hear their seductive voices in my heart, and when a long time passes without the queen calling for me, I feel sad," said Victoria, finally.

"I don't like your dreams, Victoria." her husband said. "I fear that you will forget about me in that realm of beauty, and that one day you will remain there."

"Do not be afraid, Vítek. It is only for a very short while that I am allowed to visit the fairy queen and that palace I love so much. I always know I have to come back."

Even so, Vítek did not like her dreams, as they came back again and again after that night. He feared for the life of his beloved and wanted to free her from that mysterious power. He told himself that the best way to do it would be to cut down the willow tree. But he didn't want to do so without Victoria's consent. So one day, while she was basket weaving by the window, he said to his wife:

"That willow tree is blocking the light. Maybe I should cut it down."

"No, Vítek, you should do no such thing," Victoria implored. "I love that willow tree too much. If you love me, do not do it. You never know, you may regret it afterward."

But the man could find no peace. He didn't want his wife to disappear into a world that he could not enter. One night, when Victoria was sleeping, showing no apparent signs of life, he went out with an axe and a single goal in mind. With four well-placed blows he felled the willow tree and a cry of pain shot through his soul. He threw the axe away and went into the

*house. In her mother's arms, Victoria was dead. The blows of
the axe, which had destroyed the willow tree, had put an end to
Victoria's life.*

They have asked me for a report on Božena's female friends. That
means writing about Johanna and Sophie Rott. Sophie told me
delightedly about her first meeting with Němcová. It took place
a few years after Božena's definitive return to Prague. Johanna's
husband, who was then her fiancé, spoke to the two sisters about
the writer Božena with admiring enthusiasm. Johanna agreed to
meet her although she had reservations: the sisters were from an
aristocratic family and had been educated in a private school for
noble young ladies. Johanna had turned into a proud and unap-
proachable woman. For Sophie, who was younger, the idea of
meeting the famous writer filled her with panic.

The girls awaited her arrival in the sitting room of their
home, an ancient mansion furnished in a style that was equally
ancient. Both sisters wore navy blue dresses. I imagine them
with their dresses buttoned up tightly and the tension showing
on their faces. All of a sudden, Božena appeared: smiling, fresh
faced, in a comfortable sand-colored dress with a pleated skirt
and a pale hat over her black hair. At thirty, she looked as youthful as a girl of nineteen. Her overall appearance had something
of a classical air, her features and dark hair bound at the nape
in a Greek chignon, her big green eyes, her slender neck, her
long, fine fingers. The writer's appearance alone captivated the
two girls.

After she left, the sisters talked about her excitedly and so began the friendship among the three women.

At least you, Božena, at least you have friends with whom you can share your secrets. But I, what have I got?

I've got you. You are the only one who will listen to me. What a twist of fate! And then there is Herr von Päumann, he's interested in me as well, he needs me too. I shall now write to the police and tell them about your slipups and your sins both great and small. The police will keep you under surveillance, they will persecute you, they will harm you. Yes, that is what they will do. But, even so, you will have lived better than I have; your life will always be more meaningful than mine.

Do not cease to watch Němcová's every step, and every meeting."

"With scientists and men of letters too?"

"Naturally!"

"She has many admirers . . ."

"Her readers and literary admirers do not interest me at all; they are a shameless crowd and a bunch of idiots, that's what they are, to admire a woman who writes in Czech. Czech, a dead language!"

"Do you think so, Herr von Päumann?"

"I most certainly do, and if it hasn't died off altogether, we will take the necessary measures to make sure it does so soon. You would not, surely, be comparing Czech to the greatness of the German language?"

"*Jawohl*, Herr von Päumann, *natürlich*. Without a doubt. Now, then, is there anybody else I have to keep an eye on?"

"You have talked of her admirers. Is it possible that she has any lovers?"

"*Bitte?*"

"Do you know anything about this writer's possible lovers?"

"Well, I'm not altogether sure. Even though . . . I would say . . ."

"You must clear up this doubt. It is essential. Quickly."

"You know . . . In fact, I . . ."

"Auf Wiedersehen, Fräulein."

Němcová has friends who are important scientists. She has close female friends who are ladies from rich and influential families, and who knows if some of these people might not also be lovers of hers. And with all of them she is scheming against the Austro-Hungarian Empire. Very well. People must either be coddled or thoroughly annihilated. They would take revenge if only slightly wounded, but would be unable to do so at all if wounded seriously, which is why the wound that we inflict on a person must be of the sort that prevents him from taking revenge. That's what Machiavelli said. Accordingly, we shall put an end to Němcová's friendships. She will have no more financial backers, nobody to give her enough change to buy a loaf of bread. Her lovers, if she has any, will abandon her. Her female friends will want nothing further to do with her. You have underestimated us, my dear. In fact, we don't have to do anything except have the police keep a protective eye on you. We don't have to lift so much as a little finger and your Czechs will end up helping us achieve our goals, the same Czechs for whom you always sacrifice yourself. Yes, the Czechs, those cowardly people! Nobody will be left, only this informer, she'll be there for you! And for us, naturally. To achieve final victory, one must be implacable, that was Napoleon's motto.

What a disagreeable creature, that Fräulein Zaleski. Had she been born in another era or into another family, she would not need to earn her living as a spy, and could dedicate herself entirely to culture and to writing, like Němcová. But she was born into a nation without a future, into an impoverished family. You only have to look at her, a glance even. A horrible sight. Like watching an insect squirming in a cobweb.

Why does she always blink nervously, look away, and shiver all over whenever she hears the word "lover?" It can't just be envy. Clearly, she must be planning something.

I should get rid of her as soon as I can. Misfortune is as contagious as cholera.

The doctor is late. It is a full half hour since the appointed time. She had taken off her clothes, then put them back on again, and is now on the lookout for him, her forehead resting against the windowpane. Even the milk and the post have arrived. On the street there is a boy looking up at her window, as if he were searching for someone. He is carrying some sky-blue object, like a bunch of forget-me-nots, or a shawl given to him by a lady breathless from dancing at a society ball. That sky-blue paper in his hand troubles her. Yes, the boy enters her house, climbs the staircase, knocks at the door.

"Good morning. I am to give you this."

She invites him in, but the boy doesn't have time. He is already running down the stairs and she will never know who ... what ...

The blue envelope burns her fingers as if it were a lit match. She passes it from one hand to the other before placing it on the table.

She picks it up firmly and goes out, to throw it into the Vltava. She is in a hurry to get rid of it. She knows only too well what is in it. A message: the treatment is over. And a cold wish: stay healthy. Instead of a signature, two initials: H.J. They are so clear, as if printed in a cloud, with calligraphical ornamentation at the end. She is standing on a bridge, and inside her who knows what awakens ... who knows what kind of animal. Yes, an animal that stretches its neck out of curiosity and whose paws reach for the letter. She doesn't want to give it to the beast, but it grabs the envelope so fast that she doesn't have time to protest. It removes a sheet of paper out of the envelope: the initials H.J. are the first thing she notices. The beast takes the sheet of paper in its claws, unfolds it, and against her will her eyes run over the lines. When she has finished reading, the beast looks at her sarcastically, as if to say: Can't you see, you fool! It yawns, lazily stretches its limbs, and returns to its lair inside her.

She didn't understand what she was reading, ignorant of the meaning of those long letters that leaned off to the left like cornstalks bent hard by a strong wind. But suddenly her surroundings lit up and she started to laugh. A few rays of sunlight made their way through the dense clouds, spreading light onto the golden tips of the bell towers and the Gothic steeples, among which she liked so much to fly in the company of the ancient sage. The leaves of the trees brightened with gold and purple, their dead flowers blossomed forth once more, giving off a sweet scent. Out from among the flowers stepped trumpeters, holding up their instruments: pah-pa-rah, pah-pa-rah! she heard. Between the snapping of the flags and the thunder of the trumpets, she could hear these words: I'll be back . . . I'm going to the village to care for someone who is dying . . . how I look forward to seeing you again . . . an unusual, extraordinary woman . . .

Darkness had fallen some time ago and she went back home. Without thinking anything, she made dinner, patted her children's heads, and quickly closed the door of her room behind her. Her husband was grumbling about something on the other side, but she couldn't hear him because in the middle of the room, surrounded by Bengal lights, there was the flute player leading a train of followers. She sat at the table with a cup of tea and picked up her pencil.

She wrote nothing, not that evening, nor the day after. She took all kinds of old clothes out of the cupboard, tried them on in front of the mirror, which was too small to see herself full length in, and started to mend them. She decorated her hats with new ribbons and paid special attention to the undergarments, to which she added lace, both new as well as some that was still serviceable from old blouses. On the table she placed the garnet necklace, inherited from her grandmother, and the earrings that were a gift from the Duchess von Sagan. After a few days, when she was once more able to write, she would get up from time to time, look at herself in the mirror, and hold the jewels next to her face. She did not watch herself with her own eyes but with a masculine perspective. Her eyes were as lively as they were when she was little Miss Betty, and the mirror offered her the face of a beautiful and resplendent young woman.

A week went by, then another, then a third one. She spent whole nights writing, and when daylight spoiled her concentration, she stretched out on the sofa and took a nap. After which she prepared breakfast. She had fallen in love with a strong blend of black tea, taken with a little sugar.

To write a report on Božena's lovers. On the prefect's lips, the word smelled like a tiny, poorly ventilated room. For me, this word is beautiful. In themselves, words mean nothing; meaning is given to them by one's own experience.

The first lover was Celestial. He showed her the way. In a professional sense, of course, but also in another way. He accompanied her through Šárka, and Betty, the forsaken dreamer, turned herself into a lady who knows what she wants, into a writer with talent and discerning of admiration. And into a passionate woman. Later came her friendship with young Doctor Čejka. And with Ivan, that man from Brno . . .

Yes, Ivan. I remember a pretty story that Božena once told me a pretty story about a very special night that she had spent with a man, with a lover, in the mountains. I would give my entire life for a night like that. But she is even admired by Ivan's friends, Klácel and Hanuš. Both of them are jealous. I saw one of the scenes Hanuš made; he gasped, red-faced, and kicked the walls and the furniture with almost as much fury as Božena's husband does. On another occasion I saw Hanuš, that ultrasensitive man, had puffy red eyes, just like me when I can't sleep at night and cannot cope with the sadness of my useless existence.

Božena, I could ruin you, that is to say, your dreams, like Vítek when he cut down the willow tree! But I'm not going to do it, there's no need. The police will take care of it.

You also received many passionate letters, often from men who you didn't think much of. Not long ago, your husband showed me one of them. I had to make an effort not to burst out laughing when I saw the veins in his neck popping and those feet of his in worn-out house slippers. When he gave the wall a good kick he yelled ow ow ow ow! like a piglet and grabbed his big toe. I can imagine the scene he must have made with you when he found the letter. He reckons that that graceless letter was from one of your doctors, from Lambl, when in fact it was the work of that dolt from the beer factory who you keep at a distance. Lambl was a bright spot among the men with whom you became intimate, Božena. Were you aware of that? I suppose not, because even though you liked him, you didn't feel the same passion for him that you did for some of the others who treated you badly.

Lambl helped and defended you. He invited you to meet his mother and then you went almost every day to their home on

Saint Francis Quay and read aloud to them from your recent work: Slovak folktales; *At the Castle, At the Village,* a novel of which even George Sand, whom you admire so much, would have been proud.

Lambl clung to you more and more tightly while another man entered your life, the young doctor who is looking after you now, the one with the Oriental air about him. Johanna and Sophie were jealous of your relationship with Lambl; I envy you your new friend, though I do not envy you.

One morning, he was at the door. His eyes shone, his mouth was laughing. He said: "Strong as life, sweet as love, bitter as death and oblivion. What is it?"

She and Vítězka, who had opened the door, were having a cup of tea. She sat at a low table made from a drawer. She had wrapped herself in a dark blue velvet dressing gown tied with a wide sash. She wore her hair loose.

"What is it? Beautiful words, a poem. But I can't guess the answer."

"It's tea. It has to be that way, according to an Arabic proverb. I would have a cup of it with you ladies, if you would allow me to do so."

"Well, I . . . I'm going to fix my hair; I look a fright."

"Don't go anywhere. Yes, it's true you look a fright. A beautiful one. Too beautiful."

Božena didn't know how to react. She shook her head. How he's changed! Is it him? What's happened to him?

Suddenly the animal lurking inside her emerged, bristling.

"Do have a cup of tea, friend. My friend Vítězka will keep you company," she told him, icily. "Unfortunately, I have to go. I'm late."

He was bewildered.

"I was joking. If you want to fix your hair, please do so. If you want to tidy yourself up, tidy yourself up, and I will happily wait for you. I have come back several days early, just for you,"

The strange beast opened its mouth to bite.

"I cannot possibly stay. I have a meeting with my publisher. But Vítězka is excellent company."

No, those words were not hers. That wasn't she.

But it wasn't he, either.

While she changed clothes and combed her hair restlessly, the beast still squirmed.

Later, hurrying along the street as fast as she could go, as if fleeing from something, she felt a touch of satisfaction blended in with her desperation. But this satisfied sense of pride grew weaker and weaker, until it disappeared altogether, and despair occupied all the available space on the throne.

Guten Tag, Fräulein Zaleski. Do you know who Father Štulc is?"

"Of course. The priest who writes patriotic verse with a strong Catholic bent."

"What are his verses like?"

"Dull, superficial, rhetorical."

"Who does this priest see?"

"I know, above all, who he can't stand: Frič and the revolutionary's circle of young literati."

"That is to say, the same circle that is also frequented by Němcová, even though she is older?"

"That's right. Father Štulc has admonished her bitterly."

"What is there between them, exactly? All Prague is talking about it, but it seems that nobody can say for sure what's going on."

"Somebody showed Father Štulc one of Němcová's letters, addressed to one of the members of their circle."

"Who?"

"To Mr. Jurenka, a student of medicine."

"Do you know what was in the letter?"

"I have made a copy. It is a love letter."

"*Ach so!* And what else happened?"

"Father Štulc used the letter to put moral pressure on the writer. He upbraided her time and again. And that isn't all. The Father tried to oblige Němcová to accompany him publicly in an open carriage, all the way across Prague, to confess at the castle."

"Like a heretic?"

"Precisely. To make a show of her failings and of her shame before the inhabitants of Prague."

"Father Štulc's intentions were excellent. Němcová is a kind of heretic. Of the same type as that dog Havlíček. I see that the Catholic Church has not altogether forgotten its inquisitorial past. Fortunately, the Catholic Church is on our side, and our regime depends to quite an extent on its support. What else happened?"

"Father Štulc threatened to make public the contents of Němcová's letter if she didn't ride with him in an open carriage to make her confession and show that she was renouncing the vanities of this world for ever more."

"And Němcová?"

"She refused."

"She wasn't afraid of the threat?"

"She was certainly afraid of it, as anybody would have been. But she refused to give in."

"I will now read your copy of the letter in question. It is addressed to that young man who is soon to be a doctor. Wait for a while in the lobby, Fräulein. If I need you again, I shall call for you."

The following day the young doctor ordered her to undress and untie her corset. He had always helped her. This day, however, he was distant. He cleaned the glass cups coolly. And so the days passed. She didn't dare to so much as open her mouth; he remained stubbornly silent, as his palms and fingers moved with the same professional skill over her body.

I like to dream that we will go to some place together, to the mountains, for example," says the difficult-to-read copy that Fräulein Zaleski made of Němcová's letter to her man friend, "to spend a few happy days together. But as reality is not within my grasp, I take pleasure in my dreams." Can this be of any importance to the police? I shall read a little more. "When I don't have reality, let me dream! How many times have I satisfied my longing for the sea, in dreams? How many times have I dreamed of joyful landscapes? Dreams have brought me people I love whom I will never see again. In dreams I can live as I wish and be happy. Why complain about them only being dreams, if these feelings will be with me for the rest of my days! I am grateful, deeply grateful for this kind of dream."

No, I am ashamed to read on. I do not wish to eavesdrop. But I am a defender of our Austro-Hungarian fatherland. How many enemies it has!

About Němcová: she is a sensitive woman. How must I go about destroying her? It isn't easy. When her son Hynek was dying in a Prague hospital, while she was on a trip to Hungary, we re-routed the letter from the doctor that was meant to inform the mother of her son's critical condition. We were hoping that the son would die without his mother being able to take her leave of him. But at the last moment she found out about him, rushed to Prague, and during his last forty-eight hours she held her son in her arms. Fräulein Zaleski gave me a report about Němcová's period of mourning. But even that wasn't enough to crush her spirit. She goes on writing; her novels and stories continue to be published, and people like them. I see that Fräulein Zaleski has marked a passage in one of them: "The ignorance of woman is a whip that she entwines in order to hurt herself. Until women are aware of the tremendous importance of their mission, men will not be able to build the future on a solid foundation either. If this building process is to succeed, women must work together with men. Women have to raise themselves up and sit on the throne, governing side by side with men."

Time and again, I can see that this woman is a danger to everyone. To annihilate her, we will have to seize everything that is of value from her, everything that she treasures, that she loves. First of all, her children. Those who are still around will be crushed by misery. Second, the man she loves. What is his profession? Fräulein Zaleski says that he has just qualified as a doctor of medicine. Excellent! We will send him to Galicia, to deal with cholera there. If only everything were so simple! As far as her husband is concerned, she isn't at all close to him, but just in case we'll send him to the Tyrol. That only leaves her friends. Here we need more detailed information for this campaign I am in the process of launching. Fritz, send in the informer!

The door was opened by Božena's daughter Dora, who was in the kitchen doing the dishes. She pointed to the bedroom; her mother had locked herself in. I could hear her voice and that of a man, low and coarse. Lord only knows who that was. Dora made such a racket with the pots and pans that I couldn't make out a single word. I decided to wait.

My eyes wandered over the different colored glasses and bowls standing on the kitchen shelf, inexpensive objects that Božena valued greatly nonetheless. Every day she dusted them and rearranged them differently, depending on her mood. The blue vase was usually placed at the back. Today, however, it all but hid the gray and cream-colored bowls and glasses, standing apart from the rest as if shouting, "Look at me and nothing else!" The sight of the collection of glasses strengthened my conviction that Božena was upset, that in her agitation she had played with her favorite objects without bearing in mind the aesthetic impression caused by their arrangement.

Finally Dora stopped washing the dishes; the voices coming from Božena's room could now be heard clearly enough. The man's voice was Němec's, saying: "What are we going to do to get winter clothing for the children? Haven't you noticed they're trembling from the cold? The only winter coat we have, the brown one, is worn by me. I don't have anything else, and even then I look like a straw man. My underclothes are falling apart; nobody darns them. You're the one who does the least of all. You wander about the place with your head in the clouds."

She replied: "When you were off in Hungary and I was alone with the children, I felt very lonely and even got to the stage of desiring you, but I learned to do without a lot of things."

"I keep having the most terrible dreams," he broke in which was when I realized that her husband wasn't listening to her. "The other day I dreamt that I'd died and that the coffin you'd had made for me was made of our beds."

"Since I was a young girl," Božena said, without knowing what he had just said, "I have yearned to learn, felt a desire for something higher and better than what I found around me, and felt an aversion to everything coarse and commonplace. That is the reason why we do not succeed as a couple, and the reason behind my misfortune."

"What does this studying, what do books, papers, and pens

offer you? Nothing. They don't even provide you with enough to eat. You'd be better off forgetting about all that silly nonsense and start learning how to be a good housewife."

She replied, "Few women have had so much respect for the dignity of the institution of marriage as I had and continue to have, but I was soon obliged to lose my faith in it. How could I have done otherwise? All I see around me are lies, cheating, gilded servitude, obligations; that is to say, vulgarity. You have had my body, but my desires are always elsewhere."

Then something fell to the floor and broke. The mirror? A glass? The medical cups? It was as if Božena's words had been validated. I put the blue vase behind the light-colored glasses. Then I left.

She summoned up her courage and complained to the doctor: "For weeks I've had a pain here at the foot of the spinal column."

He didn't seem to have heard her, although even she had spoken quite clearly and in a raised voice.

The next day, the doctor carried something in his left hand that looked like a wrapped plate. He left his medical bag on the floor, untied the string, and indeed, it was a plate, deep and full of ointment.

"I prepared it for you. It's the best medicine for bones and muscles."

She was so surprised she didn't even say thank you. He turned his back to look for something in his bag and then took out a book: *Stories* by Božena Němcová.

"Would you be so kind as to sign this book for me?"

With her face practically touching the pages, she wrote a most sincere dedication.

"My handwriting is like an old lady's! The truth is I'm not used to writing in this position."

They both laughed and he moved his chair closer to her and told her how, many years ago, he had helped his grandfather, a village doctor, to write prescriptions. Instead of a doctor's unintelligible handwriting, the prescriptions were written in a child's clumsy scrawl.

One or two weeks went by. He brought her plates of ointment, and sat next to her, not taking his eyes off her. Only from time to time did his gaze slip across her shoulders, her lips. He takes care of me as if I were a newborn baby, Božena told herself. The beast began to rouse its limbs, shake off its sleepiness, and howl. She made an effort not to pay it any attention. Stubbornly, she repeated to herself: like a newborn baby.

One day, when he was applying the salve, she noticed that his hands were trembling. He decided to leave off with the ointment and sit next to her, his eyes on her. Today his eyes are full of fine red veins, Božena told herself, and are more moist than usual. He looked at her for a long while and his hands didn't stop trembling. The beast inside her yawned, got up on all fours, and started to sniff. Then it gave out a strident, protracted howl. A white membrane covered the doctor's eyes.

✦

You sent all your admirers packing because of this one . . . Oh, Božena! A student of medicine, eleven years younger than you! You clung to him with the desperation of a woman who is aware that this is her last chance to be happy, or rather, the last opportunity to dream of happiness. Not long ago you wrote in a letter about that young man, good-looking but haughty, empty, and common: "For you, he is nothing special, but for me he is unique, I would rank him before any one of you all. I would like to weave a crown of stars to place on his head so that everybody might appreciate his brilliance. I do not seek to know if he deserves it or not, because I love him. Perhaps in the future, more than one woman will love him, but none with such sincerity, such devotion as I. I suppose that one day he will know how I loved him, although he will never know the depths of my suffering."

Yes, he is a conceited, superficial, and a coarse man. But despite everything, do I not like to dream of him, too?

The student of medicine became a frequent visitor. She is happy. Her inner bliss is written all over her face; she seems younger and more beautiful. In the afternoon, she shares the leftovers of a frugal lunch with her young friend; at the table in her study, adorned with flowers, she offers him biscuits to go with tea. She has taken pains to tidy up the small, damp apartment, and those of us who visit her are so dazzled by her enthusiasm that her beaming smile blinds us to her poverty and hardship.

The doctor usually sits at her table, clumsily handling her treasures with his peasant's fingers—a little bust of Goethe, which Purkyně gave her; a framed portrait of George Sand, from Doctor Čejka—and keeps helping himself to biscuits until he's full to bursting. As he now lives close by, he waits to see when Němec heads off, then invites himself into Božena's home. If there's something to eat, that cheers him up at once. She watches him eating, adoring him as if he were a deity.

Her happiness has lasted for two months. For two months this apprentice doctor has been proud of the attentions of this woman whom his friends adore and who enjoys such tremendous prestige in Czech cultural circles. The fool who has concocted a story about knowing the Orient, has moved to a place close to the block of apartments in which the Němecs live and has turned their marriage into hell. Němec, always sensitive, always jealous, has sneaking suspicions about the relationship. The inhabitants of Prague really have something to talk about now. But she doesn't give a hoot for their gossip. She trembles at the thought of losing her happiness.

One day, when I was also present, the young man appeared and said: "Why don't you put a different dress on? Doesn't it bother you that I've seen you like this so often?"

She answered that outward appearance was not the most important thing. Then she spent entire nights mending her old blouses.

The following day the student arrived, sat on her old patched-up sofa, smoked a cigarette, and got up to go. Božena looked at him, completely at a loss. When he had his hand on the doorknob ready to leave, she finally brought herself to ask where he was going.

"I can't sit on this horrible sofa. I'm going to the cafe."

He slammed the door on his way out.

Since then, this kind of scene has repeated itself often. What are you, Božena, if not his slave? You yourself wrote: "His image accompanied me wherever I went. I slept with it, and woke up with it. In front of him I kneeled as if he were God." You, who is admired, proud, who fears neither slander nor the police. Is this happiness?

This is being in love. "Love is a sickness, but one doesn't want to be cured of it." You wrote that and you've proven it.

But you have your own world, which I do not have, nor does the doctor and nor does Němec. The other day a lamp with a white glass shade came in the post. You placed it on the table of your study, mad with joy. You looked like a little girl.

"Božena, how do you manage to be so jubilant in the middle of so much hardship and misfortune?" That's what I wanted to know.

"In the evening I like to retire to my room, with a cup of tea on the table, and the oil lamp gilding everything. Then before my eyes appear invincible heroes and beautiful princesses, winged horses and terrifying dragons."

That's your prescription, that's your secret.

That is your willow tree that nobody can cut down and destroy. Not the hardship, not your husband with his eternally vexed face, not the police, not even the doctor, the person you love most.

She jumped over the puddles of water. She would have liked to go flying off into the sky again. What a pity that when it rains, one cannot fly! The soles of her shoes were soaked through, as were her coat and large chenille head scarf with fringe, complaining in silence, longing for a heated, dry room. But she didn't hear their protests; she had ears for nothing but her inner voice, which at this moment was singing an ode to joy backed by a twenty-five voice choir. The church bells were chiming, but she didn't hear them either; the choir was singing too lustily. The streetlamps on Kampa Island glided in the air like Venetian lanterns, gilding the threads of rain. Then, in the darkness between the streetlamps, she couldn't make out where a puddle ended and splash! She fell right into the water and burst out laughing.

A bell started chiming. This time she heard it and told herself that he must be in class. Poor boy, it's hard work studying medicine. And she remembered how, the other day, he had arrived much later than the agreed time. He found her writing. He placed his bag on top of a half-written sentence and sighed. She went into the kitchen to make tea and he went after her like a cat. He took her in a brutal fashion, right there among the pots and pans. The massages, the philosophy, and the ointment were no longer of interest to him. When it was over, he watched as she smoothed the folds of her wrinkled skirt with the palm of her hand, how she buttoned up her blouse, and put a needle in place of the button that he had torn off.

"You're tidying yourself up to go out, aren't you?"

"I have an appointment with Pospíšil, my publisher."

"And do you not have an appointment with me?"

"You got here two hours late, my love. I thought that—"

"Then stop thinking and do as you promised. You had an appointment with me and you shall keep it."

"I have to talk with my publisher about the money he owes me, my love. I haven't got a penny left to buy anything for the children's supper. Please understand."

"You are being unfair to me! I moved from Hybernská Street to be close to you. When I arrive a little late, despite wishing more than anything to get here earlier, you're not even waiting for me. You are busy writing, as if we had arranged nothing. And finally, when we've been together for only a quarter of an hour, you're already in a hurry to answer the call of literature, the only thing that matters to you. What do I mean to you? Tell me! I suppose I am only useful to you as an inspiration for words and more words and nothing else, the miserable spark that lights up a story."

His protest seemed to her then to be an unfair accusation. Today, in that damp winter dusk, in the middle of a street in the rain, she saw things quite differently. She drew back the silvery curtain of rain and, quick as lightning, a sudden realization struck her: he had moved close to her home not to pester her but to be with her as often as possible. However for her the situation was different: she didn't need his constant presence, she carried it within her and wrote about him. She transformed him into the paladins of her folktales and into the tender lovers of her novels. She wrote tirelessly, she slept only three or four hours a day, she ate little. She was nourished by a feeling of joy.

The church bell started ringing again. She imagined herself embracing him as they walk under that streetlamp next to the oak tree. With each new chime she became aware of more details: his hat, always worn at a slight angle, his pitching walk, his cane swinging upward. She felt such a strong desire to really be with him that she even felt his coffee-laced breath on her cheek. No, he hadn't appeared yet.

Again the bells chimed, as if there were an emergency. *Are they tolling non-stop? Is it possible that I could have spent the last hour and a half in the rain? I'd better go back home. He's probably been delayed somewhere and can't get away. Poor man, he must be fretting; he must be thinking about me.* She increased her pace. At home she would make a full pot of tea, in case he dropped by and was cold and hungry. She passed Archers' Island, Sofia Island—not a soul anywhere, everything shining clean as a whistle, the rain had cleansed it all. Home wasn't far now.

Suddenly, in the light of a streetlamp, she recognized the couple she had dreamed of a moment ago. A tall, broad-shouldered man, with a hat tipped to one side, swung his cane into the air. He was walking arm in arm with a woman who was fragile-looking and so stooped she might be a hunchback. They stopped in the darkness between the streetlamps, the woman's face was transparent, her fingers, which now stretched out to the man's hair, were translucent, like those of a corpse. He embraced her . . . He embraced her with that familiar movement of his right hand, with that mixture of possessive instinct and desire to defend. No, there was no doubting it, that was him. Now he was kissing the woman. She recognized the woman as her friend Antonia Zaleski, now called Vítězka.

With an effort, she walked back home. For a good while she

struggled with the lock because she found it difficult to turn the key. Until she realized she was at the wrong house.

Božena will turn up any second now. She's gone to the drugstore to buy a little tea," Němec says disgruntled, as he continues to read his newspaper.

Alone in her room, I dare to take a look at her desk. There is a half-written letter but I can't find the opening page, so I don't know to whom it is addressed.

" . . . this is good weather in which to die of desperation.
When I look at the thick gray fog that crushes us like
a nightmare, the naked trees from which all the leaves
have fallen as our hopes are falling from us, when I see
the empty, opaque atmosphere, sluggish and sad and
suffocating us, I feel melancholy and desolate; I get the
shivers and would like to have a pair of wings so as to fly to
countries in which a warmer, freer air blows."

I think she is talking not only of these sad winter days, but of the grayness of our country after a failed revolution, the grayness that, like mud at the bottom of a lake, has seeped into our lives.

Once more, with a column of light coming through the door, I go into the kitchen. Božena is sitting there, waiting for the water to boil to make tea. She wears a black dress and a white apron, and is sitting with her head bowed and her elegant coiffure combed upward. The nape of her neck suggests frailty, but also strength, exhaustion, and sadness. The water has boiled; she heads off with the cup and the teapot. Now she's seen me, she moves her lips in a way that is barely visible, and gets another cup. In her room she puts my cup on the bedside table and without another word goes to her desk. I have the feeling she is so sad that she cannot speak. And that she is escaping into her writing so as not to have to think. She stands in front of the desk, the tray in her hands. I observe her from behind and see that she is not reading what she has just written, that she is staring into space. One day she had told me: "Vítězka, you and I have to be strong because we are fragile." The gray light falls from the window onto her shoulder, her arm, and a curl of hair that has freed itself from her coiffure. She sits down and adds words to her letter. Then she gets her coat and before going out, whispers to me: "Today I can't give you any of my time, Vítězka. Finish your tea and go. Don't ever come back."

Her voice, always so smooth, has dealt me a hard blow. I cannot move. The sound of the door closing behind her is like a sigh.

What has she added to the letter?

"If I could choose, I would like to be reborn two hundred years from now or perhaps even later, when the world will be, if such a thing is possible, just as I would like it to be so as to able to live in it with pleasure."

So yes, it was she who saw us embracing.

How can she write in such an elegant way after having made a discovery of this kind? She wishes only to be reborn when the world will be a better place. A place in which there will not be people as mean as I am, I who have joined the police in their games designed to ruin other people's lives. But what could you expect, Božena? I need the money, just as I need love, even if only for a moment, even if it is handed to me on a platter by the police.

"I am at your command, Herr von Päumann."

"Fräulein Zaleski, how fares that campaign to isolate Božena Němcová from her friends and potential benefactors?"

"Mrs. Eliška Lambl, a friend of Božena's, the sister of one of her doctors, told me yes, I have it here in writing: 'There are many days when there is no food in her house. Nothing whatsoever. One day Božena complained to my brother that she had but one coin left and didn't know what to buy with it; whether a little tea to keep her awake, a candle to write by all night, or a little ink, which was also nearly finished.'"

"Has she spoken to other people of interest?"

"Yes, to the poet Jan Neruda, who went to see her with his companion Hálek. Jan told me: 'We visited her to ask for a contribution to the first issue of *May* magazine. We stared incredulously at the flaking walls and the shabby furniture; the tablecloth especially fascinated us, being half ripped and patched up, yet there on the table. I don't mean to say that it was the first time we'd seen such poverty, but to find it in the home of a person who had become a celebrity thanks to a lifetime of work left us speechless and open mouthed.'"

"Does our writer continue to get help from her friends?"

"When she fell on hard times she was ashamed and didn't want her friends to know anything about it. But her doctors let people know about the true nature of her situation, so that those who didn't have any money borrowed some to buy her food. During the periods in which she was confined to her bed by the illness in her lungs, which sometimes lasted for months on end, her friends returned to her side, to try and keep her mind occupied. But when they realized she was under police surveillance, their attitude changed. I don't know to what extent you have been informed about this."

"Tell me everything you know."

"Božena is obliged to ask for, and receives, hand outs. She can't expect much from the great ladies of Prague because they've distanced themselves from her. They claim that Němcová has deserted her husband—something that she's never done—and that instead of living like a humble serving woman, she frequents the company of peculiar young people. By which they mean, above all, that young friend of hers who's a doctor, or rather, a student of medicine. Many others have the same opinion. And those who don't believe it pretend that they do."

"What about the behavior of her closest friends?"

"Johanna Rott told me that she is keeping her distance from Němcová and trying to persuade her sister Sophie to also avoid the writer's company. Sophie confessed to me that Johanna had written to her in a letter: 'I don't like those people who have it said of them that they are kind hearted.' Since then Sophie has been mulling over this sentence, but hasn't managed to understand what it means. Němcová has noticed the coldness of the two sisters, but as she wants to keep her desperate plight under wraps, she behaves as if it was of no importance to her. One of her most faithful friends, Mr. Ivan Klácel, from Brno, said not long ago that he is 'avoiding Němcová for political reasons.' Božena has found out, of course. Her friends are afraid even to write to her. The poet Erben, who until recently was a firm supporter of her novels and had written highly of them in the newspapers, has now limited his relationship to the writer to chance meetings on the street. The only ones who are unconditionally loyal to her are Purkyně and Palacký."

"So the Němec family doesn't have enough food?"

"Sometimes they go for a whole day without eating. I've seen it with my own eyes. Božena, sick in bed, sends her children with messages to friendly families: 'Please, give me a little food.'"

"Has she sold all her jewels?"

"She has kept only the garnet necklace, as a memento of her grandmother."

"She prefers to go hungry rather than pawn it?"

"Mrs. Němcová believes that her life is bound up with that necklace, and that if she gives up the necklace, a curse will fall upon her."

"We will force her to sell it then. You are quite sure that Němcová's friends have abandoned her?"

"Yes, and not only them. Her husband is also disassociating himself from her. I have here a document that he wrote and signed:

It is my wish that my wife, Božena Němcová, abandon my apartment and live as she pleases, always bearing in mind that she has no right to expect any kind of maintenance from me. The causes that have led me to take this step are as follows:

1. The aversion that my wife feels toward me.
2. The violent arguments with which the aforementioned woman confronts me.
3. A difference of opinions regarding the education of our children.
4. The negligent way in which my wife looks after our home.

"Thank you, Fräulein Zaleski. That is all for today. You will receive your payment in a few days' time. From now on we will almost certainly be dispensing with your services as regards the Němcová case. Once you have completed Němcová's biography, have it sent to us at once. Auf Wiedersehen, Fräulein."

"From now on we will be dispensing with your services." Very nice. He won't see Božena's latest letter, that hopeless dolt! "Fräulein Zaleski, please stop talking about yourself." "Fräulein Zaleski, don't waste my time!" "Fräulein Zaleski, such useless whining, so typical of women, does not interest me at all!" "Concentrate on what I ask of you, Fräulein Zaleski, we will only pay you if your work for us is of any use." Scoundrel! I shall read Božena's letter by myself. She at least has wonderful memories, enough of them to build a cathedral with. The only memory that has stayed with me is the brilliance of the ring on the finger of my fiancée. And my romantic dreams about good-looking young men, about doctors and sensual cures.

No, I'm not going to read Božena's letter. It would hurt me too much. I have persecuted an unhappy and defenseless woman, as defenseless and unhappy as I am myself. With one huge difference: my legacy to posterity will be a few police reports, whereas Božena's work will always be read. Maybe they'll even be reading her stories a hundred years from now or more. No matter how much they spy on you, Božena, no matter how much hunger and misery they subject you to, and how much they distance you from your friends, people will always admire and respect you. You are important for the simple reason that they pay you such attention, that they create these piles of paper full of reports about your life, that you merit the cost of informers and spies like myself. What will happen when I am gone? Why, look, there will be a burial attended by my father and siblings and nobody else. Afterward they'll have lunch in a restaurant and will raise a toast, perhaps, to the memory of poor, unhappy Vítězka, who reveled in her fifteen minutes of glory when she worked as a police informer. Maybe somebody will shed a tear. Then they'll go back home, and the next day everything will be as before and Vítězka? Vítězka will gradually be forgotten.

And how about for you, Božena? Your readers will organize a funeral worthy of a queen. Hundreds, perhaps thousands of people will turn up to say their farewells. They will mourn you for months on end, publicly and in private. Later, they'll write books about you, they will delve into your parents' lives and will take such an interest in you that you could well be a planet spinning in the universe. Perhaps someday one of those shining stars will even bear your name. For men and women both, you will always be Mnemosyne, an untouchable goddess, mother of the muses, the most beautiful statue in the ancient world. That is the difference between we two wretched women: I am common, banal; and you, surprising, prodigious, unique.

Deep down, are you as unhappy as you seem? No. You have dreams that you believe in with an obstinacy made of steel. In the letter now in my hand, you write to your sister, I suppose about this most recent doctor and lover of yours: "Although he has hurt me, I believe in him. I believe in him, even though it might all be nothing but a sham. Don't break up my dream, don't spoil my poetry."

Yes, Božena, you have your dream world, full of beauty, love, and poetry, which nobody can take from you. Your dream world, as attractive as the real one is ugly, gives you strength to keep going. You are not afraid of human evil or police harassment. Like the girl in your folktale who gets her strength from the fantastical world hidden in a willow tree, your folktales are full of supernatural powers that bring harmony and justice to the world. You, in turn, give sweetness and consolation to the world, but above all you give it to yourself! I, too, dream. And I dream of love, but do I know any men except those who are already your admirers, Božena? Do I have any other choice but to imagine myself with your devotees? Do I have any other possibility beyond that of projecting myself onto you, of projecting you

onto me? Of an attempt to become you? And to write about. . .
about your lovers, about my lovers?

It doesn't stop raining. We are at the tail end of winter; the
snow makes a slushing sound when trodden. It's better not to
go outdoors unless absolutely necessary, or to do so only in the
evening when merciful darkness hides all that dirt. She ought
to be happy: she has managed to get her publisher to pay her
some money. She should buy something for dinner, at least for
her children. But she doesn't have enough strength to do so.
She would prefer to sit on the pavement or in front of a church.
Yes, in front of a church like that ancient sage with whom she
had flown between the chimneys. What would he advise her to
do now?

After days, weeks, of sadness that she found all but unbearable, under the weight of which she had collapsed, now she feels
completely empty. She doesn't want to even think about writing.
Her health has deteriorated; she is coughing and spitting blood.
Aside from her cough, there is nothing else left inside her. Not a
single thing to look forward to, not a trace of joy when she sees
something beautiful. Not even hope.

She passes the lit windows of the cafe frequented by her
friends. Perhaps through the glass she will see the face of somebody to whom she can explain her sorrow. She is empty but
the weight of her sadness has not left her, she's aware of that.
Only to speak, to let herself go! But what can she tell them? *I
have lost love? I have lost everything? I have lost life?* All of them,

absolutely everybody, would laugh at that. She knows that they don't care for her lover and consider him a charlatan and a fraud. Those who would listen to her would be running off to share this latest gossip with their friends a moment later. This has happened to her before. But what does she care? She needs to speak, to get rid of the weight pressing down on her, to hold someone's hand and tell them. Tell them what, really? Tell them her life is over.

That woman sitting over there isn't. Indeed, it is Vítězka. She approaches her window. Vítězka is sitting among some friends who are in the middle of an animated discussion, but she doesn't seem to understand their words. Her eyes are frightened, big brown eyes like . . . Like a deer's, like a wild goat's. . . No, like a little donkey's. Vítězka is like a tender, timid donkey who was born to be used by others. Vítězka is made of that same stuff, as are all those who have to hide their suffering in order to give the impression they are getting ahead in life, in order to make the world look like a happy place.

She taps the glass, close to Vítězka's ear. The young woman who seems so distracted looks through the glass out into the street and Božena realizes, suddenly, that Vítězka looks somewhat frightened and perhaps a little compassionate.

She leans on Vítězka, who had come out to say hello, and took her over to the Vltava. There, next to the water, she looked at her sideways. Yes, with those big, innocent, sad eyes she looked like a little kind-hearted donkey. For the first time in a long while, Božena saw tears in the other's eyes and she put her arms around the neck of that little donkey looking about without understanding a thing, her big eyes blinking. With her head on this young woman's shoulder, eyes bright with tears, she began to let herself go, saying she had lost love . . . that she had lost everything, that she had lost life. She spoke and sobbed, and her words fell like drops of slow autumn rain.

Vítězka was about to open her mouth to say: "But your lover hasn't left you! He doesn't want anybody else! His love is sincere. What he couldn't stand, and I find hard to put up with too, is that you are so great and famous, as well as being so beautiful, whereas he is just a mediocre student, one of many. It also riled him that you could escape from him, that you fled into the books you were writing, into your willow tree. And he couldn't cut it down like Vítek does in the folktale. That's why he ran off with other women, not with the most stunning ones, but with the ones who were easy to ditch, the ones who had nothing memorable about them, who could feel nothing but uncritical admiration for him. Once he had filled his cup of self-esteem with them, he came back to you. Then one day he definitely did not come back because the secret police, who were after you, moved him away from Prague. They sent him far from the capital to a practice in a distant place, and they did that because they didn't need him anymore. Your wise Czech friends had already distanced themselves from you, shocked by your relationship with him, and by getting him out of the way the police did you additional harm. They were afraid of you because you dared to proclaim in public that you are Czech. You are proud of it, you do as you please, and, on top of that, you are brilliant. All these things together are unforgivable."

Vítězka was about to say all that, but at the last minute she did not. She couldn't. She remained silent. This was her most heartfelt rebellion against the person who was better than she in every way, even as she now cried in her arms.

Božena talked and cried and talked. Her words fell upon the gray waves of the Vltava and the river carried them far away.

This was Vítězka's final revenge.

One day in May, Herr Anton von Päumann, the prefect of Prague, sat down at his work desk in the prefecture, and found that two items had been delivered to him. Both were from the same sender: Fräulein Zaleski. The first, a large envelope, contained a pretty sizable text, dated December 1854—March 1855; and the other one, much smaller, clearly contained a letter. The prefect picked up the first envelope. The note accompanying the text said, among other things: "You contracted my services in order to reveal the existence of a conspiracy, to ensure that the bad would be punished. I have sent you a detailed report on the current relationship between Němcová and her latest lover." Anton von Päumann started to read:

The woman, still young, accompanied the doctor to her bedroom. His eyes, shy but glinting, gave the room a once over.

"I'm just a medical student, but I hope that . . . "

She smiled. "Everyone has had to learn sometime, even Purkyně."

"Yes, even Purkyně, you're quite right. I'm fairly well-acquainted with Central European medical methods and procedures, but not with those alone. I've travelled in the Orient, where I learned lots of things; I discovered their methods.

At this point, von Päumann skipped a few pages, then went on reading:

"Do you know" the doctor said unexpectedly, in a changed voice, as he put away his medical instruments in his case and she buttoned up her blouse, "you once asked me about my travels. Deep down, I don't really believe in travel as a way of discovering things. Do you follow me?"

When Herr von Päumann finished reading, he smiled. He didn't quite believe it all. To the contrary, he was convinced that Fräulein Zaleski, with that sick mind of hers, had invented a great deal of it or rather, had made it all up. But as he now had the story in his hands, Herr von Päumann selected the most believable extracts for police use with a view to demonstrating the moral degradation of the writer Božena Němcová. Not long afterward, the abridged version of the story that Vítězka had written started to circulate by word of mouth among the most notorious gossips of Prague, and confirmed the rumors with which Božena's "friends" had justified their distance from her, thus leaving their consciences clear.

Then the prefect of Prague picked up the little envelope, which contained a single sheet of paper. He read:

Antonia Zaleski to the Illustrious Prefect of Prague, Herr Anton von Päumann.

May 1855

Most Illustrious Prefect,

Given that you can now dispense with my services, as you put it on the occasion of our last appointment, I consider that my most sacred obligation is now to inform you about the meeting between Božena Němcová and the Czech writer and journalist Karel Havlíček, an object of police concern.

As you know, the police released him from his confinement in the Tyrol and just recently that feared revolutionary and fighter for the rights of the Czechs and the Czech language has shown up in Prague. All his friends avoid him and when they see him they cross over to the other side of the road so as not to run into him. They fear him, knowing he is an outlaw. A few days ago, Božena Němcová was walking along Avenue Na Příkopě and spotted Havlíček there. Pleased, she ran over to him and gave him a most cordial welcome. She was the only one to do so. He warned her not to appear in public with an exile and outlaw such as himself, but Božena made a gesture indicating that none of that was of any importance whatsoever and said, laughing: "Come on! I don't give a hoot what the government says or does!"

Most sincere greetings,
Vítězka Paul
(previously Antonia Zaleski)

Vítězka Paul died in May of 1856 at the age of twenty-four. Božena Němcová went to her funeral, and afterwards wrote to her son: "Vítězka's death fills me with pain; she was truly a noble girl."

Božena Němcová died in January of 1862, not long before her forty-second birthday. Shortly before her death she had to sell her grandmother's garnet necklace because she was in abject poverty. Thousands of people went to her funeral. At the head was Father Štulc, who spoke in a tearful voice at the writer's grave in Vyšehrad Cemetery of Prague. Also present was Pospíšil, Němcová's publisher, who was one of the people responsible for the material poverty she lived in, as he had not paid her the full royalties due from her book sales, knowing that the more extreme Němcová's poverty, the more likely she would be to accept any payment he saw fit to give her. The poet Hálek declared that the circumstances surrounding Němcová's death were a shame on the Czech people, who had allowed their great writer to sink into extreme poverty, and added that the nationalists and the thinkers, "an intellectual rabble," had distanced themselves from her so as not to have to give her any money.

A volcano on Venus and a planet between Mars and Jupiter bear the name of Božena Němcová.

IS LIFE GOING TO WAIT?

ONE

The French live in the moment, whereas we prefer to philosophize about life. That is what I thought when I heard the noise, laughter, and music that were coming from the Bullier, the wooden dance hall. The painters were holding their annual charity ball there and I went out of curiosity. I recognized Derain and Braque among those who were dancing. But the Paris summer, with its pleasures and distractions, meant nothing to me. I left that gay place and decided to drop by Larionov's place. He had invited me to a party and there, at least, I could have a couple of beers.

I entered a dark apartment, which a few candles barely managed to illuminate. The shadows made one think more of fall than of the brilliant light of summer, but I felt at home. In the dark corners and in the middle of the veil of cigarette smoke, I started to recognize all kinds of people I knew: painters, writers, philosophers—the splendor of our Russian exile culture in all its misery. The guests drank and argued in groups and pairs. They weren't having a good time; they weren't happy, which also made me feel like I fit in. There was no beer, but someone offered me a glass of white wine that refreshed my fingers pleasantly. I moved from one group to another. The circle around Larionov talked about Russian passports that now were in fact Soviet ones. In time, when everything had settled down, a few people said they would go back to their country.

"Go back? But why?" Larionov asked with a grimace.

"I want to give my support to our new, young country," said a bald student from the shadows.

"And how exactly are you going to do that?"

"Through art. I'm a painter."

"You know what I think? You go and give your support to the land of the revolution, and when you're behind bars some place in Siberia, I will weep for your misfortune from a cafe terrace in Montparnasse and will toast your health with champagne."

I moved away. This type of conversation was very much in vogue among the Russians and bored me to death. I sat down in an empty chair, letting myself be swayed gently by the talk around me. Bunin was holding forth that the tsar was at fault for the atrocities that had taken place in Russia after the revolution, for he was too soft and had a weak character. Everybody pretended noisily that they were in agreement with this.

I preferred to dedicate myself to the white wine. I had a look around the shadows and, from the best lit spots, I caught sight of a hand holding a glass or some smiling lips or a worn out shoe . . .

My eyes came to rest on a very young girl who had the air of something Chinese about her, like an oriental princess. Someone must have brought their daughter. She was sitting in a corner as if she wanted to melt into it. Next to her, a dark-haired woman was snoozing on the sofa. She woke up and addressed the girl. I recognized her as Natalia Goncharova and went over to say hello. She introduced me to her young friend, pronouncing her name for me slowly: Nina Nikolayevna Berberova. Then she started to complain, the way she usually did, that she had to work hard, that she often worked fourteen hours a day whereas Larionov, her husband, only painted when he felt like it.

"But he's a great artist."

The voice came from the corner, a voice with a contralto tone to it that I would never have suspected from such a young girl.

"Yes, indeed he is," Goncharova sighed, and when she bowed her head, I noticed the thick net of white threads that embellished her black hair. "Sit down, Igor, if Nina doesn't mind," she told me. "I have to look after the other guests for a while."

I sat in her place. But maybe because the young girl had such a fragile air about her, I sat on the sofa as far as I could from her, until I was rubbing up against the knees of some noisy young man. The girl kept giving furtive looks at a corner on the other side of the room, which was so dark I was unable to see if there was someone there or if the corner were empty. When she looked at me, Nina's wide eyes had a touch of irony in them, but when they looked over at whatever was in the corner, they shone, dewy. The candlelight revealed a look of surrender. But, to whom?

"Which of Natalia Goncharova's paintings do you like best,

Nina Nikolayevna?" I asked to break the silence that had risen between us.

"I never tire of looking at her pictures of Moscow in the snow. But the one I like the most is that blue cow that looks like a pet. It seems as sweet as a teddy bear. If I had money, that's the painting I'd buy from her."

I started to talk about the The Donkey's Tail, the group of painters that Larionov had founded when he still lived in Moscow ten or twelve years earlier, but Nina, clearly uninterested, only answered me in monosyllables. So I tried more philosophical subjects: freedom, my freedom, the freedom of one who depends on no man and no woman, on no government or ideology. The more she listened to my words, the more restless the girl got, and I realized that her face expressed a rejection so strong I lost the courage to go on. We fell silent. She must have gone on thinking about something while I wondered what else I could say. The silence made me feel uncomfortable.

But, as if she had read my thoughts, the girl said, "I like silence and solitude. I prefer to be silent, you know? But I want to tell you that I don't agree with what you have just said. Because freedom, once obtained, is not difficult to bear, don't you agree? In any event, it shouldn't be for an adult person capable of reflection."

Once again, it seemed to me that her words didn't match her youthful appearance, and even less with the teddy bear she'd mentioned just a moment earlier. I wanted to protest, but Nina went on:

"I'm one of those people for whom the place where they were

born has never been a symbol of safety or refuge. The awareness that I do not have this refuge, I find satisfying; I can even say that I like it. I have no homeland or political party, family or tribe. I don't look for any, I don't need any."

Young people obliged to live without a defined set of values, often substitute theories for values. However, I didn't want to initiate any controversy, not least because I wasn't quite sure of my own position on this topic. So I limited myself to saying, "You live in Paris, you have a new homeland, new friends. Isn't that a refuge?"

"We are just passing through Paris. The day after tomorrow, we go back to Berlin. But Berlin will not become home for me, I'm sure of that."

I looked at her, perplexed. Nonetheless it felt good to be next to her. Maybe in her company I could even manage to enjoy being silent. I felt respect and a little fear in her presence. But above all I needed to think about everything that we had said. While I shifted about on the sofa, restless, Nina sent another look into the darkness. I followed her eyes: a man's figure moved in the corner on the other side of the room, a head was shaken, and a mane of long hair spread over the back of the chair.

"*Monsieur, ce métro va à Billancourt?*"

"*Oui, monsieur.* But there's nothing interesting in Billancourt. Just factories and immigrants. The Russians were there before the war, and recently a lot of North Africans have moved there. I would suggest that you . . ."

"Vous êtes très gentil, monsieur, mais je connais Paris assez bien. Bonne journée!"

Why tell him that my destination was the Renault factory? In any case, he wouldn't have believed me if I'd told him I was going there to work; engineers usually travel by taxi. It is difficult to make someone understand that, after so many years, what I want is to savor the Paris metro. It hasn't changed. I find the same weird characters as always: little old ladies heavily made up, who look like clowns giving their last performance; drunken and ever-courteous clochards. The only difference now is that there are more, and louder, tourists.

So this is Billancourt. The working-class outskirts that didn't belong to Paris in our time and where, ever since the time of the Commune, the streets have been named after the leaders of the workers' movement. I recognize a cafe; it had been a Russian dance hall and is now decorated with marble and mirrors as in the belle époque. But, as far as I can see, it doesn't have many customers. Today people prefer to get out of the city, which has become disagreeable and inhumane; back then it was the city itself that didn't accept people. It was very expensive. That is why Tsvetaeva lived in Meudon, Berdyaev in Clamart, Shestov and Remizov in Boulogne.

Here we have the Place Nationale, there the rue Nationale. And here . . . Yes, here is the rue des Quatre-Cheminées, it was here that she lived! This is the street, and there is the Renault factory. I passed through that door every day. If I turn left, I'll reach the Seine. It was on this bench that I used to sit and let my thoughts flow freely, following the pace of the river. I would always end up thinking about her. To me, this bench is dedicated to her, as is this part of the Seine. In Billancourt, even the river is brown, like the firmament supported by four chimneys as if they were celestial pillars: those are her words and I imagined a kind of Greek Parthenon in which, instead of Ionic columns, the smoking chimneys of a factory rose up.

She was sitting in the first row of the audience: a twenty-year-old girl, with black hair and slightly Asian features, probably Armenian. She went to listen to poets often. That night her body was wrapped in a white lace dress. But an attentive observer—or even one who wasn't—would have noticed that the young girl's elegant dress was made from the cloth of a curtain. And the fact was that in 1921, Saint Petersburg had suffered revolution, hunger, and civil war. Most of the once-ostentatious cafes and restaurants along the boulevards were closed.

The poet who began the evening with his verses was Gumilyov, Nina wrote to me many years later, in a letter in which she answered my questions about her literary beginnings in post-revolutionary Saint Petersburg. It was a long letter, like the ones I received later in our friendship; apparently she liked to take stock of her past.

After Gumilyov, Georgi Ivanov read, and the last to read was a young man with long hair and a velvet jacket. He was known as Vladislav Felitsianovich Khodasevich; everyone present addressed him with respect. He read poems such as "Lida,"

"Bacchus," and some others. With sensitivity, without
the histrionic pathos that characterized the performance of
the first poet.

Then came the turn of the candidates for membership of
the Association of Artists and Writers,

Nina went on.

There was only one applicant.

And I can see her. It was the girl with that dress made out of
a curtain, that is to say, Nina.

I positioned myself in front of the audience, sitting on the
ground on an oriental carpet. And I recited my verses:

> Decorated amphorae and water jugs
> I will rinse under a flow of warm water.
> And my still wet hair
> I will twist above the smoking stove.
> Like a playful little girl,
> With my pigtail well plaited,
> I will take a heavy bucket
> and I will sweep everything
> with a monstrous broom.

They applauded. In the audience, a woman who was
thirty-something years old stood up, beautiful and sure of

*herself. It was Anna Akhmatova. Before leaving, she wrote
something in a book and without saying a word handed me the
volume with its dedication, "For Nina Berberova": it was her
collection* Anno Domini.

*The poem about the broom surely captivated the venerated
poet, in part because it had been recited by a girl who looked
Japanese, charming and elegant even when wearing curtain
fabric. Nina. Only she knew how to be attractive in the middle
of the greatest misery, as she would demonstrate at other times.
The letter continues:*

*"I found your piece about the bucket and the brush
amusing," said the young man who had recited before me, that
Vladislav . . .*

*"I didn't mention any brush; you weren't listening
properly. It was a broom!" I corrected him.*

Instead of answering the man kissed my hand.

*Who was this man with a long black mane and old-
fashioned manners who still kissed women's hands, and whom
everybody admired? Was this Khodasevich? I decided there
and then I would read something of his.*

*When the readings were over, the first reader, Nikolay
Gumilyov, came up to me.*

*"Nina Nikolayevna, the committee has decided to accept
you as a member of the Association of Artists and Writers," he
said and handed me my membership card. "Tomorrow I will
meet you, right here," he added.*

The next day, both of us were sitting in a cake shop.

"It was I who discovered Akhmatova, and also

Mandelstam, and I have made them what they are today. If you wish, I would do the same for you."

He was not an attractive man. Each of his eyes peered in a different direction, but without a doubt one of them was sliding its way over my shoulders. We looked calm enough, but under the surface the animosity between us stretched out like a minefield.

"I am most grateful to you, Nikolay. I will follow your teachings religiously," I answered with apparent cool. I didn't feel free in the company of that man, but I kept saying to myself: he's a great poet!

We headed for the Summer Garden, and then turned into Gagarin Street and went along the bank of the Neva to the Hermitage. In one of the bookshops, Gumilyov bought a few volumes of poetry. Bowing, he offered them to me. I was trembling with pleasure at the generosity, but I controlled myself.

"I'm sorry, but I cannot possibly accept your gift."

"I have bought these books for you."

"No, you mustn't."

"No? Well, if that's the way it is . . ." and with a decisive movement of the hand the poet threw the books into the Neva. The waves closed over them.

When we stopped in front of my parents' home, he recited a poem that he had written inspired by me, so he said. He placed his hand on my head and let the fingers slide down over my face, onto my shoulders. I took a step back.

"How boring you are!" he said in a loud voice. "Go home, I am going too."

I saw a weak orange light in the window of my parents' bedroom.

"Good night, have a good rest," I said calmly, by way of goodbye.

"I won't sleep, Nina. I'll spend the night writing poems about you. I can't sleep. I'm sad, deeply sad."

Ah! The pathos of poets! I had always thought that they exaggerated, that it was a pose.

He left. It was the second of August.

Early on the morning of the third, they came for him. They arrested him, accusing him of being a monarchist sympathizer. It wasn't true. A short time later, they executed him.

The wind off the Seine makes reading difficult. On this bench where I have come back years later to reread her letters again, it is always windy, with wet blasts that make me shiver. I don't know if I can spend much more time here, with this cold coming in off the river and my memories . . . But still, it was in this letter that Nina wrote to me about the poets who had died after the revolution.

It was winter. The new year of 1922 was not far off. I left the university and stepped into a snow-covered street. After the revolution, Saint Petersburg had become a dark, abandoned city, illuminated only by snow. I was feeling desperate about the deaths of Gumilyov and Alexander Blok, who had died of hunger, and about the exile of Bely, Remizov, and Gorky, along with dozens of other artists. I did not know then that Yesenin, Mayakovsky, and Tsvetaeva would kill themselves. I told myself one era had ended and another was beginning. The silence and emptiness filled the square. Saint Petersburg looked like the city the visionary texts of Gogol, Dostoyevsky, or Blok had predicted: an abandoned, ice-covered ship that moves and can barely make its way through a tempest of snow. I started to run in my oversized boots. I slipped. I got up again after my fall, and stumbled and fell once more. On the corner of the boulevard Konnogvardeiski they had erected a statue of Volodarski, the Bolshevik. During the bombing of Saint Petersburg the sculpture had cracked. It was then covered with a canvas sheet which snapped in the wind. It seemed as if the statue was shifting restlessly, crying out, threatening someone. I crossed the square and walked along the boulevard up to Morskaya Street. Not a light was visible, not a sound could be heard, just the howls of the wind and the snow, more and more snow that connected the sky to the earth. And the ghosts that had started to dance in the fantastic winter night.

Suddenly, a shadow appeared from around the corner.

"Careful, the ground is slippery!"

It was Vladislav Khodasevich.

◆

I'm cold. It would be better if I went into the cafe on the corner and had a cigarette while finishing reading this letter. I remember how I too had wanted to surprise Nina like that, when we were together in Paris. I waited for her at the door of the *Poslednie novosti* newspaper offices where she worked as a staff writer. But she wasn't startled the way she was that night in Saint Petersburg. As if my waiting for her at the door of her workplace was the most normal thing in the world, she said when she saw me: "Let's go for a coffee."

That New Year's Eve, in the enormous Baroque palace that was home to the Saint Petersburg House of the Arts there was wine and food, joy and warmth, and even music and dance, that is to say, everything that the city had been missing for the last three years, given the shortages during the civil war. I sat between Rozhdestvensky, my friend who had invited me to dinner, and Vladislav Khodasevich, who knew that I would be coming along to the party.

"White or red wine, Nina?" Rozhdestvensky asked me.

"First white, then red, and then lots of other colors!"

A sculpture by Rodin presided over the blue room. There was a light on and a few candles to illuminate the table. The pianist played the waltz from Eugene Onegin, and then a ballad by Glinka and then . . . No. I lost count of the pieces he played afterward. I conversed with Rozhdestvensky but was attentive, above all, to the man on my right. From time to time I asked something of Zamyatin or his wife; I answered Kornei Chukovsky's questions. But altogether everything was a dance

*of lights, colors, and sounds; warmth came from my right hand
side. Vladislav was drinking red wine; Rozhdestvensky, white
wine; during a toast he broke the glass.*

"Take mine, we'll both drink out of it," I suggested.

*"In that case I beg of you that you also drink out of mine,
otherwise it would be unfair," said my neighbor on the right.*

"I have two glasses; I've come out the winner!"

*I clinked the two glasses together and drank out of them
both at once.*

"Nina . . ."

*Irina, who had come in Fedin's company, bent down to me
behind Rozhdestvensky's back. She whispered something in my
ear. I giggled, red as a tomato.*

*"I'm not telling you," I answered Irina, "but I'll write
a poem about it. It'll be a futurist poem because I'm totally
drunk."*

After a moment I read aloud:

*Joyful and drunken, with our hearts in our hands
we stagger as we sing,
drinking into the small hours
three out of two glasses.
"Is it true that they are sharing you?"
my timid friend asks.
I blink and look sideways at both of them,
am confused by what I see.
I live on the bank.
What more can I desire!*

Applause. I let myself fall back into the chair.

Vladislav Khodasevich leaned over to me from the right, asking in a quiet voice: "What are you referring to when you say you live 'on the bank'?"

Rozhdestvensky leaned over to me from the left, wanting to know what we were talking about.

"'On the bank?'" I answered, "That's where you find yourself when the boat leaves without you."

Vladislav waited until the moment when Rozhdestvensky got involved in a conversation with Fedin to whisper to me:

"I am not one of those who stays on the bank."

A bell tolls. Midnight! Nineteen twenty-two has started right now.

"Happy New Year! Happy New Year! For you! For Russia! For your novel! For us!"

Exclamations, toasts, the clinking of glasses, laughter.

"For the ship, Nina," said Vladislav, touching his glass to mine. Without smiling, serious, very serious, he looked me straight in the eyes.

I stepped away from him. I felt that this man had power over me. But even though I went over to the farthest end of the room, I realized that the only thing, the only person I perceived was him.

It was well into the small hours or the morning when the door opened suddenly. Dozens of buoyant people burst into the room. In the middle of the swarm I recognized Anna Akhmatova. They had even brought an orchestra with them! They occupied the largest room in the palace, the room of mirrors, and the orchestra set to playing dance music. Vladislav made me sit down on the sofa in front of the great mirror and settled down next to me. Across the room, couples moved to the rhythm of the tango and the fox-trot; the women had perfumed themselves with dried thyme and oregano; from time to time someone spoke a few words in French or English. What inspired us was the desire to show ourselves that after three years of fear and hunger, we were still alive and able to enjoy life.

Vladislav took my hand.

"Fortunately, in this country the imagination of the heart still exists."

Ah, Russian sentimentalism! But at that moment, the phrase stole my heart. I sat with my head resting on the back of the sofa, my feet stretched out in front of me, and my eyes closed as I let myself be carried away by the rhythm of the music and his sweet voice speaking to me. Next to me a low lamp with a shade of pink silk cast its light only on me and the man who was leaning toward me; it singled us out from the rest of the people in the room. Couples happy as could be were moving around as if they couldn't see us, as if they knew that they were in our way, that in some way they were too much of a crowd.

We walked, one next to the other. It was the sixth of January, the eve of the Russian Christmas. Vladislav walked with a light step. He was slim, tall. His overcoat, hat, and gloves—everything he wore was borrowed, but he knew how to keep a natural elegance about him despite everything. The snow *whipped his face, but he moved forward with his head held high and a mocking grimace on his lips, as if he were forever protesting against something.*

Yes, that gesture of Vladya's . . . Rather than protest, I would say it was derision. It was as if he was laughing at everybody, and many people couldn't stand him for that reason. But those of us who knew him knew that the grimace was the mask of a timid man.

A tune more suitable for dancing than for celebrating Christmas filled the snowy air of Saint Petersburg. Any excuse was good for an improvised party. We crossed the square in front of the Mikhailovsky Theater; the snow was crisp and shiny. Against the light of the enormous spotlights in the square, wide bands of steam, like cigarette smoke, emerged from our lips. Invisible workers were hanging a hammer and sickle on the façade of the theater; gigantic symbols already crowned the neighboring buildings. The spotlights illuminated those hammers and sickles, which were so easy to spot, red and futuristic. From time to time as we walked their light came to rest on our happy faces. We crossed Politseisky Bridge, buried under the snow, and we were already in front of the House of Arts where Vladislav lived. In the corridor we said hello to a roommate who was half asleep, Ossip Mandelstam.

A pity that Nina doesn't describe the meeting with Mandelstam in more detail. To me he is the greatest Russian poet of the twentieth century. I would like to know what he was like when he was half asleep, though I suppose he was just like anyone else, with a grumpy face.

Vladislav put wood into the smoking stove heater and made me sit down on a chair next to the window. He brought his own chair as close as he could. The Nevsky Prospekt was empty; there were just mountains of snow that shone and dazzled. On Sadovaya Street a single lamppost was flickered, and even that one was about to go out. Daylight was approaching. The aura of January radiated polar light and hurled it at the river and canals. When the cold, pale sun flooded the boulevards, I headed home.

After that night, in which the heat of Vladislav's hands and body passed into mine, I was not the same. Never until then had I said the words that I said that night to Vladislav; never until then had I heard sentences such as those he had whispered into my ear. And I have never heard them since. As if the icy black air of the Saint Petersburg night had converted them, as soon as they were born, into another piece of ice in the street to be shattered by the boots of those who would run to face so many struggles.

We moved forward in rhythmic shudders on the Petersburg-Berlin goods train.

"Nina, I didn't want to tell you earlier so as not to influence your decision to come with me. I have found out—did you know?—that my name is on the list of intellectuals that the Commissariat for the Interior plans to have removed from the

country. *Berdyaev and Zaytsev are also on it. In fact, there are hundreds of names."*

I shrugged my shoulders a little and smiled as if to say: "We're leaving anyhow. Now they can't do anything to you."

We were heading for exile. For a short while? For a long time?

I was not yet twenty-one; Vladislav was fifteen years older.

He handed me a piece of paper, but refused to let go of it. I read:

They order us to bow under the yoke,
or to live in the bitterness of exile;
but I, I carry in my suitcase
all of my Russia.

"Your Russia?" I asked, my eyes fixed on his suitcase.

Vladislav took out the eight volumes of Pushkin's complete works. He placed them on the floor of the car, around us.

"Like that. And far away though we may be, we will always find ourselves in Russia."

I shrugged again. There was a certain mockery mixed with my laughter. My eyes said, "Do you really need to deceive yourself in this manner?"

"We will always be together. We have to survive, Nina."

I stretched out my hand.

"What's on the other sheet?"

"It's just a beginning. I don't know how to finish it."

My eyes passed from one line to the other.

Here there is a story. I have seen it
clearly, perfectly outlined
while I had your gentle palm
in my hand.

I took a pencil and added:

And so, from your burning palm
the blood began to pass to mine;
it gave me life and a clear look;
I was filled with tenderness.

I sat as comfortably as I could on the suitcase and watched
the wooden walls of the freight car, as if there were a window
through which I could contemplate a cheerful landscape. At
that moment we left the Russian frontier behind.

A spacious summer villa with balconies and a wide terrace. A
huge garden. An evening drenched in the color of an old silver
moon. The paths of lime trees that lead out to the fields, beyond
the garden. Fields of corn that stretch away to the horizon, the
golden light of which is broken from time to time by patches of
woodland or by streams. In the summer, this was my world: the
house, the garden, the fields. While I let myself be lulled by the
regular jolts of the train, I saw them before my eyes. Vladislav
was next to me. This time the car had windows and we were
both sitting on comfortable bench seats. We were poor, as poor
as before, but now weren't fleeing and we didn't have to hide.
We were travelling from Berlin to Prague. My eyes rested

on the fog that prevented me from seeing the landscape on the other side of the glass, and my mind was submerged in the images of that last summer at the family villa in the district of Tversk. How many years had passed? Seven? Maybe eight? Without knowing it, that summer I had said goodbye to the house for good. I walked past it, slowly, through the garden. I ran along the paths of lime trees, and revolution was in the air. In the evening the peasants came to walk in the owners' garden. Who would have thought then that in a couple of years, flames would bring down those balconies of carved wood and that the bodies of caretakers would swing from the branches of the apple trees? How was it that I didn't suspect all that would happen, when every evening I saw the shadows drag themselves through the flowers and hang around the fountain where goldfish swam? How is it that I was unable to foresee it, when at the end of the summer those shadows dared to enter the dining room to see how my parents ate? My lack of awareness then was unforgivable. But those immense fields of corn, vast and infinite, have kept me company all my life as a vision of happiness, more beautiful than the sea, more mysterious than the unreachable peaks of the high mountain land.

After half a year of living hand-to-mouth in Berlin, a city that did not welcome us and in which we always felt like strangers, we headed for Prague. We sensed that our exile could become permanent; we followed the news that came from Russia and tried to lengthen our period of uncertainty, before we would need to decide on a fixed place of residence.

Prague—thick, November fog. Low, heavy clouds. A
tough, shadowy lid over everything that silenced life. Old
honorable Russians with their ever-so-chaste wives. A gray,
impenetrable city.
We stayed at the Beranek Hotel, that is to say the hotel of
the lamb. There were lambs everywhere: embroidered on the
cushions, printed on the menu and the bills of the restaurant,
painted on the walls and doors. It was four o'clock; outside it
was starting to get dark. Marina Tsvetaeva and her husband,
Sergey Efron, had just entered the hotel. Marina had lived in
Prague for quite some time. She had thick, red hair that fell
onto her shoulders with fringe that covered her forehead down
to her eyebrows.

I remember Marina Tsvetaeva; I ran into her once in Paris, at
the home of some friends. We didn't understand each other, as
if we spoke different languages. She saw the poet as an occult
being, as someone who lives on a desert island, in the catacombs,
in an ivory tower. Nina thought this romantic vision of a creator
was sterile, even dangerous. Marina was a proud woman who, in
the Paris émigrés, always seemed out of place. From the 1920s
onward, nothing that was written outside Russia ever managed
to get inside the country, and she could not stand living apart
from her readers. She couldn't live in Russia either, as she dem-
onstrated later with her suicide.

Now that I think of the way Marina wore her hair it strikes
me that she did so in a way similar to Vladya. Their hair was a
little weird, but attractive. What else does the letter say?

Her elegant brown dress was worn thin in many places. Marina never took off that indelible stamp of poverty. I had prepared tea on a little petrol burner, and I served thin slices of ham and cheese on a platter. We spoke of literature. In Prague, Vladislav and I had discovered Božena Němcová. We admired her life, her novels and stories, and with the help of friends we looked for those places in the Czech capital where the writer had once lived, where she had met with her friends, and the theaters that she had frequented. But more than anything our conversation turned to the experience of exile.

"I can't get used to living outside Russia," Marina complained.

"But have you tried to, Marina?" I remember Vladislav asking.

"It isn't that I can't. I don't want to!" she exclaimed with the expression of an obstinate child.

"Marina always stresses that she can't," Sergey Efron said with a grimace, by way of explanation.

"You know what I think?" I reflected. "That you say this, Marina, as if it were a positive attribute. Like a demonstration of loyalty, of faithfulness!" I smiled at her, putting my palm into her hand.

"You are hard—you really are—but hardness becomes you," she smiled at me.

I took my hand away.

"Your lack of adaptability, Marina, is a sign of your mental and existential failure," I remarked, while keeping calm.

"You are still so young! And young people, of course, need

theories, words," Marina said, sipping her tea and watching me with unblinking eyes.

"This kind of failure," I went on, "is typical of a person who does not know how to accept the times and the society that surround her."

Marina fell silent; she was looking at my shoes now. Then she said with a sigh, "You are not under threat, my dear. You can go back to your home, to your town, and put flowers on the tombs of your loved ones."

She was playing with her white cup and saucer, without looking at anyone. I sighed.

"But Vladislav can't go back, and I can't go back either. And I do not devote myself to the cult of the tombs of my ancestors or to any other kind of relic in order to bolster myself during difficult moments. I give no importance to family or blood relations, and I live without defenses and without weapons, as I haven't got a skin as thick as that of a hippopotamus or the claws of a tiger."

"You have your lover. Look how he has taken your hand. He only has eyes for you; he sleeps every night in your arms. It is easy to talk then. Whereas I . . . I have the feeling that I always have to fight against something and that wears me out."

"Marina, isn't it rather that it is difficult to bear up under the weight of your desire to always look different, to be a stranger everywhere?" asked Vladislav.

"Vladislav is right, Marina," said Sergey Efron in a quiet voice, "although—"

"The poet always bears the special mark of discontent. Why is that so difficult for you to understand?"

"I understand perfectly well what you mean, Marina," I interrupted her, more than anything because the hysterical tone of her exclamations was getting on my nerves. "I also feel that the forces that I am fighting against are impossible to define. We are faced with something difficult to describe, with enemies that have no concrete form."

"I have loved everything in life," said Marina, quietly, slowly, as if only addressing me, "but each love has been a confrontation rather than a friendship, a farewell instead of a meeting, a breaking off rather than a union, death rather than life. That is how I am."

"If you really need a homeland, Marina, look for it in what you write," I answered her in a low voice.

"But in exile I have lost my readers! Only in Russia can they understand!" she exclaimed with desperation in her voice.

"And us, your friends?" said Vladislav while he stroked her hand.

Marina laughed in a crazy way, at something only she understood. Then she switched off the light. In the darkness she threw herself at me, caressed me, hugged me.

The lights were put on again. Someone knocked at the door. On the threshold Roman Jakobsen appeared. He had come to talk with Vladislav about metaphors and metonymies.

✦

Prague is a majestic city, as inaccessible as its castle with its towers that point, black, toward the sky. We felt like strangers there. At the eating house for the Russians, people turn up with coupons; dozens and hundreds of Russians who go there to eat watered down borscht.

We went to Venice. Vladislav would relive his youth there.

"Zhenia."

"I'm sorry?"

"Zhenia."

"You mean Nina."

"Here, you are Zhenia to me. Zhenia Muratova. Zhenia, my first love, my great love."

"No, I'm not."

"Don't you like being both my past and my present?"

"The past never has the same value as the present. Not even my own past does. Only the present is important."

"Zhenia, this time I won't let you go. No, Zhenia, you are everything to me."

A few days later, I found out that Zhenia had been the first wife of our mutual friend, Muratov.

"Nina, I've written a poem about you here, in Venice." Vladislav said in a reconciliatory tone. When he decided that it was time we made up, he expected me to accept it all without a protest. But I remained silent. Vladislav went on: "A poem that speaks of your arrival at the Piazza of San Marco and of the doves that take flight at your presence."

I said nothing. But I was excited by the poem. Vladislav took it badly that I hadn't made up with him as soon as he *offered me the possibility. In Venice he never stopped talking about Zhenia. The exile always lives like a sub-letter. In love, too, my fate was that of the exile—to live like a sub-letter.*

We reached Rome, where we wanted to see some Russian friends, especially Muratov. Vladislav felt more defeated with each day that passed. He showed me the remains of ancient Rome and said, "These ruins will soon collapse completely, like me. What am I, if not a ruin? What are we if not that, you and I?"

"I would rather say that you and I will remain standing for a long time, like these ruins," I said lightly.

Each morning, Vladislav got up fearing the disasters of the afternoon. Each evening, I looked forward eagerly to the joys of the day to follow.

"Which subject do you prefer most in Renaissance painting?" I asked during one of our visits to the Vatican museums.

"Saint Jerome," answered Muratov.

"The Annunciation," said Vladislav.

"The thoughtful ass of Bethlehem," said Muratov. "And you, Nina?"

"Tobias with the fish and the angel who guides him."

"Why, Nina?" he asked me, when we passed into another room.

"I feel that I recognize myself in both figures. I am Tobias, who carries the fish and moves forward slowly and with confidence, his shoelaces firmly tied and with a ribbon around

his hair so that the wind won't ruffle it. But I am also the angel,
I walk with a challenging face like the prow of a ship that plows
through the waves, confronting rough weather. The face of the
angel radiates sureness, courage, and resolution. It is my face. I
lead someone by the hand, I guide him. I am not afraid to lead.
The clouds gather in the sky, but I pay no attention and move
forward. The progress of these two characters represents my
own path through life.

"Are you guiding someone, Nina?"

"Yes, I am guiding someone by the hand."

The different stages of our exile. Sorrento, just after sunset,
lights up for a moment like a flare. In the end it goes out, giving
way to a salt-impregnated air that burns our lips, and to the
smell of fish, both dead and alive.

In the dining room of Maxim Gorky's house, a table was
laid for twenty people. Baroness Budberg, friend and secretary
of the writer, served the soup. Vladislav was listening to what
Andrey Bely was saying to him, and then they both started
laughing. Vladislav filled me with tenderness when he laughed.
It was so difficult for him! But if I took his hand, he took it
back. As if he wanted to prove that he was the strong one, that
he despised my sentimentalism, that he didn't need me. Poor
Vladya!

"Do you believe in God, my dear?" Maria Fyodorovna,
Gorky's second wife, asked me.

"Each of us believes in his own god, don't you think, Maria
Fyodorovna?" I answered with some reticence.

"And what do you think is best, my little pigeon: to live in Russia without freedom, or to live in freedom without Russia?" Maria Fyodorovna didn't want to give up.

I didn't think twice.

"In freedom without Russia."

"It isn't so obvious, my dear. To live so far away, so many miles from home . . ."

I began to observe Semyon Yushkevich, the writer who dealt with Jewish themes. His eyes gazed around him in melancholy fashion while he murmured, "Nothing serves any purpose; death is at our heels. Death, who cannot be put off or rejected, and it is high time we started to think about our souls."

I picked up the spoon to start eating the soup, little by little. The song of a cricket came from the garden and I couldn't understand how it could be singing already, at the beginning of April. Then the company of so many strangers began to tire me and I felt a desire to walk in the garden, all alone, just Vladislav and me, even though that meant doing without dinner. But recently Vladislav had been so distant. In the garden it was almost dark already, and a cold, wet breeze blew in through the open window. I wanted to ask Andrey Bely, who was sitting in front of me, to close it, but he had his eyes fixed on his dish because they had forgotten to give him a spoon.

The conversation was growing stale.

I saw the host wrapped in a silence heavy with annoyance. He stared at a spot on the wall above the heads of the guests and drummed his fingers on the table to let everyone know that he was in a very bad mood.

"The chicken hasn't come out well; it's too dry," Maria Fyodorovna informed the eaters.

At last! As if obeying an order everyone started up animated conversation: all present tried to cover up the hostess's inconvenient remark, to make out that they hadn't heard anything, to laugh, to make noise.

For the third time that evening, Bely explained to Vladislav how he had fallen in love with Liubov, Alexandr Blok's wife. When he was about to do so for the fourth time ("I forgot certain details"), Vladya jumped up and excused himself by saying that he had to leave for a moment. Gorky was hurling tirades against Dostoyevsky and then at Gogol, as if all the Russian writers of the last century were his personal enemies. No one dared contradict his opinions; only I, who had not considered the situation properly, mentioned the name of Tolstoy. At that moment I didn't have Vladislav by my side to tap me on the shoulder by way of warning. In a few brief words, Gorky recognized his talent, but quickly moved the subject, moving it into the territory of hatred by dwelling on Tolstoy's personal weaknesses.

The next morning, taking advantage of a walk with Gorky while Vladislav still slept, we discussed the subject once more.

"Do you, Berberini, also reproach me for my book of memories of Lenin?" the writer asked me while looking at the orange-tinted sea.

"I understand your intentions. You want to go back to Russia and you are paving the way."

"I will confess something to you. While I was writing the book I couldn't stop crying."

I smiled. I don't like grandiloquent sentiment. I wanted to say, "You were crying like an old peasant woman," but I didn't dare.

Gorky continued.

"Twenty-five years ago Lenin explained to me his concept of the world, of life, the only coherent concept I have ever known. Without his vision I am lost."

"You will go back to Russia, won't you, Alexei Maximovich?"

"Here, in Italy, I am writing more than ever. This week I will read to you *The Artamonova*, a novel that I have just completed. In Russia they are trampling on the principles of human dignity and of freedom. But . . . "

"But?"

"But without Lenin's conception of the world, life has no meaning for me."

"So you will go back. Be careful, Alexei Maximovich. I am worried for you."

We sat on a cafe terrace. In the square, the children of Sorrento started to sing, not Neapolitan shanties, but the latest American hits. Then they passed a hat for the tourists to put money in.

The day came when we ran out of money. With difficulty we gathered enough to buy two train tickets to Paris. We left Rome on a sunny April afternoon, and ended up standing, *the following morning, in the Gare de Lyon in Paris. It was raining; gusts of wind cut through to our bones and the city was covered in fog. Everything there was gray: the sky, the streets, the people. Instead of the castle of Sant'Angelo standing out against the blue of the sky, we saw a clock tower pointed up toward a sky the color of dirty lead. We felt strange in that unwelcoming atmosphere. We felt that we had arrived in hell, from which the path of return is a difficult one, if there is a path of return at all.*

We found a small flat on the outskirts of the city, in Billancourt. Vladislav spent his days stretched out on the bed, staring at the ceiling. I sat at the table and looked out through the only window at the wall of the house in front of ours and at a scrap of Parisian sky, almost black. We didn't have enough money even to eat, and no hope of a steady job. When someone came to see us, I ran to the bakery on the corner to buy a couple of cakes. Out of decency the visitors didn't touch the food.

And here this long letter comes to an end: a few questions about my health and my work, and then a greeting and signature. Where did I put the matches?

Here they are. My cigarettes have gotten wet. One day, it must have been in the early 1930s, when I was wandering through the streets of Paris, from the rue de l'Ancienne Comédie to the boulevard Saint-Germain, I suddenly saw Zamyatin coming from the opposite direction. Once he had walked past me, I turned around and followed him out of sheer curiosity. He headed for the rue de l'Éperon, went into a Russian bookshop. I did the same just a moment later. He looked at a few books and then went into the second room. A young woman, engrossed in a book, stood next to one of the shelves that filled the room. The writer looked at her inquisitively several times, as if she reminded him of someone. To me, her slightly Asian traits also looked familiar—she was slender, attractive, with a plain dress and a long pearl necklace around her neck. Zamyatin went up to her and lowered the book she had in her hand.

"Don't you recognize me?"

The girl was confused. He reminded her of their meeting.

"We met at the New Year's Eve party in Saint Petersburg, at the House of the Arts, remember? In 1921. We had dinner together, with some other people. You were sitting next to Khodasevich."

They left together. And I remembered a room full of cigarette smoke, the kind of mist that always surrounds Russian intellectuals, the light from a candle, and an Oriental princess. How she had changed! Her way of being, defiant and independent, stood out even in the way she walked, lightly but full of aplomb, even self-satisfaction, and in the way she held her head high and in her mildly ironic smile with which, as they walked, she turned to Zamyatin, who was gesticulating theatrically.

They sat down in the Cafe Danton. I like these Parisian cafes where people sit facing the street, like in a theater. This way people sitting together don't have to look at each other if they don't want to.

The girl with the pearl necklace talked for quite a while, but in such a low voice that I was barely able to make out anything at all. The writer lit his pipe and rested his chin on his hands, all set to listen. Zamyatin, who was living in Paris at the time, didn't want to see anybody. He, who had been a member of the Bolshevik party in the time of the tsars, avoided the company of Russian exiles. He hoped that one day the Communist authorities would give him back his passport and he could go back to his country, in which he had lost confidence a long time ago, as he showed in his novel *We*. Then, he started to speak. He clearly wanted an optimistic tone to accompany his optimistic words, so he spoke loudly.

"Nina Nikolayevna," he said in an affected, almost military manner, "one must wait patiently and keep calm, like certain animals that, instead of coming out and fighting, remain patiently in their lair."

"But is life going to wait?" the woman interrupted him.

I will never forget it. It was an outcry.

"Life? What life are you talking about? In any event, life forgot about me a long time ago."

"Life only forgets those who forget about it."

"What kind of life can a writer have when he is condemned to silence? It's been a long time now since I frightened off my old comrades, in the publishing houses, in theaters. Any publisher interested in my work is making itself a candidate for the firing squad."

"But you're talking about Russia. Things work differently over here."

"I want to serve the great ideals of literature. And to do that I need readers in my own language, in my own country, a Russia in which it is possible to create literature without having to be the lackey of worthless people."

"We exiled writers also form a part of Russia. And here everything depends on us."

Zamyatin looked at his hands, which had fallen onto the table like dead weight.

"I am afraid that it will never again be possible to serve our literature. I am afraid that Russian literature has only one future left: its past."

He frowned. That was to be expected. His previously ecstatic face became ever more solemn. Zamyatin was beginning to look more and more like a walking automaton. Or rather, a walking corpse.

For a long while they sat in silence. The silence of the writer was heavy, long, painful. He knew not only that the girl was right, but also that she was aware that he knew. Zamyatin hated the ones who had stayed *over there*. As for the ones who had come *over here*, he despised us, too.

"Among the exiles, Russia exists," Nina Berberova said emphatically, as if to convince Zamyatin as well as herself. "It is a poor Russia, a pitiful one, pathetic and provincial, but it *is*, all the same! Maybe it's true that my generation of exiles won't do anything worthwhile and the previous generation will soon disappear. But over there in Russia, over there they are killing people! Over here we are alive. Life goes on! That's the important thing."

After a moment, she calmed herself and added, "That is why it is better to opt for a clear and precise alternative."

The writer had stopped smoking for a while and his silence was increasingly painful. His companion felt sorry for him, wanted to erase the effect of her words. She said, as if to herself, "Life goes on and wears away the trivial events as well as the important ones. Famous names and whole epochs are turned to dust. As somebody once said to me, we are like the people of Pompeii, you, me, and all the exiled Russians—buried under ashes."

The writer was silent. Both remained silent for a long while. Eventually they got up to go, without even having understood each other.

They said goodbye in front of the cafe and each began to walk in the opposite direction. Suddenly I felt as if I didn't know where to go. So I followed the writer. I caught up with him at an intersection.

"Mister Zamyatin, I just wanted to say hello to you because I admire your work. Allow me to introduce myself—"

"I am not Zamyatin," he said in a metallic voice. I certainly hadn't expected that. "I am not Zamyatin; you've made a mistake," he repeated and moved on.

I was stunned. The traffic lights shifted from yellow to red, from red to green. After a while, mentally I heard another voice, impatient: Is life going to wait?

Yes, here is rue des Quatre-Cheminées, a street destroyed by bombs during the Second World War. The house where Nina and Vladislav lived doesn't exist any more.

Quatre cheminées. Four chimneys indeed, but in my life there was only one woman. That cry, "Is life going to wait?" changed me forever. It tied me to her. That was it. My path was laid out before me: it was hers. Pursuit of that woman took me across Paris, into the French countryside during the war, and then on to America. It could be said that I had fallen in love, although now I think it was a matter of obsession, full of self-deception, one of those passions that help one stay alive, to live in a dream. This obsession kept me chasing after her and even had me investigating into her private life. Someone in love is worse than a spy.

During the roaring twenties, which for us exiles were rather on the miserable side, there was a Russian cabaret here instead of this cafe where I am now. We called our cafes "cabarets." It belonged to Boris Stepanovich—I don't remember his last name. Maybe Amfiteatrov? No, he was called Kozlobabin. We went there after finishing work in the Renault factory—Petrusha, Kostia, and I—to have a beer—Russian beer, as Monsieur Kozlobabin used to proclaim. Originally Petrusha was a cellist, Kostia a student of philosophy. I was an engineer, but I wanted to be a writer. In Billancourt we were all simply workers, some of the ten thousand Russian workers to whom Monsieur Renault hired in the 1920s so that we could manufacture his cars. In the evenings, Dunia, that stocky platinum blonde, used to sing in the cabaret:

Billancourt, new homeland,
a lair for young lives.

Every night, in a little corner,
Russia cries its eyes out.

Unforgettable. Another pudgy platinum blonde presided behind the bar—the wife of Boris Stepanovich, Madame Kozlobabina. She laughed with the regulars and made sure that nobody slipped away without paying. When a Frenchman came in by accident, no matter what he ordered, Madame Kozlobabina served him that cat's piss she claimed was vodka, and even added, with all the cheek in the world, "*C'est typiquement russe!*"

One day, as if she were an apparition, Nina Berberova turned up there. She was wearing an elegant suit jacket—at least that's how it struck me on that day; at that time I didn't suspect the degree of misery she was in—and had her short, black hair combed back. She sat at one of the tables and ordered a coffee. She pretended to be engrossed in her cigarette but I noticed that her big brown eyes were running over the faces, over the walls decorated with Russian balalaikas; she was scrutinizing people's gestures and digesting snippets of conversation. She was probably looking for material for the stories and chronicles that she published at that time in the *Poslednie novosti* newspaper.

Petrusha, Kostia, and I sat by the bar, still with our work overalls on. I wanted the ground to swallow me up when that elegant woman approached to say hello to Petrusha, who was one of her friends. She didn't recognize me after our first meeting in the darkness of the Bullier. Petrusha introduced me as a writer who was starting out and Nina winked at me, as if to someone who is taking part in the same conspiracy.

That day I found out that she too lived in Billancourt. I walked her to her street, rue des Quatre-Cheminées.

The stamp on the next letter that Nina sent to me is also American, which means that she wrote it several decades after our meeting at the cabaret.

"Waiter, bring me another beer!"

It was muggy. Dust and smoke came into the room through the open window. With difficulty, I managed to get Vladislav out of bed, and we both left the flat. We wandered through the streets without any particular destination. The city was just waking up from its summer lethargy, and in the coolness of the twilight hour, it was reaching a frenetic pace. We stopped at a Montparnasse bistro for a coffee, and then we headed for the other end of Paris, for Montmartre, where we lost ourselves amid the smelly streets. We entered a house of ill repute, then a dance hall. In a little theater located in a cellar, a music hall show was being performed; the cardboard sets were more pathetic than ridiculous. We watched a sideshow hermaphrodite, and then went over to the bar, where we were served drinks by fat naked women. Euphoric, Vladislav was planning the poems he would write about this other side of Paris.

But the following day Vladislav didn't get out of bed, not even to have his morning tea. He said, "Why me? Why is it I who must suffer among all the people in the world? Why has this had to happen to me?" He blamed me for things. He kept telling me that I wasn't as interesting or attractive as I had been at the beginning of our relationship. It fit perfectly into his logic that because Vladislav had lost interest in me, he had fallen into a depression. What was more, this situation paralleled his feelings about being in exile, the loss of Russia. The contrast between the misery in which the Russians lived in Paris and the opulence and arrogance of the Parisians kept me so busy that I wasn't even trying to experience, for myself, the wealth of culture that was all around me. I felt buried under the poverty I was suffering, and the difficulties with the French language, which in Paris turned out to be completely different from what I had learned in school.

I couldn't stand the sighs that came from his bed, day after day, without a word of explanation.

One day Vladislav received a letter.

"What do they say?" I asked him.

"I'm on the list of the one-hundred banned writers in Russia. My books can't be sold there."

I sat down on his side of the bed.

"Well, so what? Your life, our life, is here now."

Vladislav covered his head with a pillow. I did what I could to uncover him, and we struggled with that for a while. Then Vladislav relented. With the face of a child who is at once capricious and hurt, and with a voice altered by anguish, he said, "Here I am not able to write. There I am banned from doing everything: writing, publishing, and living.

"You will learn to write here."

I had no doubts. Like Tobias, I spoke with confidence,
without realizing that he was dragging me into his hell.

"I can't live without writing."

"Then write! I'm always telling you."

"I tell you I'm not one of those people who can write
anywhere. The flower of writing does not bloom everywhere.
Now I know that in order to write I need Russia. And I can't
go back."

"We have brought our Russia here."

No. He didn't make any effort. Like an obstinate child, he
covered his face with a pillow again. I took it away from him
once more.

"Hey, Vladya . . ."

"I've walked into a dead end. I can't go forward and I can't
go back."

"There is always a way, it's just a matter of finding it."

"All right, all right . . . I know what it is."

"And?"

"Put an end to the whole thing with a pistol."

I took his hand.

"Don't talk like that, you're not Anna Karenina. Come
on, we'll go out and walk for a while. You'll think about other
things."

"I don't want to think about other things. I don't want
anything."

"Nothing? You don't even want me?"

"You, yes. You will die with me. First I will kill you, and
then myself."

Ah, what a letter! What times those were. I must take a break. Almost all the signs on this street were written in Russian then. And the air smelled the same as in Russia: garbage and dust; the perfume of lilac was added in springtime.

After our meeting in her neighborhood, which was also mine, I saw Nina in the offices of the Russian newspapers and magazines from time to time. She went there to remind the editors that they owed her money. One day I found her there and I noticed immediately that she didn't look too well. Instead of the usual coffee that day she asked for a glass of wine, which helped her open up a little more than usual in conversation. Hearing one detail after detail of her situation, I got a good idea of her life with Vladislav.

"I've managed to get tickets to the Russian ballet for tomorrow," I told her. "Would you like to come with me, Nina Nikolayevna?"

"But he won't want to come . . ."

"Come on your own."

"I can't do that to him. What's more, I'm afraid that . . . "

"Perhaps Vladislav doesn't feel so well?"

"He suffers from something I call Russianitis. He can't stop saying that without Russia he is unable to write."

"So he doesn't write."

"But without writing he can't live, which is to say, he can't live without Russia."

"But he's got Polish and Jewish blood, not one drop of Russian."

"Blood is surely not the most important factor. The important thing is where one has been brought up. We Russians are not like the English, who think nothing of travelling thousands and thousands of miles away from home, as if it were nothing. We Russians lose our balance after a thousand miles, and then we can never get it back."

"Are you one of those who cannot live without writing, Nina?"

"Me?" For the first time that day she laughed openly, and I also beamed, as if mirroring her. "I write with great pleasure, but I would not exchange one single minute of life for the written word, my balance for the manuscript of a novel, or a tempest raging inside me for a poem. I love life too much."

The next day, before the performance, I went to see them. The first thing I caught sight of was a man's head, with black hair, caught in the sheets of the bed. Nina was resplendent in an evening dress, and was getting ready to leave for the theater.

"Are you not coming with us, Vladya? We've got tickets for the Théâtre des Champs-Elysées, and you can't tell me you're going to miss that."

His defeated head didn't move.

At the theater, I stopped to observe Nina among the mirrors in the foyer: a dark blue, sleeveless dress, which flowed from the Chinese collar down to her knees without marking the waist; large black eyes full of curiosity; slim arms, thin along her body. I had never seen her naked arms before and their fragility moved me more than all her desperation and misery.

I took her by the elbow to lead her to the seats. It was a performance of Stravinsky's *Rites of Spring*.

I see they have artichokes. I'll order two or three. What do artichokes remind me of? Where was it? Yes, in Paris, one day Nina and I were having a coffee at La Rotonde as usual. She was thinking with her cup up close to her lips, and I watched her eyes as they wandered in circles. As if she had read my thoughts, she said, "What is love for you?"

I went red as a beet. But she wasn't expecting an answer. Without noticing anything, she went on, "Love is sharing an artichoke leaf. Knowing how to do it, wanting to do it, and being able to do it. There are very few people who are prepared to do this."

I murmured something. I wasn't ready to talk about this subject; I hadn't thought enough about it. "Waiter, bring me two or three baked artichokes. Yes, warmed up. Thank you."

Nina shared an artichoke leaf with Vladislav.

Then she told me how one day the first wife of Georges Annenkov—who danced in the evenings at La Chauve-Souris— went to see them and left a piece of cloth that needed embroidering on Nina's knees.

"It has to be ready by tomorrow."

And she left.

Nina started to embroider. "If I manage it," she said to herself, "I can earn up to seventy centimes an hour." She spent the entire night embroidering; in the morning only a few stitches had yet to be done. That night, unusually, Vladislav slept like a log. In the morning he woke up and said, "The poor little thing is doing needlework! She's spent the whole night working by candlelight until her eyesight has gone poor. Oh, that's been described by Dickens and Chernyshevski. Who does that interest today?"

"Thank you. The artichokes smell wonderful. And a glass of red wine, please."

I will finish reading her letter.

At first I didn't know where I was.

"Wake up, Nina, we'll have some tea together," said Vladislav.

"What time is it?"

"Half-past two. Do you mind me having woken you?"

"On the contrary, Vladya. Aren't you going to put on your pajamas? I had them close to my breast while I slept to keep them warm for you."

"No, I'm not going to bed yet. I'm writing something that is half finished. Nina . . .

"What is it?"

"Yesterday evening I lied to you when I said I'd spent the day at home. I spent the afternoon going around to the offices of newspapers and magazines."

"And?"

"I went to the Dni and they gave me eighty centimes for that long essay on Russian poetry in exile. 'You must understand that we can't pay you more than we do Lolo. People eat him up. Do you think the readers can't live without an article on Russian poetry in exile, brilliant though it might be?' An Sovremennye listy *the secretary told me there was no*

one to receive me, but she warned me that in the next issue, instead of my poem they were going to print Mrs Teffi's story because it was unbelievably funny. I also dropped into the offices of Poslednie novosti. I spoke with the editor, and you know what he told me, that Milyukov of yours? Guess."

"That you should write a novel for him that he would publish in installments."

"All I need is for you to laugh at me too. He made it clear that he can do perfectly well without my contributions."

"Vladya . . ."

"Wait, the story isn't over yet. Afterward I had an appointment with Olga."

"Don't speak to me about it. I've already told you, it's not my business, so I don't want to know anything about it."

"Don't shout! I mention it for another reason. She showed me the magazine Na postu, which someone must have smuggled out of Russia. One of the major figures of Soviet literary criticism, whose name I forget, talks about me in this issue."

"And what has this major figure written?"

"He says, 'Vladislav Khodasevich, a typical decadent bourgeois, describes seeing his mirror image in the window of a train car:

I penetrate alien lives
and suddenly I recognize with repulsion,
beheaded and without life,
my head in the night.

"And so? The verses are good. Do you want a little more tea?"

"You know what the poem's about, don't you?"

"As I understand it, in the glass you saw something like the features of contemporary Russian literature. Texts that have a body, but from which the head is separated. A literature without readers."

"More or less. Give me a little more tea to calm me down. Well, the major figure ends his article with this sentence: 'It is high time that all these Khodasevichs and other crybabies who profess mysticism and decadence were liquidated.'"

"Vladya, listen. Do you not have an opinion of your own? There is no one as closely linked to the cultural renaissance in Russia in the first quarter of the century as you."

"As I?"

"Yes, you. You can talk about the deaths of Tolstoy and Chekhov as events that have taken place in your lifetime. You were a friend of Blok, of Skriabin."

"But they've destroyed me."

"Not you. They're trying to destroy something bigger. You are only one of the pillars of this grand building that will soon be reduced to rubble. And, despite everything, it will be necessary for you to live. And to write."

"Thank you for your words, Nina, but I don't believe you."

"They are not just words. Come to bed."

"Nina, I want to put an end to the whole thing. Will you come with me?"

✦

I didn't leave him alone. I was afraid that he would open
the gas tap or throw himself out of the window. I didn't have
money for studies. I didn't think about the Sorbonne, but
about practical things: learning to use a typewriter, doing the
most ordinary secretarial jobs. Vladislav was so downcast that
he almost never got out of bed, saying that everything loaded
him down. Vladya didn't eat any fruit or vegetables, or fish or
cheese; he only liked meat and macaroni. There was no money
to buy meat, so he preferred not to eat. He sank even further.
And me? I felt desperate but the more worries I had, the more I
looked forward to the start of each day. I was obsessed with life,
with the earthly and the day-to-day. What else could I do?

Vladislav had a chronic cough and chronic stomach pains.
Doctor Golovanov visited him for free and declared that all
the problems had to do with his liver. Vladislav would have
to go on a strict diet. But he wasn't able to put up with any
diet, and for that reason he didn't improve. He suffered from
boils. The doctor gave him injections, but they didn't have any
effect on him. His bed had to be changed every other day, and
sometimes daily.

It was a rough day, with gusts of dry, biting wind, when I
walked to the offices of the periodicals that owed Vladislav
money for his articles. He had visited two editors but neither
of them had given him anything. I offered new articles and
poems by Vladislav, but they didn't want them. I felt that they
were starting to avoid me as well. When I came out of the last
office, I took the metro and got off at Glacière Station; I ended

up heading for rue Dareau. My cousin Assia wasn't home, so I sat on a step and waited for her in the cold and darkness. After two hours she finally she appeared. I asked her if she could lend me some sheets. We sat down at her table to have a cup of tea.

At nightfall, I opened the door of the flat with my key and saw that Vladislav was dressed, leaning against the wall, and could barely keep himself upright.

"What are you doing dressed?"

"I was about to go to the police so they could look for you."

Exhausted, I collapsed into a chair. I was dizzy. I rested my cheeks in the palms of my hands. Then I raised my eyes, in which, I imagine, shone flashes of sarcasm.

"'We French are convinced that all the inhabitants of the rest of Europe are nothing more than a poor bunch of idiots.'"

"Who said that?"

"Stendhal, and he was right."

I made his bed. Vladislav got undressed and slid between the clean sheets. He took my hands and kissed them for a long time, and laughed out of happiness that he did not have to go and identify my corpse in the city morgue. I lay down beside him, observed his thick hair, and told myself that all this, his self-destructive moods and his sarcasm, all formed part of that long conversation of ours that had started one winter's night in Saint Petersburg, in an empty square piled high with snow, dominated by the half-ruined statue of a Bolshevik.

The next day he left. At home he left me a note saying that he had gone to study historical material in the Versailles library;

he didn't say how long he would be gone; it turned out to be a week. During those days I didn't work. There was no way I could concentrate on anything. I couldn't sleep. I waited for him. But nothing came, not a message, not any news, not a greeting.

I thought that Vladislav had left me without a single word or maybe that he had died; I visited our mutual friends and asked them about him. No one would give me any answer, until Mark Vishniak told me that Vladislav had come to see him to tell him that he had decided to commit suicide. The Zaitsevs confirmed this.

At the end of a week he came back as if absolutely nothing had happened, accompanied by Olga Forch. I knew her from Saint Petersburg as a writer who was a friend and admirer of Vladislav. She had just arrived from the Soviet Union to make a brief visit to her daughter, who was exiled in Paris. Her visa had nearly expired. I was shocked to see her, older, with gray hair, but I was grateful for her presence because this way I could put off the questions and reproaches that were burning on my tongue. We had tea. Olga explained the policy that the Soviet Communist Party applied to writers; she chose her words with great care, constructed her sentences cautiously. She was noticeably nervous, and became more restless as time went on. Suddenly she exploded.

"The only thing that helps us live is hope!"

"Hope of what, Olga Dmitrievna?" I asked.

"Of some kind of a world revolution which will put an end to our suffering under the Communists. Who knows!"

"It won't take place," said Vladislav in a low voice, calmly.

Olga fell silent for a moment. Her serious face became even more somber, the corners of her mouth turned downward, her eyes misted over.

"If that is the case, then we're lost."

"Who is lost?"

"All of us, those of us who are in Russia."

She promised that she would come back the next day, but she didn't appear either on that day or the day after. After four days had gone by, and Vladya and I had made up, we went to see her, thinking she might be ill. It was a pleasant summer twilight; the sun was flooding the windows of the place where Olga was staying, at her daughter's home. We went in. Olga was lying on the bed, her hair a complete mess, her cheeks red. She said that the day after she had been with us she went to the Soviet embassy, where they told her that it was strictly prohibited for her to see Vladislav Khodasevich, the enemy of the Soviet people. From time to time she could see Berdyaev and Remizov, but not Khodasevich under any circumstances.

"Go," she said, "you can't stay here."

We were left standing in the middle of the room as if someone had thrown a bucket of cold water over us.

"Go," Olga whispered, making an effort, "and forgive me, Vladya."

A sob shook her enormous body. We stayed for a moment behind the closed door and saw the sun playing on the dust. At the moment we both realized that our exile would be a long one, that perhaps it would last all our lives. A little later

I received a letter from my parents asking me not to write to them if I didn't want to cause them great difficulties.

"I had a dream tonight. Afterward I was unable to sleep," Nina answered me when I asked her why she was so restless. We were walking along the rue de Vaugirard toward the Luxembourg Garden. It was raining a little. We sat down in one of those wooden art deco cafes. I ordered two coffees, then lit Nina's cigarette and my own. It began to rain heavily. Contrary to her usual habit, Nina's hair was a little untidy that day.

"In my dream I found myself in the train station at Saint Petersburg, or rather Leningrad," she continued. "I was waiting for the Paris train. It was a goods train that was bringing the coffins of the dead from exile back home. I ran along the platform past the endless rows of cars that were gradually entering the station building. On the first car, inscribed in chalk, were the names of Rachmaninov, Liliukov, Chaliapin. On the second, Zamyatin, Lunacharski, Diaguilev. I asked in which car they were bringing Khodasevich. With a wave, they indicated a point a long way away, toward the end. Then the car passed with the names of Remizov and Shestov. I ran on. I discovered Vadislav's coffin in the last car. The door to the car opened with a loud noise and ten railway workers came running, each of them was pushing a trolley. 'Unload! Unload!' I heard behind me. At that moment I woke up."

I offered her another cigarette; she took it from the packet with her long fingers. I held up a lit match for her.

"What does this dream mean, Igor?"

The waiter, wearing an apron that was long and as white as milk, brought us two little cups of coffee.

"What does it mean?" Nina insisted.

"I don't know. I have to think about it. I don't believe in premonitions."

"When I thought that I'd lost him, I desired so, so much to have him back with me again."

Nina had to go back to the office of the newspaper where she sometimes worked as assistant editor. I stayed in the cafe to read the latest issues of *Poslednie novosti*, which Nina had taken out of her briefcase and placed on my table before she left. I read one issue and was about to pick up the next one when I realized that the folded newspaper contained inside it a sheet of paper. A letter. Creased, clearly read many times. You shouldn't do it, you mustn't do it, I told myself, but my eyes were already passing from one line to the next.

Nina,

I will be staying a few weeks more here in the south of France. I have found out something about you, or rather about you and Milyoti. I ask you in earnest not to have any more dealings with him. I don't mean that you should have it out with him. But I beg of you, most insistently, that after all that has been said of him, after the ambiguous and stupid position in which he left you and me deliberately, do not appear with him anywhere and do not receive him at our home. Do what you want with your reputation but bear in mind that I have mine.

Vladislav

What do I do now with this letter? If I give it back to Nina, she will know that I have read it. And if I don't give it back to her, she will be sure that I have kept it.

I gazed at the branches of the chestnut trees through the little window; they were silhouetted, black, against the sky. It had stopped raining, the clouds had broken and given way to a blue sky that shone now, fresh, bright, almost springlike. A drunken clochard was walking through the park, the passersby avoided him with a disguised but nonetheless noticeable disgust, and he regaled them with a repertory of epithets that he made up on the spot. He is a poet of the day-to-day, I reflected.

Suddenly, Nina appeared in front of me, her hair done, smiling, a little distant, independent, as always. She handed me an envelope with my name on it. And as suddenly she went off, saying farewell with only a light movement of her fingers. A ghost.

Igor Mikhailovich,

You surely found a letter among the newspapers. I owe you an explanation. There are situations in which it is easier for me to write than to speak.

Little by little, almost imperceptibly, something in me began to fall apart; and now this has even affected my relationship with Vladislav. Our being together, which until recently was a joy and a consolation to both of us, has turned into a routine. Everything is going badly. In the morning I wander around the flat like a specter. I yawn and do nothing. Vladislav usually sleeps until midday. In the afternoon I am unable to read or write. Our evenings have always been somewhat melancholy, but now they are downright somber.

I am washed up; I feel that nobody needs me. Little setbacks that before I would have ignored as insignificant, now make me furious. They also irritate him, but he hides the fact. What can I do when he is in such a mood? I know the answer: to see him just once a week. In that way I would rediscover my identity and I could once again be the person who, a long time ago, he loved.

Life has taught me that even when there is nothing happening, nothing stays as it is. Everything changes, all the time. Between dawn and dusk humans change ceaselessly. These are enigmatic processes from which new transformations, variations, and mutations emerge.

I do not know if I am making myself clear.

N.B.

I thought that I should go and see them, to see it all with my own eyes, to talk with both of them. Maybe I could do something for them! I didn't want to admit that what I really wanted above all else was to sit again in that little room that Nina had decorated so well with some old engravings of Saint Petersburg and a few yellow carnations in a milk bottle. Yes, just to sit in that little room, full of her voice, that somewhat somber voice, which was such a contrast to her fresh laughter.

I went there one day at dusk, after Vladislav had come back from the south of France. Nina was about to prepare dinner.

Vladislav was sitting at the table with a pack of cards. We shook hands, he mumbled something incomprehensible. Nina had me sit down and served me a cup of tea. You could have cut the tension with a knife. To break the silence and give the impression that everything was all right, I said the first things that came into my head, silly things. Commonplaces are usually a good remedy for depression and provide a certain relief for bad moods.

"Do you know what Jean-Michel asked me the other day? If there was a samovar in every Russian's home."

Now, for the first time, Vladislav raised his eyes from his cards.

"Have the French any idea how much a toy like that can cost?"

The silence of this couple was re-established at once, and made me furious. So I ranted about the fact that the most prestigious western intellectuals filled the newspapers with articles that praised the "new Russia," its "'interesting experiment'" and its "highly personal experience." When the pieces in question are signed by names such as H.G. Wells, G.B. Shaw, Romain Rolland, Thomas Mann, and Stefan Zweig, what can we do? Write, of course, write about the persecution of intellectuals in the Soviet Union, about the repression and the censorship, the arrests and the trials and the labor camps, of course, but who will publish us? And if it is published, who will believe it?

"There is nothing else to do but to sit in a corner and keep quiet, like good children. *Sois belle et tais-toi*," Vladislav said, and he took another card from the pack.

Tying her apron on, Nina said, "The other day I couldn't help laughing like a lunatic. Any French intellectual worth the name inevitably quotes Jean Cocteau's phrase: 'Dictators foment protests in artistic circles; without the spirit of protest, art would die.' Would this phrase be just as viable if under such a dictatorship, Cocteau was shot through the head?" she laughed.

Vladislav was irritated by her laughter, which bubbled forth like a mountain spring. He rested his head in the palms of his hands and concentrated on his cards, as if taking refuge far from us in a world that was only for him. Nina also got nervous then and went off to finish preparing dinner. I felt restlessness fill the entire room. I noticed that the bed wasn't made, that cobwebs hung off the ceiling, and that there wasn't a trace of a flower. Dust covered the engravings that hung on the wall, and in the middle of the room there was one worn-out boot of Vladislav's; I couldn't find the other one. We devoured macaroni in silence so as to get it over with as quickly as possible. Even when he was eating Vladislav didn't stop testing our patience. I only felt a sense of relief once I was out in the street again.

What else does Nina say in her letter?

Vladislav had returned to the south of France when I decided to leave him. I spent whole days waiting for him at home, but ultimately I started to get my things together: two packets of books, a shelf, several dresses, and a few folders full of papers. All the rest stayed in its place as if nothing had happened, from the teapot to the engravings of Saint Petersburg.

When Vladislav arrived and listened to what I had to say to him, it didn't occur to him to ask anything else other than, "Who are you leaving me for?"

"For nobody."

After half an hour, once more: "I want to know who he is."

"On whose name do you want me to swear the truth? On Pushkin's?" I smiled.

I went to make a borshcht so that Vladislav would have a few meals after I left. He followed me into the kitchen.

"You know how we'll kill ourselves? With gas."

I saw him standing at the threshold of the kitchen, in striped pajamas, with his arms open, propped up against the doorframe. As if he'd been crucified.

In the afternoon I left. He followed me with his eyes through the open window. On the table he had an enormous saucepan full of soup, which would soon stop steaming.

TWO

I found a room in the Hôtel des Ministères, Nina wrote to me in the following letter:

On the boulevard la tour-Maubourg, between the Seine and the École Militaire. I had always found that neighborhood attractive. I went up the tall, narrow staircase to the sixth floor and opened the door with my number on it and entered a room at attic level; a folding screen hid the sink and the little gas cooker from sight. From my sixth floor room there was a view of Les Invalides, of the metal mesh of the Eiffel Tower, and of the long tree-lined avenues, which at that time of day were still silent.

In the afternoon, after my arrival, I put my books on the shelf, hung my dresses in the closet, took out my notebooks, ballpoint pens, and fountain pens, and laid them out on the table, which wobbled a bit. Then I washed myself. When darkness began to fall, I felt totally exhausted. I collapsed on the bed. I lay there without moving, without even turning on the light. I stared at the window which darkened gradually. My thoughts too were dark ones.

I was thirty-one years old; after eleven years of living together I had just left my partner. What must he be doing now? He probably had the cards on the table. For the first time that day, this image aroused a feeling of tenderness in me. Mentally I saw his sad face. Don't think! Don't think either about the fact that I am thirty-one years old and completely alone. Don't think! My fatigue helped me to empty my mind. I fell asleep before it was completely dark.

I slept until the afternoon of the following day, when I was woken by a knocking at the door. Vladislav! He had come to ask me how I had spent my first night alone. Then we went to have dinner together. Afterward I went straight back to bed and once more I slept until the afternoon.

I remember the evening—after finding out her new address—I went to see her and invite her to dinner. At night, I took her back to her hotel. We walked past a Russian cabaret; the singing, the shouts, and the laughter could be heard a mile away. Nina hummed "Two Guitars," a ballad they were playing on a balalaika inside, and said, "Young French people get drunk praising the Soviet Union and proletarian literature full of optimism and the builders of the great tomorrow, but it doesn't occur to them, not in their wildest dreams, to ask why Stravinsky lives in Paris and not at home, or why Diaguilev died in Venice, heavily in debt instead of becoming the director of the Bolshoi ballet."

"They don't ask us anything," I said, "because they don't need to, they have everything clear in their minds: we are children of the revolution and we are not busy building Communism, so it is logical to assume that we are the reactionary children of dukes and princes. Do we live in misery? That's good for us. We got what we deserve."

"They adore Russian folklore almost as much as they do the Bolshevik revolution and the building of Communism," laughed Nina.

A few gypsies were singing in the cabaret and the Cherkessians were dancing with Astrakhan hats on their heads.

"The French go wild over that type of hat. They say: 'C'est typiquement russe!' smiled Nina.

"The French and the Americans," I said, "as well as the English, sing Russian ballads with drunken voices, weep, and embrace each other."

"And above all, the glasses they've just emptied they smash

against the floor," said Nina, laughing so much she swayed as if she were drunk, "and like that, in the middle of the broken glass, the tears, and the drunken singing, they imagined they've turned into Mitya Karamazov, whose name vaguely rings a bell."

Only on the fourth day did I get up at my usual time, between eight and nine, Nina goes on writing in the letter. *I looked around me, realized where I was and why, and I was flooded by a great wave of happiness. Through the window I saw the streets of Paris and the chimneys of the roofs in front and I said to myself: "All of this belongs to me, and I don't belong to anybody!"*

This feeling of freedom made me go out onto the street. I walked through the parks observing the fruit trees that were about to blossom, in Champ-de-Mars I felt as if I were again in Russia, in an infinite field of corn. Under the bridges, the river murmured; in the Tuileries fountains, children sailed boats they had made themselves. Then I entered the Louvre as it was about to close, but I still had time enough to go through the Egyptian rooms that I hadn't seen. I went back to the hotel and ran up the staircase to the sixth floor. In the attic room I already felt at home; I ran my fingers over the dresses hanging in the closet and I told myself once more: "All of this belongs to me and I don't belong to anybody!" I took Kafka's The Metamorphosis, *got into bed, and read it through to the end. Then I fell fast asleep.*

I spent the whole summer reading. It was muggy. In the morning when I got up, I chose a book and read until midday;

then I continued with my reading in the Champ-de-Mars, on the terraces of cafes, where I ordered coffee and ice cream, poured the black liquid over the ice cream and read. In the attic room it was so hot that I couldn't sleep there, so I read; not the books that Vladislav had recommended to me with paternal solicitude, but things I had chosen for myself—Virginia Woolf, Joyce, Gide, Kafka, Proust.

"Look, Igor, there are some friends of yours over in that corner!"

"Who?"

"Nabokov, with that woman who I'd like to paint the way Goya did his duchess. There is something of *The Maja* about her, haven't you noticed?"

I pretended I wasn't interested. Nikolasha liked to talk like that, probably because he knew that it irritated me.

In a corner of the Russian bistrot called l'Ours, Nina was sitting with Vladimir Nabokov. It hadn't been such a long time since Nina had left Vladya. It didn't surprise me that the couple had attracted the attention of my painter friend: Nabokov was blond and tanned, with a fine face, slim, athletic, dressed in a white shirt; Nina, vaguely Oriental looking, in a pearl-colored dress. There was something about the couple that was noble, aristocratic, that made them stand out in the crowd, at least for someone with a sharp eye.

They were eating Russian pancakes—the cook of L'Ours made exceptional *blini*—with smoked fish and imitation caviar, and they were washing it down with vodka. Later the waiter also brought them a bottle of red wine. As Nabokov knew the owner of the premises, without a doubt it was he who had invited Nina to have lunch with him. They were laughing a lot; they didn't stop making toasts, and it was clear that they were getting drunk, and not only on the wine but also, especially, on each other. Nabokov's frenchified rrrrrrr, so typical of the Saint Petersburg aristocracy, he repeated again and again.

"Where do you write, Nina Nikolayevna?"

"At home, on a little wobbly table, with a view of the chimneys of Paris, or at a cafe table. Like everybody, no?"

"No, not quite like everybody. I write exclusively in the lavatory, if I might dignify that little room in my hideaway in the outskirts of the city with such noble terms."

"Why in the lavatory, Vladimir Vladimirovich?"

"Mainly because it is sunny there all morning. And also for the not insignificant reason that my apartment is unfurnished."

"You live in an empty apartment?"

"Completely empty. When my wife or my son want to go the lavatory, I have to take a break. But they know this and are respectful. They drink very little."

Nina laughed as if she never wanted to stop. They made a toast to that original form of writing desk.

"It is a table or a chair, as I please, but is never the two things together. I'll give you a piece of advice, Nina, even though you don't need any. Don't forget that the lavatory is usually the quietest place in the apartment."

The waiter comes up to refill their glasses. Nabokov pays

and apologizes to Nina saying that he hadn't noticed how time had flown in her company and that unfortunately he simply had to attend a meeting of the editorial board, which had started half an hour ago. Nina said that at least she could quietly finish enjoying the exquisite dishes that they hadn't had time to finish while they conversed. He kissed her on the cheeks, one, two, three kisses, and was off.

Now my moment has come, I told myself. I said hello to Nina and she invited me to sit at her table. I signalled to my companion.

"Nina, let me introduce you to my friend Nikolay Vassilyevich Makeyev, painter, student of Odilon Redon, and also a journalist and politician, the author of the book *Russia*, published in New York."

"That is to say, a Renaissance man," Nina smiled wryly. Nikolasha also smiled and looked at Nina without blinking. She noticed it and took hold of the bottle to offer us a glass of wine.

"Isn't this friend of yours, Nabokov, a bit arrogant?" said Nikolay.

I had never seen my friend behave like this. Although he liked to *épater le bourgeois*, he never got close to being rude.

"Not at all. Why do you say that?" said Nina coldly.

"It is notorious that in a gathering of people he pretends not to know his closest friend; he deliberately calls a man who he knows perfectly well as Ivan Petrovich, Ivan Ivanovich. Be careful with him, Nina Nikolayevna: one day he will address you as Nina Alexandrovna, you'll see! And in order to show his superiority he likes to mangle the titles of novels, with his hallmark sarcasm. For example, apparently without thinking and with all the pretense of innocence, he calls a book titled *From the East Comes the Cold, From the East Comes the Fart*.

"I don't know what you're getting at with all this," Nina said, very distant. "Vladimir Vladimirovich has his eccentricities, as does everybody. In 1929, when *The Luzchin Defence* came out," she went on, and although she was looking at me in particular, I sensed that her words were meant for Nikolay, that the painter interested her, that she liked to argue with him, "I read it twice in a row."

"Twice?" Nikolay said, surprised.

"Yes. I found it to be a demanding work by an author who is meaningful, complex, mature. I suddenly realized that from the fire and ashes of revolution and exile, a great Russian writer had been born."

"You say that with so much pomp."

"Of course. Because at that moment I felt certain that our existence, that is to say that of Russian writers in exile, would have meaning. At that moment I felt that my entire generation had been vindicated."

"Nina Nikolayevna, I am familiar with the articles and the stories that you publish in *Poslednie novosti*. How can someone like you talk of generations and vindications? Haven't you your-self said on more than one occasion—and if I may say so with a self-assuredness that irritates readers—that not only every writer, but that every individual in the end is alone? Does Nabo-kov care at all about his generation? Nabokov has earned his place in literature and no doubt he will keep it for a long time, but does this mean that the others, you among them, will survive only in his shadow?"

"One thing at a time. I am convinced that each person is a world, a universe, a hell in his or her own right. I don't believe at all that Nabokov could drag a mediocre person along with him, into his immortality. But Nabokov represents the answer to the doubts of all the humiliated and wronged people, all those who have been unjustly ignored, those who have been pushed into the background in exile."

"Perhaps you include yourself among those humiliated?"

"I include myself among those who love life too much to have the right to be inscribed in people's memory. I prefer life to literary fame, the mad inebriation of an action to the results, the path toward the destination to the destination in itself."

"Bravo, Nina! To the mad inebriation of an action by Nina Berberova, who with this speech has just entered the kingdom of immortality! Allow me to give you a kiss: mwah-mwah!"

Nina wrote to me, *How did love come? From the outside. A smile lit up the serious face that a moment before still seemed strange to me, and then the eyes began to speak to me. I discovered a charm in him unknown to me before: the parting of his hair, the warmth of his hands, the smell of his body and breath, his voice. I have always been sensitive to voices and the expressiveness of faces. Then, thanks to the power of love, when I had penetrated his inner life, when I had made it mine and it became for me a source of happiness.* Then I realized that I had lost Nina. And that life does not wait.

At our meetings for coffee, Nina would tell me how she came to know Nikolay, and of the outings and excursions on which they went together. They visited the L'Orangerie and the Jeu de Paume, for the exhibitions they admired by Matisse, Dérain, and Bonnard. On bicycle outings they rediscovered Corot in the trees next to a lake, Courbet in a river flowing between two rocks, Pissarro in the winding country lanes lined with plane trees and poplars. Sisley was everywhere: in the kiosks and the little bridges, in all the lanes and cornfields. Nina was transformed. She was less sarcastic and became more spontaneous. And I could barely recognize Nikolasha. He discovered within himself a kind of goodness that he must have kept well hidden. He was painting more than ever. Nina and he chose the paintings that he would exhibit in the Salon d'Automne.

One morning he went to look for her at the hotel with a bottle of champagne in one hand and a sack of piroshki in the other.

"Let's go to the notary! There's a house . . ."

From the notary's they went on bicycle, through the countryside, to Yvelines. The bag with the bottle of champagne swung on the handlebar. They reached the village of Longchêne; there, in front of a half-ruined grain barn, Nikolay jumped off the bicycle.

"This is our home!"

And he was already leading her in. Here we will make a little kitchen, here we will have the bathroom, this will be the living room. You can choose wherever you want to have your study. In the attic, among the beams, they found a date: 1861.

He uncorked the bottle of champagne, opened the sack that contained the piroshki made of meat and cabbage. While they had dinner they made plans about the fruit trees they would plant in the garden. Nina wanted to have beehives and a vegetable patch.

A neighbor brought them a few armfuls of dry grass that had been recently cut and they made their bed with that. Through the window they looked at the stars. It was May, the cool of the night entered the building, and the hay gave off a strong smell, but the perfume of lilacs in the garden was so delicious that it didn't even occur to them to close the window. They pressed tightly against each other, buried in the hay.

"And time came to a standstill," she told me then.

It was spring. And Vladislav more than once, she told me, asked her friends about her, looked for her, wrote to her.

> *My love,*
> *Nothing, nothing can change the great feeling that you inspire in me. It will always be the same. You know perfectly well how I reacted when someone wanted to do you harm or put some distance between us. It will be this way forever: whoever wants to be on a good footing with me, must be on one with you too. Take care of yourself. Now I am going to sleep, it is almost four in the morning. I kiss your hand.*
>
> > *Your Vladya*

It was spring. Vladislav went to see her at the offices of *Poslednie novosti.* They had lunch together; in the afternoon they walked along the Seine, and when it rained, they played billiards in a brasserie. Often they sipped wine and had some cheese at the George V Cafe, close by the offices of *Vozrojdenie*, where Vladislav was now making weekly contributions with his book reviews. Then they took long walks through the side streets of Montmartre, and Nina accompanied him to the rue des Qua-tre-Cheminées, to the apartment that was now his alone. They prepared tea and drank it slowly, until well into the night. Nina wrote to me later, *I kissed his beloved face, his hands. He also kissed me, so moved that he couldn't even speak. When, by sheer magic, I managed to make him laugh, I felt it to be a great success.*

Time came to a standstill. That is what she told me and that is what happened. Several times a week, Nina cycled from Longchêne to Paris. On the way back she took the main road—I cycled with her many times—and then an unpaved lane, and from a long way off she peered into the distance trying to see the green patch that was the roof of the grain barn that she and Nikolay had turned into a home. She liked to receive guests. Many couples went to see her: Kerensky and his wife, the Zait-sevs, the Bunins, Goncharova and her husband, Larionov. I most enjoyed her dinner parties when we gathered with just a small circle of close friends. In the summer we had dinner in the gar-den under the trees. Nikolay was a good host, the home radiated well-being. They had decorated it with Nikolay's paintings and a few engravings by his master Odilon Redon. The guests walked through the garden and the meadows that separated them from the neighbors. For Nina, time came to a standstill.

275

It was in the winter when she received news that Vladislav had become seriously ill. She wrote to me:

February 25, 1939
Diagnosis: obstruction of the biliary tubes. The treatment is barbarous, cruel. Vladya said: "If I could always be with you, I'm sure I would be cured." He feels better.

May 3, 1939
The latest diagnosis: cancer. For the whole month of April he suffered cruelly and has lost twenty pounds. His hair has grown back (during the treatment it had completely fallen out), but has turned gray. He shaves rarely and has a white beard. He doesn't put in his dentures. The pain in his abdomen makes him suffer day and night. Sometimes they give him morphine injection, but he becomes delirious: he meets Bely, the Bolsheviks are after him, he worries about me. In one of his dreams he saw a car accident in which I lost my life (that fact is, I'm learning to drive). For hours he couldn't calm himself. The next day, when I went to see him, he started to sob and see visions again.

At the end of May and the beginning of June, Vladislav was in the hospital, in the worst conditions that can be imagined. None of us had enough money to pay for a private clinic for him.

June 15, 1939
On June 8 he came back home, exhausted by the tests they

*had carried out on him, and by life in the hospital. On the
twelfth they had to take him back to the clinic again for a long
operation. On the thirteenth he didn't recover consciousness.
On the fourteenth, at half past seven in the morning, I arrived
at the clinic. He had died at six that morning, without having
regained consciousness. Before he died, he kept raising right
arm."*

In death, Vladya reached out to somebody with a hand that
"held a trembling flower." Alive he had written in one of his
poems.

Nina was under the influence of death. She didn't go out, she
didn't want to see anybody. Visits did nothing to cheer her up;
the look on her face made that clear enough to her visitors. A
few months after the death of Vladislav, she published this cry,
which shot through the world of the Russian exiles like a bolt of
lightning:

*Miserable, stupid, stinking, deplorable, disgraceful, worn-
out, hungry Russian emigration of which I form a part! Last
year, Khodasevich died, thin as bone, unshaven on a sunken
mattress and in torn sheets, without money to pay for medicine
or a doctor. This year I go to see Nabokov and I find him
in bed, ill, and in a pitiable state. (I brought a chicken for
Nabokov. Vera started cooking it at once).*

✦

"A little more wine?"

"Certainly. The dinner was excellent, Nina."

"Bring another bottle of wine, Nikolasha. We would like to drink a little more."

She was thoughtful, melancholy. She hadn't been herself for a year.

We sat on benches around the table, under a walnut tree. In that curious turquoise light of the pure June sky, we were silent more often than we spoke; that evening was conducive to silence and reflection. Even the acacias and the plane trees around us were motionless and didn't make so much as the slightest whisper, like they were statues.

"The premonition of summer floats in the air," said Olga with a dreamy look. In the shade her teeth flashed like white lightning.

"More like the premonition of a long war, not that I want to spoil your illusions, Olenka," retorted Boris Zaitsev.

"Here in the country one can easily forget about war," sighed Vera Zaitseva.

"Here in the country?" said Nina in a low voice, to herself, "In September of last year I stretched myself out on the lawn, there at the bottom of the garden. It was the first day of the war. The grass started to grow around my veins, while flower buds started to open between my toes; the ivy embraced me as if it wanted to throttle me. I don't remember anything else."

We fell silent again. Only at a distance could the song of a cricket in the neighboring meadow be heard, and from time to time, a frog jumping into the stream behind the house.

"Last year at this time the stars also shone this way, with a green hue," said Olga.

"Last year at this time . . ." sighed Nina.

Nikolay looked at her attentively and poured more wine in our glasses, which looked pitch black in the shadow of the walnut tree.

"Last year at this time we finally bought ourselves a secondhand radio," said Vera Zaitseva, "For a year now we've been listening to Mozart and Boccherini. At least we had something ideal, even though happiness was not ours for the asking. And now? Now for a month we have heard nothing except the horrible news about the German invasion."

"I'll write a story about you, Vera," said Nina, "about you and Mozart, about happiness and how difficult it is to obtain."

"A sheet of paper and a pencil for Ninon!" exclaimed Nikolay, but nobody was in the mood for his humor. Nobody laughed.

"I will write about having ideals as a substitute for having happiness. Like your Mozart, Vera," said Nina in a quiet voice. "Last year at this time . . ."

Nikolay drank a little wine.

"Ninon is remembering that Vladya died exactly a year ago."

Again, he drank from the glass that he hadn't put down on the table between sips. He got up and went to the house. We didn't say anything. He came back with a sheet of paper and a pencil, he placed these objects in front of Nina, who listlessly started to draw stars with twelve or fifteen points. When it was almost impossible to see anything, she added a crescent moon, identical to the one that was at that moment emerging from behind the acacia.

"I try to cheer Ninon up," Nikolay went back to the earlier subject, keeping a firm hold on his glass, "by telling her that they will meet up some day, there . . ." he pointed upward.

Nina interrupted him impatiently. "I'm not a believer. What's more I don't try to deceive myself with prayers the way you do. But above all, why do you expect me to desire to meet him again *in that other world*? Half the time we couldn't put up with each other when we were alive."

"Nina's right," said Vera in her favor. "After so many years people don't even want to see each other down here. Time passes and people end up having nothing to say to each other. Maybe I wouldn't even recognize my poor Aloysha, and that'd be a good thing."

Vera sighed.

"The other day I saw him in a dream, Vera . . ." said Nina.

"My dead son?"

"No, I'm sorry. I saw Vladya. There were a lot of people in the room and nobody else saw him. He had long hair and he was thin, almost transparent, light as a ghost, but elegant and youthful. We found a way of being alone together. I sat next to him. I took his hand, fine and light as a feather. I told him, 'If you can, tell me how you feel.' He answered me with a peculiar gesture that I interpreted to mean 'not too bad.' Then he filled his mouth with smoke, bent his back, and said, 'How can I put it? One doesn't always feel comfortable . . .'"

"How strange," said Olga, shaking her golden head and looking around at the others. "Do you make anything of it?"

"It's strange, the whole thing is very strange. 'My solitude begins when I am two steps away from you' says the lover of the main character in a Giraudoux novel," Nikolay said, blowing cigarette smoke out of his mouth.

"It could also be said that my solitude begins in your arms," Nina said in a harsh tone of voice, staring at a spot beyond the fence.

"Ninon reckons," Nikolay continued as if he hadn't heard what Nina had said, "that in his poems Vladislav predicted what would happen and that this, according to her, is already starting to happen—"

"Olenka, where would you like to be now if you could choose?" Nina interrupted him, uneasily.

"Here, in the freshness of the night under this walnut tree, in 1941, a year from now, because then the war will be over."

"And you, Vera?"

"Me? It's rather banal, I'm ashamed to tell you, but I would like to be in the tsar's court in Pushkin's time. To be able to hear him reciting his poems. Pushkin, I mean, not the tsar."

"Another ideal as a substitute for happiness?" Nina smiled sadly, "And you, Nikolasha?"

"I would like this to be the first day in this house. I would like to eat piroshki and wash them down with abundant quantities of champagne, and I would like to look forward to our first night on the dry grass."

Nina was drawing her stars. Suddenly she looked up.

"I would like to be in America."

"The truth is," Nikolay went on as if he hadn't heard her, "that Vladislav couldn't have chosen a better moment for dying. He isn't forced to see the Germans and human cowardice, as we are. And who knows what else we're going to see."

"And when I say that I would now like to be in America, that means that one day I will be there," said Nina, while continuing to draw something on the sheet of paper.

"You are the exterminating angel, Nina. Would you really punish us with your departure?" said Boris Zaitsev.

"I'm more of a Lady Macbeth," said Nina.

"Why America?" I asked out of interest while I tried to get rid of the fly that had fallen into my glass of wine; at each sip it slipped between my lips and then reappeared.

"I'll tell you a story," answered Nina after a while." A very old man, called Andreyev, a few days before his death in 1919, heard the enemy bombing raids in his home in Finland and at night he dreamed of America. I have the feeling that between his nights and my own there is no difference at all, as if no time had passed. And, apart from that . . ."

"Apart from that?"

She didn't answer.

"Apart from that, what, Nina?" I asked again.

"I simply meant that I don't like life to be too easy."

Vera and Boris Zaitsev burst out laughing.

"You don't have to worry about that, Nina. You haven't been

granted an easy life, and I don't think any of us have been threatened with one either!"

Nina didn't laugh. She was thinking.

"Probably when I was little, I began to think in this way by reading Nietzsche, and it's stayed with me since then. In a nutshell, I like the complexity that is part of human life."

Olga sighed and shook her head so that her golden hair flew around her head like a halo.

"Nina, what blasphemy, how awful . . ."

As if to confirm her words, suddenly some artillery fire was heard. Then a detonation, an explosion, and silence. A long silence, different from that which had preceded it: heavy, a bad omen.

"Let's go, it's late already," said Vera, and Olga was already putting on her hat. Her teeth, white as a sheet, were shining in the darkness, when she said, "What most agreeable company, it's a pity we have to go home. Come and see me very soon, Ninochka. Bring her, Nikolasha."

The car shuddered along the lane full of potholes.

I took hold of the tablecloth so as to shake it. A piece of paper fell from it, on which Nina had been drawing stars. I folded it and put it in my pocket. I also said goodbye and went to the guesthouse. I didn't feel like getting on my bicycle and going home in the dark.

At night, by the light of a lantern, I read what was written on the sheet of paper that had fallen off the tablecloth. I already knew those words. But Nina had added more.

Miserable, stupid, stinking, deplorable, disgraceful, cowardly,
worn-out, hungry Russian emigration of which I form a part!
Last year Khodasevich died, thin as bone, unshaven on a
sunken mattress and in torn sheets, without money to pay
for medicine or a doctor. He lived in Billancourt. Billancourt
is a drunken worker, the fifteenth district, a vale of tears, of
trivialities, and dreams of glory; the sixteenth is a starched
collar around the wrinkled skin of a mundane crook, with a
fur coat, venereal disease, debt, gossip, and cards. And there's
Meudon and all the suburbs full of orthodox churches, where
they barely tolerate us and where soon we will fill entire
cemeteries.

The bombing continued during the night. Sleep was impossible.

In the morning Marie-Louise came, who helped in the garden and around the house. First she started weeding the vegetable patch. While I prepared coffee for breakfast, I watched through the window as she took a basin full of weeds off to the woods on the other side of the fence. Suddenly I heard her cry for help. I was by her side in a moment. In some brush in the woods lay a boy who was about twenty years old, maybe younger, and he was looking at us with eyes full of fear. He looked like a wounded fawn; his large, brown eyes looked as if they were made of glass. His parachute had gotten stuck on one of the branches. We wanted to help him up, but he couldn't stop moaning. He didn't understand French. I touched his legs and he shouted out in pain. Both his legs were broken. Marie-Louise brought him water, I held his head up; he drank and moaned. We washed his face that had been scratched by the branches, and wrapped him in a blanket. Later, they came looking for him to take him as a prisoner of war. He was German. When they carried him away like a wounded animal, I saw his eyes dilated in fear and full of tears. I saw those moist fawn's eyes in front of me all day long, while we hid in the house and Nikolay wrapped Nina up in jackets and jerseys. She was shaking all over although the temperature was that of high summer. Nina wouldn't have any of it; she kept repeating that she wanted to be left alone, that all she wanted was to leave for America.

The strawberries that grew in Nina's garden were already ripe, but had blackened. A huge curtain of soot fell onto the garden and flakes of black snow covered the lawn, flowers, and fruit. The soot couldn't be washed off and the strawberries became inedible. We spent whole hours together lying in the bomb shelter that we had dug at the bottom of the garden. The boom of the guns was deafening. The children didn't stop trembling. Some people from the village came to share our shelter. There were only seventeen of us left; the others fled with the exodus out of Paris that occurred after the German occupation. The abandoned houses were looted.

✦

Hitler was in Paris. The village of Longchêne began to fill with Germans who were no longer being made prisoner. They marched in triumph while the conquered looked on, who calmed themselves and dwelled on all kinds of favorable details: the Germans were clean, courteous, and paid in real money (they printed it back home in Frankfurt, day and night). The conquered told themselves that this hardship wasn't the fault of these people. They were just carrying out orders.

One afternoon, sometime after I had gone to live in a neighboring village, I plunged myself into the summer mist to see Nina. Nikolay was in the kitchen making bread, Nina was out with a spade, working on the garden.

"Nina, you're still not complaining about having too easy a life, are you?"

Nina was peeling a turnip; she cut it in half and offered the half to me.

"How do you expect me not to complain when I'm living with a man who is healthy and indestructible in body and soul?" she was laughing with her mouth full of turnip. "He is sensible, generous, sincere, and tender. Wouldn't you complain? He knows how to do everything. After lunch he fixed the fuses; now he's preparing cornbread; later he will draw a self-portrait; and in the evening he will sit at the piano and play Schumann's *Carnaval* for us. Tell me, is it possible to live with a man like that? Come on, we'll listen to the news of our heroes."

"Now people are saying its better to be a living coward than a dead hero."

"I'm a coward too."

We went into the house. Nina put on the radio, and a quartet could be heard playing, probably Brahms. Nina went on, "Yes, I'm a coward. When the Russian revolution was going on, I told myself: 'This is a problem for the tsar and the nobility, for the counterrevolutionaries and the bankers. I'm sixteen years old and have nothing to do with any of it.' Now a new catastrophe has come along and what do I do? Just repeat the same old refrain: 'This isn't my business. This is a European thing. Who am I? A Russian exile, half Asian, that is to say, a nobody.' But the other day I told myself, as I was looking at myself in the mirror: 'It doesn't speak well of you, this attitude of yours.'"

"It's difficult for us exiles to grow roots and that's why we end up feeling that all problems are alien to us."

"We all write, paint, compose music, and philosophize with a single hope: that we will go back to Russia after we're dead, in the form of our work."

"And you say that, Nina? You, the little westerner? For whom life is everything, be it here or there?"

"I want to be in some place where I can feel myself part of what is going on. But I know now that France is not for me."

I smiled. I wanted to ask her about her intention of going to America, but at that moment Nikolay came in.

"Nina has promised me that you would play Schumann's *Carnival* for us, Nikolasha."

Nikolay washed his hands and sat down at the piano.

Seated next to Nina, I liked listening to the way the chords summoned each other up. Outside the fog grew ever thicker and apart from us; nothing else existed. Everything had become unimportant, distant. The only thing that really existed was the foggy summer evening, the music, and us. After the last chord, I clapped.

"Did you like it, Nina?"

"A moment ago I said to Igor Mikhailovich," she addressed herself to me, "that Nikolay is a person who knows how to do everything, didn't I?"

"Yes, that's exactly what you said."

"And by that I meant that a person who knows everything, deep down knows nothing at all."

She ran upstairs to her study.

Nikolay shrugged his shoulders, attempted a smile, and followed her.

I took my bicycle home. The fog had become so thick that not a single star could be seen.

During the whole of autumn I didn't go to see them even once. For a time I thought that my falling in love was a chimera, a fantasy that I had created for myself in order to make my life easier. That is why everyone likes to be in love, isn't it? Sometimes I went to Paris, but my main concern was survival. When Nikolay came to see me, he brought me fruit from his garden, or bread that he had made himself. Generally speaking, there wasn't any other kind of bread. One morning it snowed a little, but as the day drew on the snow melted in the rain. That evening, in the darkness next to my door, a bicycle stopped, some wellington boots could be heard, splish-splash, and there was Nina coming into the house.

"I have to tell you while it's still fresh in my mind! Today I have had a meeting with beauty!"

This was the Nina I had known from before, the Nina who had charmed me so! I got some dry slippers for her and a pot of tea. I didn't have so much as a crumb of bread. She began to tell me her story.

"This evening when I went to the farmhouse for milk, in the rain, walking along a path full of puddles, I made the acquaintance of Ramona. She's the daughter of a woodcutter, a Spaniard who went into exile at the end of the civil war. The girl is eight years old and lives in indescribable misery. In the cold of winter, her dress, or rather the rags she wore, were hanging off her, and you could see her body through the holes. She splashed in the puddles in shoes so worn they were covered in holes, and so big that they were practically falling off her feet; they probably belonged to her mother. Her long, black hair was arranged in two pigtails and tied with two pieces of red wool. She was going to the farmhouse; like me, she was stumbling in the dark. While the farmer's wife poured her some fresh milk, I was able to observe the little girl in the light. She looked like a figure from a Goya painting: fine, tanned fingers, huge eyes, full of curiosity, brown and shining. These tender eyes noticed me. She smiled with confidence, without knowing who I was."

"And you?"

"I felt carried away with joy and compassion. You know, I had the feeling that something had awoken inside me."

"Tenderness?"

Nina looked out of the dark window while she reflected. She was in another world.

"Igor Mikhailovich, what I am about to say now hasn't got anything to do with what I came to tell you. No, in fact it does have something to do with it. Yes, it certainly does, now that I think about it. You know, with someone who loves me, with someone who adores me, I can be bad, terrible, treacherous."

"Really? And why, Nina?"

"When I get the feeling that someone has put their hand on me tenderly, at that moment I feel like hitting that hand cruelly. It's an attack of hatred. And at moments like that it's a great effort for me to control myself."

I didn't know what to say. She had taken me unaware and I felt flustered.

"But going back to the girl. I told her, 'Come with me, pretty one. I'll give you a little ribbon for your pigtails.' In fact I wanted to give her warm clothes. But she didn't understand French. Her smile and the tin can, her ignorance of the language spoken by the people around her, the timidity that appeared for a moment in those tender and slightly frightened eyes—all this appeared before me to rid me of the rigidity that paralyzes me, to renew me, to clean away the death, blood, and the mold that lives off my soul."

✦

It was a long winter. The Germans arrested hundreds of Russian exiles and sent them to concentration camps. In town there was often no bread, and when there was some, we didn't have money to buy any. The days, weeks, and months dragged on, cold and dark. I didn't even notice that summer had arrived. The eighth of August—I remember the date well—was Nina's birthday. How old must she have been? Maybe forty, already? I walked to their house early one morning, with a bunch of wildflowers in my hand. I had nothing else to give them. Together we went for a swim in the little river lined with willows.

> A willow all of silver, on the bank
> caresses the resplendent September waters,

Nina recited.

> From the past my shadow rises up
> silently and comes to meet me,

Nikolay continued reciting the poem, and then started to sing it to the melody of "Ochi chornye."

> No matter how many lyres they hang from this branch
> there is space–it seems–for mine too

and Nina took over once more, finishing the stanza to the melody of Beethoven's "Für Elise."

And this sweet, sunny rain,
comes brim full of good news, of comfort.

"What's that you're singing?" asked Marie-Louise, who had
come to swim with us.

"It's Anna Akhmatova, who we have just recognized to be
the Queen of Poetry."

"After Pushkin," Nikolay corrected her.

"All right, after Pushkin. She writes about a weeping willow."
Nina took off her white dress with its pattern of little red and
blue flowers. "The poem starts like this:

All the souls of the people I love
are among the stars: what luck, I no longer have,
then, anyone else to lose and cry for!
The air here is conducive to repeating songs.

And straight away she began to translate the poem into French.

"You really have no one left to lose? Not even your parents?
You must have remembered the poem for some reason," asked
Marie-Louise, who was up to her knees in the water.

"I know nothing about my parents; it has been a long while
since correspondence between us was banned. But it is true that
I no longer have anyone to lose and cry for. No one who means
anything to me," she answered, testing the temperature of the
water with her toe.

She entered the water very cautiously, and then splashed
Nikolay who cried out and fell straight into the river. But he got

up immediately, even in the middle of the river the water only reached up to his knees. He and Marie-Louise tried to swim in that puddle of water, playing at being dogs and frogs, while Nina and I laughed.

Once dressed, we heard the moan of airplanes getting closer; they were fighters. When they saw us, they immediately started to come down in such a way that I thought they would crash nose first into the ground. They fired their machineguns at the willows next to the river. We threw ourselves into the undergrowth, Nina, in her white flower dress, threw herself into the river. Even after the fighters had gone away, we stayed on the ground motionless, and Nina stayed in the water. We went home, dirty, exhausted, exasperated.

Nina laid the table in the garden while waiting for the guests. With considerable difficulty, she managed to procure half a pound of sausage. She cut it into very thin slices and placed one on a slice of bread. The table was laden with three bottles of wine and my bunch of wildflowers in a glass jar. The guests turned up at eight. Nina welcomed each one of them with a cup of tea. The sugar and the milk were on the dining room table. While she served the last cups, the guests started to go into the garden.

Bunin was the first. He observed the table, done up as if for a party, then examined the plates with the bread and slices of sausage. When he had finished, he unhurriedly began eating the slices of sausage, one after the other. He devoured the twelve slices, that is to say, all of them. We sat down to dinner. In front of us were a few plates with dry pieces of bread. Our Nobel prizewinner Bunin was drinking wine, laughing his head off, and talking about a surrealist table.

"Surrealist scenes are what the Germans give us every day; what we want is food on the table," grumbled Nikolay, in a bad mood.

"In this way the dinner is more original," Bunin insisted.

Twilight was falling; we sat under the walnut tree as we had done a year ago. The light wasn't turquoise like last year; it was rather the color of a pigeon's wing. The air was misty. A night butterfly came into the dining room and vanished from sight.

"We can't complain about having only to see a few surrealistic scenes; I saw one not long ago," said Nina. "The Germans called up the Russians in order to register them: the German police wants to find out who is White and who is Red. Then they send the Reds to concentration camps. I went to the Kommandantur in Rambouillet. Russians that I saw there, in torn clothes, some of them looking like skeletons, their hands covered in calluses. They were frightened. A German official was interrogating them. He didn't understand how the Nansen stateless person's passport that we all carry is proof that we are not pro-Soviet. I spoke to him in German, too fast, anxiously, making mistakes, trying to persuade him that his persecution made no sense. I had the following words on the tip of my tongue: 'Look carefully at these men and women! Can't you see you won't get anything out of them? Can't you see that they've been suffering for twenty years, that they've been doing the hardest jobs, the jobs that no Frenchman wants to do?' That's what I wanted to tell him, and that is what I repeat to him every night while I sleep. Every night now, I'm in the *Kommandatur* saying, 'They're wrecks, because they've been living abroad like this for twenty, twenty-five years. Before, they were like you, yes they were, they were young and strong. Their children are timid and gormless like they are; their wives are exhausted from so much work and worry. They pay taxes, they go to church, they carry a stateless person's passport and sad faces. Have pity on them. They are Russian exiles.' And every day I wake up in tears."

The leaves of the walnut tree murmured above our heads; they brought to mind the waves of the sea. The black butterfly flew out of the dining room window and beat its wings against the oil lamp that we'd put on the table.

"We sat here a year ago, under this walnut tree," said Olga, quietly.

"Its branches have grown in the meantime," observed Vera Zaitseva.

"It was the evening of the German occupation of Paris and the entry of Italy into the war." said Boris Zaitsev. "Today it looks as if even greater horrors are in store for us. Dozens of planes fly above us every day on their way to Britain. London is in flames."

"Which is worse? " asked Olga, in her childlike voice that irritated so many people. "This or the suicide of Marina Tsvetaeva after her return to Russia, and the arrest of Isaak Babel, they say, that has taken place in the USSR?"

Nina answered without thinking twice, as if she'd known the answer all her life: "For me, knowing that Babel is in prison is harder to bear than the news of the sinking of ships filled with passengers."

"And if we'd been travelling in that ship?" Olga's voice was like that of a schoolgirl.

"Even if we'd been travelling in it. I'm sorry, Olenka."

"But if Nikolay had been on it, you wouldn't say the same, would you?"

"There are no exceptions, Olga."

Nina sat up straight at the head of the table. She was wearing her white dress with a pattern of little flowers, which she had had time to wash and hang out to dry in the sun. She was a beautiful marble sculpture, I told myself. The exterminating angel: "It's an attack of hatred. It is difficult for me to control myself." Her words went through my head.

Bunin whistled.

"A year ago, Boris," said Vera Zaitseva to her husband, as if she had remembered something, "at a dinner here under the walnut tree, we said all sorts of rubbish! I said I wanted to live in the time of Pushkin. And you, Nina, wanted to go off to America. You don't remember that now, do you, Ninochka?"

"I will go off to America, most definitely. I don't say things just for the sake of it."

"And what will you do there?"

"I will live. Above all, I'll live far away from Europe. And how will I live? I will get up at six to see the sunrise. Then I shall do some exercises. For breakfast I shall eat a pear with dry bread, and I will drink tea. After that will come work: translations, stories, articles. Then before lunch, a long walk in the open air. After dinner, some reading. I want to live far away from people!"

We shook our heads because we couldn't imagine Nina, energetic, sociable Nina, living in that way.

"Why far away from people, Nina?" asked Bunin, the only one of us who took it at all seriously.

"Because every afternoon airplanes fly on missions above our heads to bomb the houses of innocent people. I can't sleep. It's like an obsession. I'm afraid that this situation will last forever."

"But we're alive and we're drinking wine," Olga raised her glass.

"I drink wine, *ergo sum*," Bunin also raised his glass.

The rest of us also took part in the toast and when it was over, for a long while we savored the taste of wine on our tongues, as if that might even be taken away from us. Then we were done. Somehow we had forgotten that it was a birthday party.

When, after a few months, my brother contracted an illness that was difficult to cure, I moved to his house in Meudon so that he would have someone to look after him. From time to time I got a letter from Nina, but I don't know if I received them all. The postal service wasn't working very well.

November 15, 1941
Yesterday at eight in the morning I went to the cemetery,
to Khodasevich's tomb. They had removed the earth. Six
gravediggers came with cords and took out the coffin. One

of them told me that in the place where the coffin had been the earth was arid and that probably the deceased had not decomposed but rather had gone dry, like a mummy. They transported the bier to a new, definitive resting place. Slowly, they placed the coffin at the bottom of the tomb. Then they covered it in earth. And I . . . I couldn't take it anymore. I went to the Zaitsevs' house, which is nearby.

December 3, 1942
The bombing of Billancourt by the Americans and the British started on the March 3 at ten in the evening. Around a thousand people lost their lives; two hundred houses were destroyed. The cemetery is closed. Many graves have been wrecked by the bombing; you can see bones and skulls everywhere. All this week there have been searches for people in the cellars and shelters destroyed by the bombs. From one of the basements a child's voice shouted, "I'm here, Mother, here, come!"

March 20, 1942
On Sunday after the bombing of Billancourt, crowds of people came to see what had happened and, once there, took a stroll. The cries of those who had been buried alive could still be heard from the basements while the day-trippers laughed, played with their children, and ate toast with salt and oil.

March 8, 1942
In the bombing of Billancourt, Khodasevich's grave was spared.

The black cross of his tomb now rises up among the tombs of those who died during the bombing.

March 17, 1942
Yesterday, at eight in the morning, the Gestapo arrested Olga and took her away. I don't know if you know that on her mother's side, Olga is Jewish.

October 10, 1944
Dear Igor Mikhailovich, I want to give you the following news personally: Nikolay and I have separated. The fault is mine.

Nina

July, 1948
Dear Igor Mikhailovich, we have sold the house at Longchêne. The buyer is Mony Dalmes, an actress with the Comédie-Française. She wants to "condemn that door" and "open this window over there." Go ahead, lady, you go opening and condemning as you please. Do exactly as you wish!

December 1948
Meeting in the Pleyel room. Camus took the floor. He reminded me of Alexander Blok, both because of his physical appearance and his behavior, and because of the subject of his speech: in a sad voice he spoke about the freedom of the poet. Sartre intervened to say that by this stage in literature you can't talk about love and jealousy without having adopted an attitude about Stalingrad and the Resistance. Breton then held forth on Trotsky.

July 1949

*Dear Igor Mikhailovich, to your questions I must answer
no. I am not distraught. I feel liberated. From what? From
intellectual anarchy. From the opinions that were dictated to
me by my moods. From a sense of guilt (I have gotten rid of
it completely). From anguish. From the fear of the opinions
of me that other people might have. From restlessness. From
contradictory and indefinable emotional attacks.*

*In the moment that I achieved tranquility, I realized that
I am still able to rebel and I have the feeling that things won't
stop here, under the roofs of Paris. I have glimpsed, vaguely,
the events of the future. "Energy is eternal delight" (William
Blake).*

August 21, 1950

*I adore walking through the Trocadero at night. In the
darkness, I sense the coming of winter. The parks and gardens,
so noisy by day, are submerged in shadows and silence. Some
lampposts make circles of light that illuminate part of the path
or the wide branch of a plane tree. For an instant I forget who
I am and what is happening to me. I also forget that of which
I am always aware: the decadence of the Russian circle now,
which started the day Paris was conquered by the Germans
and continues in unstoppable fashion even now after the war.
I usually come back from my walks fairly late at night. Before
the day appears, Paris is phantasmagorical, a little like our
legendary city on the Neva, especially when the wind bends the
naked branches of the trees and gray, monotonous rain drips*

down across my eyes and lips. My legs carry me in automatic
fashion and I am aware of only one thing: that soon it will be
a quarter of a century that I have been walking through Paris,
and half a century that I have inhabited this earth. And I
know that I want a change.

August 29, 1950
Dear Igor Mikhailovich,
    I have received the following letter. Read it, please:

> *Nina, what is up with you? I do nothing. I only read.*
> *I don't even go for a swim. In my sad life there is nothing*
> *new.*
>   *Your friend forever, who embraces you tenderly,*
>   *Ivan Bunin*

You see, I haven't lied to you. We are on the way down, dying,
all of us.

                              Yours, Nina

P.S. Perhaps it will interest you to know that on November 1, I
will be getting a boat from Le Havre to New York. I am going,
and I am never coming back.

October 1, 1950
Igor, I don't want to put off the answer to your question. No, I
am not afraid.
    I am not afraid, although I feel that I am leaving behind

me not only Paris, but also Petersburg-Leningrad, Prague and Berlin, Venice and the French countryside, clear and misty at once, which I will love as long as I live. I see it when I close my eyes: giant trees watch over the roads, wide cornfields, meadows with brightly colored edges, pointed steeples of little forgotten churches, built a thousand years ago, long before Montaigne and Cervantes.

I am leaving behind me people that I love, each of whom is a long story of friendship. I am leaving behind my beloved dead. My life.

No, I am not afraid.

Nina

We said goodbye at the railway station. Fourteen of us. Nina was going by train to Le Havre, where she was getting the boat.

"You will always be present among us," said Boris Zaitsev.

"And not only because of your embroidery," smiled Vera Zaitseva.

"Don't catch cold; it's a rough day," said Nina as a goodbye to Bunin. Little did she know that in three years she wouldn't have to worry about him because Bunin would be dead.

The train started to pull away. Nina stood by a lowered window, and tears rolled down her cheeks. I had never seen her cry. I went up to take hold of her wet hand as it pressed her handkerchief. I walked by her side following the rhythm of the train as it was pulling away.

"I feel like Prince Myshkin," she said, smiling through her tears.

"And I, like Anna Karenina."

"Like Myshkin and probably like Dostoyevsky himself, for suddenly I see everything with a great clarity, with absolute lucidity. Everything that I am leaving. And everything that has left me."

The steam of the locomotive wrapped itself first around her, then around the whole car, then around the entire train.

THREE

She wrote to me in her first transatlantic letter:

> . . . a gothic cathedral that floats in the sea, a slim ship with towering masts. A long time ago, I also saw Saint Petersburg like that, like a ship wrapped in ice. Now I saw New York the same way when after a sea voyage of one week, the city began to emerge out of the gray waves and the November drizzle. Slowly but surely, the cathedral got ever closer, forming a clearer and clearer outline in the lead-colored sky; and the closer it got, the more its temple shape changed, and it became a slim city on a narrow island, a capital consisting of towers with an infinity of lit windows. I felt that I had stopped moving and that the city was approaching me across the ocean. Whereas many cities are fixed in a single place, New York and Saint Petersburg float in the sea.

*In the evening, sitting next to the window of a hotel on
the corner of Ninety-Fourth Street and West End Avenue, I
could not take my eyes off the unusual spectacle: around its
eighteenth floor rose extremely tall skyscrapers, covered in lit
windows. I was fascinated by the life in those windows, with
their different lights, and again, as I had done in the taxi that
morning, I asked myself where the center of the city was. In an
unknown capital, is the center where we find ourselves, or, on
the contrary, is it far from the place where we happen to be?
The two sensations came together inside me on the morning,
after the arrival of my boat, as the taxi was passing through
the still-dark streets full of advertisements that hadn't been
switched off yet. The two suitcases of my exile lay on the floor
of my hotel room, unpacked, but I had a copy of the* New York
Times *open on the bed, at the page with the wanted ads, and
I had already marked a few advertisements with red pencil.
After the taxi fare and a week in advance at the hotel, I was
left with exactly twenty-seven dollars.*

When I arrived in America to look for Nina, I met her friend
Alexandra Tolstaya, who spoke to me of her relationship with
Nina. She told me about their meetings, the excursions they
went on together. I already knew about them from the letters
that Nina had sent me. In more than one she wrote of Alexandra, or Sasha, as friends called her, and of her other new friends.
In one of them she writes:

Alexandra played with fire and asked me questions more often as a way of passing the time than out of interest.

"And how did you adjust, Nina?"

"I started taking the most diverse jobs," I told her, amused, "always ones that didn't require any knowledge of the language because I don't speak a word of English. In a printing shop, in a factory. Once they fired me on the spot because I began to reflect on the meaning of technology and put the envelopes into the machine on their sides, so that the addresses were printed in the air and the envelopes remained blank."

I was sitting with Alexandra and a male friend of hers on some tall dunes. The sea was roaring in front of us, and the waves were rising up with white hats, waves as tall as the ones I had only seen before in Saint Petersburg. They didn't look very inviting as far as swimming was concerned. As for us, three figures tanned by the sun, agile flames of the fire leapt up and dyed our faces pink.

The man stretched himself out. I observed his long pianist's fingers as they picked up a piece of sausage with a napkin, stuck it on a fork, and roasted it on the fire, while keeping his palms protected by the napkin. He noticed my look and quickly let the napkin fall onto the sand.

"And did you feel cheerful doing those dreadful jobs, Nina Nikolayevna?" he asked.

"What is this, a police interrogation? Now I feel cheerful and even on the brink of laughter as I watch you and your clumsy musician's hands try to stick something as prosaic as a piece of sausage on the end of a fork," I said, laughing with so much enthusiasm that no one could be cross with me for having mocked them.

Yes, Nina, how well I know your infectious laugh, how you let it out to cover up the terrible things you had just said! How many times I would like to have gotten cross with you, and I haven't been able to because of the way you laugh!

Nina's reply to the man—about whom all we know is that he is tanned by the sun—continues in her letter:

"Well I also thought to turn myself into a beggar. I took this very seriously. I even went to see the tramps and the homeless so as to negotiate a place with them and avoid putting myself where I wasn't wanted."

"Nina, as you are a beggar, do you want to ask for more alms, that is, another piece of sausage? With or without bread?"

Alexandra took it as a joke, but Nina had the idea fixed in her head that she would end her life among beggars. I understood her perfectly. She was far from being melodramatic or hysterical. Many of us were absolutely convinced of the same thing, this image of the end of our lives. We would end up as homeless people. It was a fact that we contemplated quite coolly.

"As you insist. Then together with the sausage I will also toast this crust. What do you think, Alexandra? May we ask our distinguished guest to play something for us on the guitar?"

"I would be delighted to play for you, Nina. But first I would like to know how you got to know each other, you and Alexandra."

I leaned back on my elbows on the white sand.

"I can see that you have brought an enormous case full of questions with you for the weekend. I do whatever I can to make you shut up, but it's just not possible. Alexandra will tell you, and I'll add the details as she goes along, isn't that right, Sasha?"

A handsome greyhound came running out of the sea. It stopped in front of us and shook to dry its coat. The fire was whispering, Alexandra shouted a few words, and the dog went over to the big house, with its tail between its legs.

"Nina came to see me in my office at the Immigrant Aid Organization. She didn't come to see me as the daughter of Leo Tolstoy, but the fact is that when one is called Alexandra Lvovna Tolstaya, it is difficult for one to cover up one's family connections. So I made her wait for over an hour and then I let her in."

"With a not very friendly face, Sasha, if we want to round off the picture."

"And I asked, 'Nina Berberova? Are you the daughter or the niece?' 'Of whom?' the visitor asked. 'Of the writer, of course.' 'I am she.' she answered with relief. I embraced her, and we went to have lunch together."

"In a Chinese restaurant, we had roast duck with honey."

"And on Friday I took her from Manhattan to the house, here."

"Because you saw that I didn't have a clue about fishing and, what was much worse, that I didn't know how to play cards, sing a duet, and dance a waltz just as you all did in Iasnaia Poliana."

"Just as we all had done before my father forbade us to, when he grew tired of mundane amusements."

"I learned to play canasta . . ."

"Come on, Nina. You play like a garbage collector. You'd lose the last thing you own. That necklace with the charm. What is it?"

"A dove."

The man played the cords of the guitar with the tips of his fingers in darkness. I stretched out and suddenly I lay down on the sand, watching the stars that were emerging from the clear sky, the crescent moon that shone ever more brightly. As it had so many years ago under the walnut tree at Longchêne, as it had done in Sorrento, Berlin, Prague . . . No, there was nothing else except fog, like in Saint Petersburg. Before my eyes there grew, like shining ripe strawberries, a hammer and sickle lit by spotlights, and more and more hammers and sickles that hung from all the buildings in the square full of snow. With a rapid movement I turned to one side, and supported my head with the palm of my hand so that I could see the man playing melodies by Boccherini on his guitar while the reflections of flames danced on his face, arms, and that part of his tanned chest revealed by his half-unbuttoned shirt.

✦

Alexandra has never managed to understand Nina. But, can I say that I have really come to understand her? Is it possible to know and understand somebody deep down, no matter how much in love we might be? The more I knew Nina, the less I understood her. Each time I realized with greater clarity that I did not love Nina just as she was, but rather my image of her, or that fragment of her personality that was destined to fill an emptiness inside me.

May, 1951

According to the date, she wrote these letters to me prior to the long ones I have just read.

Dear Igor Mikhailovich,
The first person I have had dealings with in the United States is Alexandra Tolstaya. I had seen her many times in photographs of her with her father, the writer Leo Tolstoy. At that time Alexandra was twenty-eight years old and almost forty years have gone by since then. She is a strong, well-built, very elegant woman. Some time ago, Vladislav wrote some things about her in his article dedicated to the death of Leo Tolstoy. Do you know this article?
I have also met Vsevolod Pastukhov, pianist, teacher, and poet, and we have made friends. Through his music I relive the ambience of Saint Petersburg, which in fact I never had the time to get to know well enough.

May, 1952

Igor,

At the teas Maria Tselina offers here in New York, I have
met a whole bunch of Russians. The ones who used to attend
her salon in Paris had known each other for years, ever since
they lived in Moscow. Here it is different. When she invites
people, Tselina doesn't keep to any given criteria. Vladislav
used to tell me that the day would come when Russian exiles,
the literati, would meet up as an association of people capable
of distinguishing an iambus from a trochee. But the ones I meet
at Tselina's place don't even know how to do that, so now I
divide the Russians into two categories: those who try to take
the maximum advantage possible of their experiences in the
west, and those who have brought along a screen that they have
placed between them and the western world. And what I do is
avoid the latter.

Nina wrote to me much later, in one of those letters that
seemed to be rough drafts written before she started her
memoirs:

In front of the fireplace, Alexandra was brushing her
greyhound. I sat in front of her in an armchair, and I told
myself that leaning back in a comfortable chair with a book in
one's hand was absolute paradise. The warm, salty air and the
smell of recently cut grass came in through the open windows.

Weakened by the muggy heat, I placed my feet on a stool while my eyes wandered from the framed photographs that were hanging on the wall to the man who was mowing the lawn in the garden.

"Alexandra, you have your no-man's-land, don't you?"

"No-man's-land? What do you mean by that?"

"Since I was little I have been convinced that each person has her no-man's-land, a land that belongs to her and her alone."

"Are you referring to acceptable and unacceptable life, the legal and the non-legal, that which is permitted and that which is not?"

"Not at all, Sasha. What I mean is that each person lives or ought to live without limits, in absolute freedom, in a private space, even though it might only be for an hour a day or an hour a week or one day a month. Deep down we live for this private life of our own."

"No, I don't experience anything like that, Nina. I know nothing of that."

"You don't have a territory where you are alone with your father?"

"My father died a long time ago."

"So?"

"And you think that . . ."

"Think about it, Sasha."

"And you have this no-man's-land, as you call it?"

"I also have my dead person."

"A dead person?"

"Yes, my dead person is alive for me; and the living, for me, are dead," I explained looking at a spot somewhere through the window, someplace beyond the garden, the sea, the horizon.

Then I fixed my gaze at a spot in the garden. A tanned man was mowing the lawn, the muscles of his shoulders were tense under his vest. Rather than a famous musician, he looked more like a Russian peasant. I thought that I liked him like that more than when he was playing the guitar or the piano. Alexandra noticed my look.

"You have charmed our pianist. He never used to mow the lawn before you came along."

"Pastukhov must be about the same age as me, yet somehow he manages to bring me back the echo of old Saint Petersburg, even though I personally never knew it, just a few of its notes at the beginning of the 1920s, when they were already fading away in the atmosphere of revolutionary Saint Petersburg."

"And that's all? Doesn't he give you anything else, this man, except these notes?"

"Yes, something else. I feel at ease with him."

"And that's all?"

"I'll help you brush the dog."

I took the brush and comb from Alexandra's hands and started to brush the coat on the firm stomach of the reclining animal.

"Nina, why do you wear a dove around your neck?"

"Why? Listen:

The doves flee frightened
from the feet of my loved one.

Do you like it?"

"Yes. Who wrote it?"

"Him . . . My no-man's-land. My dead person. A long
time ago. We were in Venice, the city of doves."

I continued brushing the dog vigorously.

Pastukhov came into the salon, shining all over, with three
glasses of vermouth in his hand.

July, 1952

Dear friend, do you remember that during the war we
sometimes spoke of certain special moments that have the
power of transforming people? We didn't speak about it in those
terms, but that's what it was: remember how I told you about
my meeting with a Spanish girl, a moment which renewed
tenderness and compassion within me? Recently I have been
thinking of this subject. In some way we all have our no-man's-
land. Within the territory of this other life, the invisible one
which is ours only and in which we live in complete freedom,
unusual things can happen. Two attuned souls can meet; a
person who is reading a book or listening to music can reach an
extraordinary degree of depth. Certain moments, lived in our
no-man's-land, either complement some aspect of our "real" life
or they have a meaning that is all their own. This inner life can
be a pleasure or a necessity.

Nina B.

September, 1952

Dear Igor Mikhailovich,

You ask me if I have got used to living in America. Yes,
I'm fine here. I try to understand America. I keep on
discovering more and more. I admire America, its youth, and
its dynamism. But deep down, you know . . . It makes no
difference to me whether I live in one place or another. I like
to have new impressions; they help me to cope with the pain I
carry inside me. But in the end, isn't it everybody's wish to snuff
out their most intimate pain with a blanket of new, different,
strong, crazy experiences? What we wouldn't do to be relieved
of ourselves!

> *Greetings from*
> *your Nina*

In an undated letter I received ten years or so after the earlier
brief ones, she wrote:

In the program there was a concert dedicated to the memory
of Dmitri Shostakovich. I was sitting next to Alexandra
in the first row of the circle and was listening to the art of
Vsevolod Pastukhov's piano. All the other instruments are
unnecessary, she told me; he alone is a whole orchestra that
fills the concert hall. I observed the pianist submerged in the
universe of the music where nothing of the outside world could
reach. But perhaps something could: the pianist's face took
on from time to time an illuminated resplendent expression,
like the one I had seen on him for the first time a few months

ago in Alexandra's house by the sea, he brought us some glasses full of golden vermouth with ice cubes that knocked against each other like bumper cars. I thought that musicians were happy beings: in music they have their no-man's-land, which fills them completely and which acts as a refuge. Both Vsevolod Pastukhov and Dmitri Shostakovich did. Before them, Schubert, Mozart, Bach. Neither the Inquisition nor the totalitarian states would ever permit anyone his no-man's-land, this other life. But with music it is possible to preserve one's inner life even under a dictatorship. It is true that Shostakovich had serious problems with the totalitarian government, but nobody, not even Stalin, could take away the music that was echoing in his head.

Applause, a storm of applause. The audience gave a standing ovation.

In the wings there was a long line of people who wanted to shake hands with Vsevolod Pastukhov. Alexandra and I were the last in line. Pastukhov saw us and offered us the place next to him. He presented Alexandra to his friends and then me as "my friend." I was stupefied; I felt my face grow severe, inaccessible. But no one was paying any attention to me, the evening belonged to Vsevolod Pastukhov. Alexandra excused herself, saying she still had work to do. We accompanied her out onto the street; she went off in her red sports car, which shrank until it melted into the flood of lights. Pastukhov called a taxi to Central Park.

On the way he told me of his first meeting with Shostakovich in the 1920s. He continued while we looked for *a place on the terrace of a cafe in the middle of the park; he told stories while the waiter uncorked a bottle of champagne effortlessly, noiselessly. Then he played for a moment with his glass, expecting me to suggest a toast. After all, today he today had had the kind of success that comes only once in a lifetime, if it comes at all! But I sipped my champagne without saying a word, so that he clinked his glass against mine, in silence, before tasting the liquid full of tiny bubbles.*

"Do you still work as a quadrilingual secretary for that old witch? And you handle her correspondence with Albert Schweitzer, Gary Cooper, and Kurt Furtwängler?"

"Mrs. Toom's latest whim: she now wants me to grow roses instead of writing her letters."

"And you've refused."

"I certainly have. So she told me to grow tulips. And if I don't want to, then I can leave."

"So you left."

"I left. The very next day she called me to tell me that the detective novel she had half-finished reading had gotten lost somewhere. And that I should help her find it because otherwise she would never find out who the murderer was. So before hanging up I told her the murderer was the gardener."

The pianist laughed his head off, and his face shone as it had during the concert, as it had a few months ago. I stopped noticing what was around me, I only saw him.

The waiter filled our glasses to the brim.

"To Shostakovich. To your Shostakovich," I said in a low voice.

We touched glasses, we looked each other in the eye, we drank a sip.

"And to you," I added in a voice that could barely be heard.

He placed a palm over my fingers and held them tightly. He raised his eyes to me in a way . . . I don't know how to put it. Like Tolstoy when he was looking at his daughter in the photo in Alexandra's living room.

I wanted to move my hand, but my fingers were imprisoned. I started to notice what was around me. In front of us there was a little artificial lake, an owl had started to hoot, and in some place nearby a popular American band began to play. Without a doubt people were dancing. I could hear shouts of happiness. I felt like dancing with them even though I didn't know that particular dance. But I didn't say anything. I took a sip of champagne.

"One day in Alexandra's house you recited some verses about doves, Nina. I heard it through the open window."

"Yes. This:

The doves flee frightened
from the feet of my loved one.

"The loved one in question is you."

"Yes."

"The doves are the men who are afraid of you. On one hand, you are attractive and they desire you; on the other, you are mature, self-confident, and intelligent. And sarcastic. And worst of all, you are mysterious. And men panic when faced with mystery, because they don't know what to do with it. That is why they flee, frightened."

I laughed without stopping, drank champagne, choked, and coughed, and with my fingers over my open mouth, I said to him: "But it's about some Venetian doves! On San Marco square!"

"Nina, let's go together to Venice! And afterward we will not separate anymore!"

I took a sip thoughtfully. Here we are, then, I told myself. This had to happen one day; once more I am in a situation in which someone wants to take away the one thing that matters to me. The owl hooted again. A gust of cold wind blew that hinted at the coming of fall.

"I prefer the path to the destination, the sea to the harbor," I answered slowly, in a low voice. "Is what we have already not enough for you, Vsevolod?"

"I live submerged in insecurity. We spend the weekends together, we go to the theater, to the concerts. But all that is insecure. And I need security."

"Either you have security inside yourself or you don't have it at all."

"Maybe you will have to think about it, won't you, Nina?"

He kissed the palm of my hand.

Instead of the artificial lake in Central Park, I saw before me the Venetian sky in April—dull clouds, a heavy downpour, and then an intense blue sky, the square of San Marco full of silky doves. I arrive, dressed in an ivory-colored raincoat, and . . . zaaaaaaasssss, dozens of doves beat the air with their wings, higher and higher, they have disappeared.

"I'm not an insurance agent whose job it is to make people feel secure," I said, and got up.

He looked at me, petrified.

The music from a neighboring dance hall could now be heard more intensely. A strident shout of joy reached us. It was a dark night, without a moon, without stars.

Suddenly my violent gesture came to an end. I caressed his cheek with the tips of my fingers.

"I'm sorry, I didn't want to . . ."

He sat, stunned, and watched as I moved away with my head down.

The letter ends here.

September, 1952

Dear friend,

Tonight I had the same dream I had many years ago in Paris. Isn't that strange? We were sitting in a little art deco cafe built of wood in the Luxembourg garden. You probably don't remember, so many years have gone by! We were walking together from the newspaper offices and down the rue de Vaugirard, I remember it perfectly well. Then we had coffee together in the Luxembourg garden and I told you about a dream, which I dreamt again tonight! The one in which I found myself in the train station at Saint Petersburg. I was waiting for the Paris train. It was a goods train that was bringing

the coffins of the dead from exile back home. I ran along the
platform, past the endless row of cars that were entering the
station building little by little, and I discovered Vladya's coffin
in the last car. The shouts of the railway workers woke me up.

Nina

The day after the concert, very early in the morning, Nina phoned up Alexandra Tolstaya to invite her to go on a long trip together through Colorado and Arizona. "The sooner the better!" she insisted.

On Friday afternoon they set off on their trip in Alexandra's red sports car. They discovered all kinds of scenery, the most varied types of people, Indians too. From time to time Nina talked of her no-man's-land; she said that sometimes it took over so much that it didn't let her live her primary life, the visible one, and that life isn't going to wait. The Kansas prairie made her think of Russia.

I didn't find out anything about this until much later, when I was in America. Alexandra Tolstaya told me about it. Since then I have only received one letter from Nina, the last one.

Igor, my friend,
You have known me almost my entire life. Sometimes I think
that if I hadn't abandoned Vladya, he might have lived longer,
he might have lived until the war, we might even have lived
through the bombing of Billancourt, we might . . . Forgive me
for saying such words. On the day of the bombing we might
have died together; you know that the house where we lived

on the rue de Quatre Cheminées was completely destroyed. Sometimes I imagine (and I am ashamed to confess it) that we are together in the cellar during the bombardment, he is protecting me with his body, he lies on top of me, and at that moment a bomb falls on the house.

Igor, do you remember my outcry, "Is life going to wait?" that day in the cafe in Paris? I knew it. Life never waits!

Don't reply; there is nothing more to be said.

Yours, Nina

In 1993, at the age of ninety-two, Nina Berberova died in Philadelphia, Pennsylvania. She had worked as a professor of literature at Yale University from 1958 to 1963, and Princeton University from 1963 to 1971. Until nine years before her death, her work was almost unknown to anyone outside Russian émigré circles. In the spring of 1984 the French publisher Hubert Nyssen of Actes Sud found a manuscript in his mailbox with a letter from the translator: "The author of this novel is Russian, and I believe that her work has not had the recognition it deserves." In a short period of time, Actes Sud released the complete works of the author in French, novels and stories, which since then have been translated into dozens of languages. Almost overnight, Berberova turned into a worldwide literary figure.

At the end of her life, after the change of regime, Nina traveled to Russia, where several books of hers have been published and where her readers adore her.